Land of

Linda Dooks

First Published in 2023 by Blossom Spring Publishing
Land of Opportunity Copyright © 2023 Linda Dooks
ISBN 978-1-7393514-6-5
E: admin@blossomspringpublishing.com
W: www.blossomspringpublishing.com

To Peter, my husband, for all his encouragement,
love and support.
Love to Richard and Emma.
Joan, Lesley and Jean, who encouraged and guided me
to finish my Novel.
Thank You.
To Laura at Blossom Spring Publishing. Thank you for
your patience and guidance.

CHAPTER ONE

In the year of 1897, on a cold, bleak moorland, I waited — for what, I was not sure. Jack had promised to come, but he had failed to materialise. How many more days must I wait? Will he come? Does he love me as he'd promised the last time we'd met?

*

Living in the heart of the North York Moors was beautiful and bleak, even in summer. The farm nestled within the valley, hidden from view, was a lonely place. Rose's only relief was Sundays when they would attend the Methodist Chapel service at Castleton. She would spend a few precious minutes there with Sally, her dear friend who lived with her parents at Calshot Farm near Hutton-le-Hole. While her mother was alive, she could visit for the weekend when it was Sally's birthday and harvest time. She had loved it there, Sally's parents were kind and made her welcome. Sally always begged her to live with them, but Rose knew that would never happen — her father refused to allow her to go. As a result, Rose only ever saw her on Sundays, as her parents always invited her to Sunday lunch.

Many parishioners felt sad for Rose; they knew life was hard for her. During the week, Rose would escape to the top of the hill near the stone cross of Young Ralph. Here, she would hide little love messages in the groove at the top of the cross, believed to have been carved out centuries ago by wealthy landowners after a pilgrim froze to death on the spot. Lost or hungry walkers could take one coin to buy food and a hot drink in the nearest town, a tradition that is now long gone.

Each day Rose returned, and today she found her note had disappeared. Had Jack been? Had he taken the message, or had someone else found it?

It was nearly teatime as she returned to the farm; she no longer considered it home. She heard her father already in the barn milking. Abel, her brother, returning from the fields, shouted at her to clean the tractor.

Life was hard for Rose. The previous year's loss of her mother had left an ache in her heart. But, while her mother was alive, Rose felt safe. Her beloved mother was always there to soothe her if her father shouted or hit her.

"Take no notice, my pet; he's just bad-tempered. He means no harm." Her mother would say.

Now, Rose was nothing more than a glorified maid to them. She was only sixteen and her whole life ahead of her; she could not stay at the farm. She hated every moment.

But then, Jack came. During last year's harvest, he had arrived hoping to find work, and they had struck up a friendship. By the time harvest had finished, their friendship had blossomed into love. Jack had promised to return the following spring and take her away, promising her a better life.

Going into the small scullery kitchen, Rose checked the stew, which had been gently bubbling on the range since lunchtime. Then, riddling the coal for more heat, she placed the saucepan of potatoes and vegetables on for cooking, knowing her father and brother would be in soon for tea. If it weren't ready on the table, there would be trouble. Her eyes fell on the mantelpiece, where she saw the note she had written earlier that morning and left on the cross. A smiley face had been drawn on the front as if it laughed at her. Rose knew it was her brother. He must have followed her and watched as she slid it into the groove, hoping that Jack would find it. Grasping it off the shelf, she threw it into the fire. I hate you; I hate you, she thought. How could you? She knew now that Jack had not come, oh, but he promised, she could not give up hope. She would creep out tonight and wait at the cross. He would come; she just knew.

The boots banging at the door told her that her father and brother had returned. Rose strained the vegetables, placed them into dishes, and laid them on the table with the large stew pot. Her father and brother sat down without a word, tucked nosily into the food, not waiting for Rose to take her share.

At last, Rose took what was left, ignoring the sneer from her brother as he glanced toward the mantle.

"No post today then," he leered at her.

"No," Rose replied. She felt her heart hammer in her chest.

"Funny, I could have sworn I saw the post boy on his bike this morning; he must have gone to Glen Farm taking a shortcut through ours." Her brother kicked her shin under the table but said nothing more, and Rose ignored him. At least he hadn't told her father, but he could think again if he was going to come to her room later tonight. After his first visit, she'd began locking her bedroom door — Abel had woken her, laying his whole weight on top of her — forcing the air from her lungs, but she had managed to grab her hairbrush from the side table, giving him a cut above his eye. He had hit her in the ribs and threatened,

"Next time, I'll have you." Then, explaining the wound to his father at breakfast, he had banged his head on the shelf while washing himself.

After they had eaten, Rose went into the scullery to wash up the dishes.

Abel had crept up behind her, hissing, "Let me in tonight, or I tell Father." There was no way he would get near her tonight. As she wiped the knife, she slipped it into her pocket. Rose would rather hang for murder than let him do that. But, no, she would be gone with or without Jack — Abel would find her room empty.

A little later, Rose put on her coat and left the farm to walk up to Old Ralph Cross — just in case, she thought. A breeze blew across the moor bringing with it the calming aroma of heather, helping Rose to clear her mind as she waited for Jack, but he never came. So she made her way to her dear friend.

*

Later that night, Rose sat on her bed. She looked at the chest of drawers pushed across her bedroom door. She knew that the lock would not keep Abel out. Her room was downstairs, just off from the scullery. It used to be Abel's room until her mother died, and Abel told his father he should have the enormous bedroom upstairs. Fortunately, Rose had collected her precious things and, thankfully, the money her mother had given her from her father's weekly allowance for food. Rose had hidden it under a loose floorboard under her bed. She had also sewn a little pocket on the waistband of her dress to keep the money safe.

She knew Abel had been in her room when she had helped her father with the milking one morning, and Rose couldn't be sure if he had found the loose floorboard. Abel denied it when she asked him, but she saw the sneer on his face. It was just after that; he had told his father, being the son and heir, it only fitted that he should have the room. But now, Rose was glad because it meant she did not have to creep down the stairs carefully to avoid those that creaked. Rose knew her brother would sleep for at least two hours before coming to her room; he invariably fell into a snoring sleep when he hit the pillow. Rose hoped that finding her door barred, Abel would not dare make too much noise by pushing it open, as it would wake her father. She would have until daybreak.

4

With layers of clothes on and one good pair of boots, she wore only on Sundays for the chapel, Rose returned the knife she'd picked up 'just in case' to the drawer and went over to the window; she had oiled the latch earlier that day, knowing she could not use the old kitchen door, as it rattled and creaked when opened. The window swung open quickly, and she climbed out and quietly eased herself down into the yard. Rose stood for a moment, her heart hammering in her chest. Still. Nothing stirred. Even the two collies just looked at her as she put a finger to her mouth — they returned to their kennels as if understanding.

A full moon helped Rose make her way across the yard, through the gate and start her walk across the field. She knew where she was going. Sally and she had spent many happy hours as children playing in Sally's grandmother's old cottage hidden away in Calshot Farm's woods. Sally's grandmother had died many years earlier, leaving the place abandoned. Now it would be a shelter for Rose until the milk wagon trundled through the bottom lane on Friday morning on its way to the main town of Pickering. She hoped to get the mail carriage to Hull and, from there, freedom.

*

Sometime later, Rose lifted the stone to find the cottage's key. Not that she needed it as the back door had rotted away and chickens clucked in the scullery. Rose saw a parcel wrapped in cloth; opening it, she found cheese and an apple, a thick slice of bread left by Sally, and a note. Rose read.

"Hi, Rose, just a little food to keep you going. Grandpa will come tonight. He says you must not wait until Friday. Don't worry; he's on your side. Please don't forget to write to let me know you are safe; send it to Aunt Ivy. She will pass the message on. Get someone to write the address so they do not recognise your writing.

Good luck. Sally."

Rose felt her heart flip. Would her father and brother find her before getting the train? Please, God, I hope not.

She was sitting on the only rickety chair in the scullery. Tiredness must have taken over because Rose was suddenly awakened by a trundling sound outside, making her jump off the chair. Was it them? Had they come? She remembered Sally's note and hoped it was her grandpa. She felt herself tremble, her breath caught in her throat and then a voice.

"Are you there lass?" Rose breathed a sigh of relief. Her tense shoulders relaxed. She grabbed the food parcel, she had decided to keep for later and ran outside to see old Mr Thornbridge smiling down at her from the wagon.

"Come on, lass, let's have you. If we hurry, we can get the five o'clock train."

Climbing onto the wagon, Rose smiled a thank you.

"Sally said you would come; please don't tell them you've seen me," she whispered.

"Nay lass, no need to worry, I've got a terrible memory," Sally's grandpa chuckled.

Within a couple of hours and still, well before dawn, stepping down from the wagon, Rose had thanked Mr Thornbridge and found herself standing on the platform just as the train arrived, belching and hissing steam, making her tremble. It would be her first time on one of these metal monsters. Unfortunately, her only companion was an elderly lady who snored most of the journey.

*

What seemed like hours later, arriving at Hull Station, she was glad to step down from the metal beast. She had been so tense during the trip that her body ached. Rose entered a world of noise outside the station, with people rushing around — even though sunrise had just happened, she guessed it must be about six o'clock. Reminded by the warning from Sally's grandpa to be careful of her belongings, not that she had any, she touched the band of her skirt, relieved to feel the pouch — also grateful for the two sovereigns he had given her.

A porter, who had just finished dropping off luggage to a waiting carriage turned to Rose, wondering if she needed assistance.

"Lass, you shouldn't travel alone," he announced.

Rose's heart quickened as she looked at the porter. Then, swallowing hard, she smiled as she told him her aunt would be waiting for her at the shipping office. She hoped the rising colour in her cheeks did not give her away; she had never been any good at lying. But, to her relief, the porter didn't seem to notice as he then suggested it was quite a walk, and she should take a carriage.

Suddenly the old lady Rose had shared her carriage with on the train appeared at her side.

"Oh, hello, dear, where are you going? Are you taking a carriage?" she smiled at her.

"No, thank you," Rose said. "I'm going to the shipping office. I can walk from here."

"Nonsense, child, it's too far to walk. I'm going that way; please let me offer you a seat." Rose hesitated. "Come child; I don't bite," the old lady smiled at her. "By the way, my name is Cybil."

Rose found herself hustled into the carriage.

*

Before too long, Rose noticed the giant cranes as they neared the harbour.

"Which ship are you catching, dear?" Cybil asked.

"Erm, I'm not sure I'm hoping to book a passage to Liverpool, then on to New York."

"On your own, my dear?" Cybil raised her eyebrows as she took in the lost and frightened look of the young woman who sat before her.

She had such a kind and gentle face, and before Rose could stop herself — she'd told Cybil of her day and why she left.

"Well, my dear, I wish you luck and hope you find happiness in your new future." Cybil smiled at her.

Then, all too soon, the carriage pulled up outside the shipping office and just as Rose was about to step down, Cybil slipped some coins into her hand.

"I wish I could give you more, but this will help," Cybil smiled.

"No, it's so kind of you, but I can't possibly," Rose said, but Cybil waved her hand and told her to go.

"I wish I'd done what you're doing now, my dear," she smiled. Cybil banged the carriage roof. As the carriage left, Cybil waved, and Rose stood alone. The kindness of Sally's grandpa and total strangers made Rose cry.

Drying her eyes, she climbed the steps into the booking office. A tall gentleman with small silver ring glasses was writing in a ledger — he lifted his head and smiled.

"May I help?" He asked.

With guidance from the clerk, she found she could afford third-class travel rather than steerage and that, much to her amazement, the ship from Hull would be leaving in one hour. She would then disembark at Liverpool and board RMS Campania at 8 a.m.

Having paid her passage that included meals on the RMS Campania, Rose left, and with the office boy's help, which the clerk suggested she needed, Rose found herself aboard the steamer. Within the hour, it had left the harbour and was at sea. Rose stood at the railings, looking back.

"Will they still find me?" she whispered. Rose hoped not. She had given a different surname to the booking clerk, who had smiled at her, knowing that that was not her name — but said nothing.

*

That night as Rose sat in the waiting room at Liverpool docks, she watched the hustle and bustle of those around her. Like her, they could not afford a hotel for the night, making the most of the warmth of the small fire, mothers cuddled children on their laps as they slept — the men played cards while some drank, but all were in good spirits, looking forward to their new lives.

At seven o'clock the following day, stewards arrived in the waiting room to assist with all passengers' health checks before being allowed to board RMS Campania. As Rose walked up the gangplank, a bubble of excitement coursed through her. She had made it. Upon finding her cabin, it had two single beds, wood flooring, a porthole allowing light to flood in and a chest of drawers with a washstand next to it. For the third class, this, to Rose, was luxury. She would also be sharing with another young woman named Agnes.

Rose and Agnes quickly discovered they were both running away from terrible home life — they soon became friends.

Hearing the ship's horn blow thrice, Rose and Agnes left their cabin and went up on deck to watch the gangplank being pushed back onto the harbour path as the ship left its moorings. Rose looked down onto a sea of different faces, crowds of people cheering, waving, some crying — some smiling. Rose waved back as her excitement and happiness started to flow. But the realisation of what she was doing, where she was going, was suddenly interrupted as she spotted the top of her brother's blond hair — his head twisted and turned to her direction, the massive scowl on his face was dark. She stepped back quickly to hide behind those waving from the rails and watched him scan the crowds. Her heart was pounding in her head as well as her chest. A sudden feeling of terror ribbed through her at the thought that he had found her.

Agnes took her arm, feeling her new friend trembling.

"Is that your brother?" she asked.

"Yes," replied Rose in a weak voice.

"Don't worry," laughed Agnes. "He can't see us."

*

Rose and Agnes stood at the railings looking out to sea that evening, having had her first decent meal in days. She had never been on a ship before and wondered how it stayed afloat. She was surprised at the smoothness as it cut through the waves — oddly, the roar of the ocean as it crashed against the ship was deafening — yet distant. Feeling the salt air on their faces, neither spoke. Instead, Rose and Agnes linked arms as they thought of their future in this exciting new place called America.

CHAPTER TWO

ARRIVAL

Rose and Agnes sat in the large dining room having breakfast on the first morning at sea — long tables filled with families, couples, and single people like Rose and Agnes. The far end of the dining room was for young and older men travelling independently.

"I can't believe we'll be in New York in six days," remarked Agnes to the family opposite them. They were a family of six, mother, father and four children, ages twelve to four; they looked a little green. Their father encouraged them to eat to settle their stomachs, as they would feel better. The youngest grizzled a little, and their mother scooped her up, offering soothing words and a cuddle. Rose looked at the children and smiled. They all had red hair like their parents.

"What's your name?" asked Rose.

"Daisy," whispered the child.

"That's a pretty name; I'm Rose, just like the flower rose." The child smiled timidly back but did not speak.

"She's four, and I'm her older brother Ian. I'm twelve. Daisy is a bit shy. And that's Daniel, he's eight, and my other sister Rebecca she's six." Rose smiled at the brother. He was thin like the rest of the family, and Rose wondered if life had been hard for them.

"You have lovely names," Rose smiled at the children.

"Do you have family in New York?" Agnes interrupted.

"Yes," replied the father with a hint of the Irish lilt. "We're joining my brother and his wife. They run a cattle ranch in Wyoming. I am unsure how far that is, but we have a few travel days before arriving. Luckily, my brother John is meeting us when we dock."

"Wow, fancy that, a cattle ranch," replied Agnes. "Just think, Rose, all those tall, strong cowboys wearing leather trousers and cowboy hats riding around the fields on horseback!" Agnes giggled.

"Plain's miss, it's called the plain, and my brother is not a cowboy; he's a cattle ranger." The father smiled at Agnes.

"Yeah, well, in England, we call them fields. To me, it's the same thing, and I prefer the thought of cowboys — sounds more exciting," laughed Agnes.

"Agnes!" hissed Rose. "Please don't be rude."

"No, I'm not. I'm just saying, sorry if that offended you. I didn't mean it to," pouted Agnes.

"It's okay," smiled the father. "An easy mistake. We shall have to get used to the names in America."

"My uncle calls our back garden the yard." The oldest boy said, looking at Rose.

"How strange," she replied.

"Right, children, time to go. We need some exercise," the mother said as she stood and ushered everyone away. "Bye for now. I'm sure we'll see you at dinner," the mother smiled. Agnes and Rose watched them leave.

Agnes dug her elbow into Rose.

"Well, that went well; just tried to be friendly," giggled Agnes. Rose smiled.

"Oh, Agnes, life is going to be so different. Don't you feel scared?"

"Scared, don't be daft. It's an adventure!" replied Agnes.

*

As the days passed, Rose and Agnes settled into a routine, but Rose thought Agnes a little forward as she chatted up the single men standing near the line on the deck, which separated them from families and young girls travelling alone.

"Oh, come on, Rose," Agnes sighed, "It's the time for a bit of fun!" Agnes nudged Rose in her ribs. Rose didn't like to think she was a prude, but it seemed too forward.

Earlier in the day, Rose learnt that a trunk of second-hand clothes was available for those who had arrived with nothing. Swallowing her pride, she investigated and chose another warm skirt in dark blue, two white blouses, underwear, and another pair of shoes with buttons up the sides, plus a battered leather brown case. She was surprised by how good the condition of the clothes were. Rose was relieved to find the communal shower room empty. She washed and changed into her new skirt and blouse, returning the rest of her clothing to the cabin, feeling fresher and more respectable.

*

One night, as they made their way to the dining room, Agnes grabbed Rose by the wrist, pulling her towards the first-class dining room's forward deck. Opening the door, they stepped inside to find themselves standing at the top of a grand staircase that swept into the dining room. Rose stood mouth agape, looking at the splendour before her.

"Agnes," she whispered, "we shouldn't be here. What if someone sees us?"

"Oh, Rose, where's your sense of adventure?" laughed Agnes. "We're only looking."

Rose saw the magnificent well in the centre of the room, which went through three decks to the skylight above its lights, twinkling like diamonds. The oak-panelled walls and thick russet carpet were soft under her feet. Velvet matching curtains hung full length from the windows and portholes. Dining tables draped in pure white table cloths, their cutlery sparkling under the lights. Ladies in elegant gowns of different colours and gentlemen in black trousers, white shirts and cravats with long dress coats were escorted to their tables by servers dressed in black-tailed coats. It took her breath away. A grand piano stood in the corner, played by a gentleman in a white tailcoat with matching gloves. The sound of laughter, chatter, clinking glasses, and cutlery filled the room. It was a world away from what Rose knew.

The door behind them opened, and a gentleman collided with them.

"Good evening, ladies. Are you heading down for dinner?"

"No," said Rose quietly.

"Yes," Agnes laughed. "We were waiting for our gentlemen friends." She smiled up at the man before her.

"Agnes, stop it. I'm sorry we shouldn't be here; we only came to look. I'm so sorry; please forgive us." Rose found herself blushing to the roots of her hair.

Before her, the man smiled and offered her his arm. "Shall we?" he asked.

Agnes grasped his other arm.

"I'm game if you are," she laughed. Then, feeling embarrassed and shocked, Rose turned and fled through the door behind her and did not stop running until entering the third-class dining room.

Sitting at the table with the family they had become friendly with, Rose tried to settle her pounding heart as she waited for Agnes to join her, but Agnes never arrived.

"Where's your friend tonight?" asked the eldest boy Ian.

"Oh, she is not feeling too well," muttered Rose and ate her meal without saying much else.

*

Later that night, as Rose changed and settled into bed, Agnes breezed into the cabin.

"You silly idiot, you missed a great meal, should have seen the look on the waiter's face; it was a picture; I think

I feel a bit tiddly after the champaign; it tickled my nose," laughed Agnes as she flopped down onto Rose's bed.

"I thought they would throw you out," said Rose.

"No, not with that gentleman. They seem to know him well; if you're interested, Thomas Blackwood is his name."

"Well, I'm not," huffed Rose. "It was so embarrassing. How could you?"

"Stop being such a prude, Rose. You must live a little and enjoy it while you can; God knows what will happen when we reach New York." At that, Agnes got up and undressed before dropping into her bed.

"He asked me what I would do when I reached New York."

"What did you tell him?" Rose asked.

"Simply told him I would be New York's finest singer, and people would come for miles just to hear me."

"Oh, Agnes, you're such a dreamer."

"Well, what are you going to do?" Agnes raised an eyebrow.

"I don't mind being in service. At least I'll have decent food and a roof over my head," replied Rose.

"A glorified maid to some posh American twit, no Rose, you can do better than that."

Rose sighed. Maybe her friend was right.

"I'm tired, Agnes," and Rose turned the light out. Sleep eluded her that night. Instead, she lay listening to Agnes snore and the hum of the ship's engines, which she usually found comforting, but not tonight. For the first time since boarding Rose wondered if she had done the right thing.

*

The following day was Sunday. After breakfast, Rose and Agnes joined the Sunday service held on the upper deck. The minister turned out to be one of the officers they had seen occasionally strolling the deck and had stopped to chat with him. He had told them it would only take six days to arrive in New York, explaining the ship's speed and the triumph of holding the blue riband for the fastest crossing. Meaning that tomorrow God willing, they will arrive at Ellis Island and step foot on American soil. It still amazed Rose that a ship could travel so fast. She was also surprised that first, second, and third-class passengers joined the service.

The minister believed in one service for all. She smiled because they would feel equal if only for a morning service. After a while, Rose was aware of a gentleman who stood beside her. Looking up into bright blue eyes and a gentle smile, she realised it was the gentleman from the night before. Rose found herself blushing and wished she didn't. Instead, he smiled as he raised his hat and wished her good morning.

"Thomas Blackwood," he announced, raising his hat. "I was sorry you disappeared so quickly last night," he whispered.

"We shouldn't have been there, but it was so beautiful. I'm glad I saw it," Rose replied as she extended her hand. "Rose Watson," she smiled. Just then, the hymn Praise my Soul, the King of Heaven struck up, and they joined in. Agnes sang, and Rose was surprised that Agnes had a beautiful voice and understood why she wanted to be a singer. But was it a good life to lead? Her parents had always said that theatre people were nothing more than painted trollops. She didn't think Agnes was one, just more outgoing and braver than her.

After the service, Thomas Blackwood invited Rose and Agnes to join him for coffee.

"Ooh, lovely, yes, please," Agnes smiled.

"It's very kind of you, but we couldn't. It wouldn't be right," Rose interjected.

"Rubbish," said Thomas Blackwood. "If you don't join me in the lounge, let's take one of these deck seats to have coffee here. Please say you'll join me, Rose; it is just coffee."

Agnes poked Rose in the back. "We'd love to, wouldn't we, Rose?

"Well, alright," Rose whispered. And at that, Thomas Blackwood took Rose's elbow and led them to three chairs with a small round table at the side. Beckoning a server, he ordered coffee for three. Before too long, they all began to relax and enjoy their coffee. The sea was calm, and although there was a cool breeze, a waiter had arrived with blankets to put across their knees, and Rose felt relaxed for the first time since leaving England.

As they sipped coffee, Thomas took in the beauty of Rose; she was tall, slender, and painfully shy, and her flowing blond hair and green eyes, which smiled as she spoke, made his heart flutter. For a moment, he felt guilty; it had only been two years since the sudden death of his dear Rosemary and the children's mother, but maybe as his friends kept reminding him, it was time to move on. He wasn't sure about her friend. She seemed a little flighty, as his Rosemary would have said. Perhaps just a little too forward. His thoughts were suddenly disturbed by Agnes.

"Oh, Mr Blackwood, this is so kind of you."

"Please call me Thomas," he smiled. "Your first time in New York?" Thomas asked.

"Yes," Agnes replied. "We're seeking adventure and fortune, aren't we, Rose."

"I'm just hoping for a new start," Rose smiled.

"Have you come together as friends?" Thomas inquired.

"No, but we are now. We met for the first time when we saw our cabin." Agnes laughed. Rose felt herself flush slightly. She didn't want this stranger to know of her escape from home with nothing but the bits and pieces she possessed. What would he think of her?

"Then allow me to tell you a little of New York." First, Thomas told them about the Statue of Liberty they would see upon arrival. "She is pretty magnificent. You certainly feel you arrived home upon seeing her." Thomas smiled. He told them of his two children Isabella, three, and Lucas, five, that he had been to England on business and was glad to be nearly home.

"Where is home?" Agnes enquired.

"Manhattan," Thomas replied.

Agnes chatted non-stop about how she couldn't wait to get there. Rose sat silently listening but observing this man, wondering what his wife was like; it was strange that he hadn't mentioned her. She felt her heart flutter as she looked into his bright blue eyes and caring face. He was taller than her, his hair was blond like hers, and she felt the urge to push his fringe away as it fell across his left eye.

While finishing their coffee, they laughed, watching the children's antics as they played shovelboard with their parents, their laughter floating across the ocean. Others strolled along the promenade, enjoying the calmness of the sea — the occasional acknowledgement towards Thomas Blackwood. The aroma of Cuban cigars and cigarettes drifted from the gentlemen's smoking room from the open door adjacent to where they sat and mingled with the salt air. Eventually, Thomas Blackwood stood.

"It is getting chilly, ladies; we should retire before lunch." Agnes and Rose thanked him and said their goodbyes.

*

Back in their cabin that night, they packed what little they had ready for disembarkation the following day. Agnes looked at Rose.

"He ain't half got the hots for you, girl," she giggled.

"Who?" frowned Rose.

"Who? Don't who me? You know who I mean, dear Thomas couldn't take his eyes off you during the service and while we had coffee."

"Don't be silly, Agnes. He was just polite," Rose said, feeling herself colouring up.

"Oh, yeh, is that why you're blushing?" laughed Agnes. "And why turn down another good meal in the posh restaurant? You're daft you."

"It wouldn't have been right; we don't know him."

"Not likely to either if you keep saying no." Agnes snapped.

"I'm sorry, Agnes, I'm not like you. I find it hard to talk to strangers."

"No, it's me that's sorry; I can't wait to get off this boat and start my new life." Agnes sighed.

CHAPTER THREE

Sailing into Ellis Island, New York, Rose and Agnes stood on deck and got their first sight of the Statue of Liberty.

"Wow, look at that. Thomas was right. She is magnificent, isn't she? So we're in New York, babe," laughed Agnes. She was hopping from foot to foot with excitement.

Rose felt her stomach flip, and a sudden bile rose and hit her throat. She leaned over the railings and threw up. Shocked, she turned to see if anyone had noticed. They hadn't. All around, people were too busy taking in their surroundings. She was here. The thought of her new life made her tremble. The sudden horn from the ship made them both jump and collapse laughing, as they held each other.

It took forever to disembark. It was already dark when Rose and Agnes walked down the gangplank. Finally, tired, weary and desperate for food, they arrived at the Immigration Station Building. Several other ships had also arrived simultaneously, and now the building was a mass of people — many from Ireland and different continents. Long trestle tables stood at the far end of the building where helpers from various charities served hot soup and bread, pasta smothered in tomatoes washed down with tea and coffee, milk, water and orange juice for children.

"Food Rose, come on, I'm starving." Agnes pulled Rose across the room until they stood before a rather rotund lady with a floral wraparound pinafore and a bright yellow crochet hat.

"There is a queue, dear!" she said with a tight lip smile.

"Sorry," replied Agnes. "Only were hungry, you

know."

"So is everyone else in this building; now, wait your turn, dear."

"Awkward old cow," hissed Agnes.

"Agnes, please, what's wrong with you? I'm sorry, my friend didn't mean it." Rose looked appealingly at the helper. Rose pushed Agnes to the end of the line and waited. "Agnes were both tired and hungry, but you don't have to be rude," Rose frowned.

"Oh, shut up, Rose; I'm not in the mood. I feel like one of your home cows herded around in pens." Rose dropped her head; she had been near to tears on arriving — without her friend being awkward too.

*

Later that night, after being shown their sleeping arrangements, Rose was glad to collapse onto her bed. She lay exhausted. A feeling of dread had seeped into her very soul. She was running away from the struggle of home to find herself in nothing more than a warehouse. Although it did look nice inside, with its pine and spruce wood walls, the outside was nothing more than the galvanised iron cladding. Rose felt anxious waiting until morning to meet potential business people hoping to get work. Maybe Agnes was right. It did feel like going to the market on a Saturday with her father to sell their cattle.

"Hey Rose, sorry about earlier," Agnes whispered as she hung over the top bunker, but Rose had already fallen into a deep sleep.

*

"No, no, leave me. Why are you hurting me? I won't come home. You can't make me." Rose struggled to push her brother's arms away as he continually shouted her name, but the shaking continued. Then, waking with a start, Rose realised she had been dreaming; Agnes was shaking her — telling her to get up.

"There's a fire. Move!" Shouted Agnes dragging Rose from her bed. The screams and yells terrified her. Quickly shaking the sleep from her head, she followed Agnes blindly through the mass of bodies until they found themselves standing on the harbour path. They looked up to see the building ablaze — smoke hitting the back of their throats, making them cough and splutter.

"Bloody hell, Rose, they're trying to kill us before we've had a chance," spluttered Agnes. Officials with clipboards started ushering people towards the harbour boats, telling them to reboard the ships they had left earlier for safety.

*

Back on RMS, Campania Rose and Agnes stood on deck and watched as hoses from the fireboats and steamers helped douse the flames as they shot up high into the night sky. Suddenly a loud crashing noise made everyone look up to see the Immigration building collapsing. Rose felt the whole harbour was ablaze at one point, fearing the ships would also catch fire.

Later, sleep evaded most people, except for exhausted children cuddled up to their parents while sitting on the deck. A look of grief and loss edged their faces, not knowing what would happen next.

The fire was out by six o'clock the following morning. Just the ironclad structure that rose scorched and twisted into the air remained. The smell of acrid smoke still lingered. Rose and Agnes sat huddled together, not knowing what to do.

"I left my case and clothes behind," said Rose.

"You and me both," grumbled Agnes. "We've only got what we stand in, and we smell of smoke."

"How will anyone take us on looking like this?" whispered Rose.

"Chin up; maybe lover boy will come to the rescue," laughed Agnes. No sooner were the words out they heard a voice shouting Rose's name.

"Rose, Rose Watson, can you hear me? Rose, Rose?"

Both girls stood and peered over the railings to see Thomas Blackwood, top hat in hand, looking up towards the ship.

Agnes waved madly, "Here, we're here, " she shouted. "Comm'n Rose, lover boy has come for us." Agnes dragged Rose toward the walkway only to be stopped by a burly chargehand.

"And where do you think you two are going? No one's to leave this ship until roll call," he stood, arms folded, blocking the gangplank. Thomas arrived behind him, explaining that the two ladies would join him — Rose noticed money cross hands. Then, with a smile, Thomas escorted Rose and Agnes off the ship to a waiting landau.

"Bloody hell," said Agnes, "talk about speak of the devil. How did you know where to find us?"

"Agnes, please, don't swear," interjected Rose, who had coloured to the roots of her hair. Thomas laughed and told them that news of the fire had reached the hotel he was staying in before heading home and was anxious to know they were alright.

As they reached the landau, Rose turned to Thomas.

"We couldn't possibly go with you; sorry, it's not right. We would be intruding on your kindness," smiled Rose.

"Rubbish, I won't hear another word; you cannot stay here; whatever would you do? No, you are welcome to join me. I'm sure the children would love to meet you, and I have an excellent housekeeper. But, please," said Thomas, "let me help you both until you can find your feet; I am not forcing you into anything you do not wish to do, but this is a large city, and there are undesirables

— you would not be safe." The girls thanked him, and before Rose could stop Agnes, she was already clamouring into the landau. Thomas gave Rose his hand as she climbed in.

The girls took in the view as they travelled, seeing buildings that seemed to rise into the sky. The one thing that Rose missed was the open fields here — everywhere seemed to be concrete and brick.

"Do you have trees?" Rose asked tentatively, not wanting the man to think her stupid. Instead, he smiled at her, his hand resting on his cane as he spoke.

"Oh yes, wait till you see Central Park; you'll love that. It's not far from where I live." While travelling, Rose and Agnes told Thomas of the hardships working the farms on the moorlands at home, its bleakness in the winter and the beauty of spring and summer, especially the heather in full bloom and the sheep that wandered freely.

"How fascinating. I have visited England several times but only to visit the Capital, London." Thomas replied.

After a long journey, the landau stopped outside an imposing three-storey building of red brick, with tall sash windows on either side of a central front door. Ten stone steps from the pavement reached the royal blue door; its brass handle and knocker gleamed in the sun.

As they stepped down from the landau, the door swiftly opened by a small boy who raced down the steps to greet his father, who then scooped him up, the sheer joy on their faces made Rose smile.

"Papa, Papa, you're back. Have you brought me a present from England?" he asked.

His father returned him to the pavement and ruffled his hair.

"All in good time, my little man." Thomas smiled. "First, let me and my guests get into the house."

"Cor, this is a bit of alright," hissed Agnes as she dug her elbow into Rose. Rose just smiled; she wasn't sure what they had come to and was somewhat apprehensive.

"Come in; no need to stand there. Welcome to my home," Thomas said as he climbed the steps, entered the house and enveloped the hug from a rather buxom woman with white hair tied tightly back into a bun — her face was round and full of smiles. Rose noticed a small child hiding in the woman's skirt as the door closed. Then, seeing her father, she rushed into his arms, burying her head into his neck.

"Isabella, my sweet, daddy's home," Thomas hugged her, kissing her head.

"I've missed you, papa," she said quietly.

"Me too, child, but I'm home now, never to leave again, I promise," her father said as he lowered her to the floor. Then, he turned to Rose and Agnes.

"Let me introduce you to my dear long-suffering housekeeper, cook, nanny and whatever else she is — Mrs Longsdon." Thomas laughed and turned. "Mrs Longsdon, may I introduce you to Agnes and Rose, orphans of the terrible fire on the docks. We all met while travelling onboard. After a few days' rest, we can help them somehow." Thomas smiled. Mrs Longsdon appeared a little reticent but welcomed them, showing them into the drawing room, disappearing to make tea, coffee and sandwiches.

While they waited, Thomas gripped his leather bag producing two gifts. Snuggled into her father, Isabella watched, fascinated, as he opened a musical jewellery box; a tiny ballerina danced in circles.

"Thank you, Papa," she whispered, taking it into her hands. Lucas couldn't wait for his and squealed with delight at the model of Big Ben showing him the time, which chimed the hour — he disappeared to put it by his bedside.

*

That night, having eaten a delicious steak with roast potatoes, vegetables, and thick rice pudding, Rose and Agnes felt exhausted as they climbed into their beds. Its comfort and feel of clean white sheets was pure heaven. Thick russet carpet and velvet curtains hung from the windows. A small fire was burning, and Rose could not believe how lucky they had been.

"This is a bit alright…" whispered Agnes, "…but I'm not staying. I want some action to find the theatres. I'm going to hit the highlights me," she giggled. "What about you, Rose? What are you going to do?"

"I don't know. I'd love to stay here forever."

"Don't be daft; there's a whole new world. Let's hit the town," replied Agnes. But Rose was already fast asleep, too tired to think what tomorrow would bring.

CHAPTER FOUR

Where was Agnes, her bed empty, and what time was it? Rose listened but couldn't hear anything. Then, finally, she got up, throwing open the russet curtains. Rose washed in the ivy-patterned bowl and jug left on the room's corner table, feeling ashamed she had overslept.

She then went to the bathroom to use the indoor closet. Rose couldn't get over that they had an indoor toilet bowl with a blue pattern design, a wooden seat, and a flush handle with a cistern above. She had heard of them but had never seen one before. After flushing, Rose waited for the cistern to fill and then flushed again. Oh, what joy. The large copper bath was boxed in with wood and a strange contraption above, which hissed noisily. Rose wondered if it produced hot water. Would she dare try it if turned on? Tonight, she thought.

She returned to her bedroom, giving her skirt and blouse a good shake, dressing and wishing for a change of clothes, the smell of smoke still present. Rose opened the door and headed for the stairs. As she walked down, she studied the pictures hanging on the wall, stopping to look at a beautiful young woman, her long flaxen hair over one shoulder and long slender hands resting on her lap — the dress of deep blue, with white-collar and cuffs and matching slipper shoes. Rose wondered if she had been the late Mrs Blackwood. So beautiful, thought Rose, how sad.

Continuing down the last stairs, Rose turned towards the panelled door she had seen the housekeeper go through the night before, hoping she might find the kitchen. Through a narrow corridor, Rose pushed open the door to the kitchen.

"Good morning, dear. Have you slept well?" Smiling, Mrs Longsdon looked up from the table and put down her teacup.

"Morning," smiled Rose. "I'm sorry I've overslept. Agnes should have woken me."

"No, I told her to leave you, I knew how exhausted you looked last night, and you needed rest. We've had breakfast, but I'll put toast on and make a fresh pot. Will that do you, dear?"

"Yes, thank you," smiled Rose as she pulled out a chair and sat down. "Where is Agnes, by the way?"

"Oh, your friend tucked into a hearty breakfast and has gone out to explore, as she called it; I told her not to get lost, but it's up to her."

"I hope Agnes hasn't upset you?" asked Rose looking somewhat apprehensive.

"No, dear, although she is a little outspoken. I suppose it's the way of the English," smiled Mrs Longsdon.

"Not all of us," Rose smiled back, thanking her at the same time for the toast and tea she had just put on the table. Mrs Longsdon sat down on the chair opposite and smiled at Rose.

"Forgive me, dear. I shouldn't have spoken out; I'm not used to strangers in the house."

"It's fine." Rose smiled. "Agnes can be a little outspoken." Rose tucked into her breakfast in companionable silence, taking in her surroundings. Looking around the kitchen, it seemed huge to Rose. She thought her old home would have fitted into this room alone. The giant oak table she sat at stood in the middle. To her right, a double range run by electricity. Its black lead surround shone. Rose was fascinated that the house had electricity. Flicking a switch on and off made her giggle for some reason. Behind her, shelves filled the length of the wall with every pot, pan and dish imaginable. A white door in the corner which Rose thought could be the pantry. In front of her is a substantial oak dresser with different size plates and cups hanging from hooks. To her left, a double stone sink in front of a large window with a view of the garden. At the side of that, another door, she assumed, led out to the back garden. Already missing the openness of the moors, Rose couldn't wait to explore the garden. After she had finished, she stood up, collected her plate and cup, taking them to the sink to wash.

"No need for that; that's what I'm here for," Mrs Longsdon stood and gently pushed Rose back to her seat.

"Where is Mr Blackwood?" asked Rose.

"Gone to work, my dear; he leaves early, around seven in the morning, and won't return until five. Before he left, he suggested you rest for a few days before deciding what to do. Then, of course, you are most welcome to use the house as your own." Mrs Longsdon smiled.

"How kind," whispered Rose. "But I really can't intrude; I must find work."

"And that would be, may I ask? So you're not another one looking for theatre life?" Rose noticed Mrs Longsdon's lips form a straight line.

"No, I'm not like Agnes, although she does have a lovely singing voice," for some reason, Rose felt she should defend her new friend.

"Yes, well, each to their own is what I say," Mrs Longsdon turned and washed the dishes.

"I'm not sure what to do," replied Rose feeling that she should think about work. "I was wondering about the position of a maid. I saw a lot of large houses as we arrived last night; one of them must need paid help. I can cook and clean, my mother taught me to sew, only basics, but I'm not bad." Turning from the sink, the housekeeper looked at Rose and, smiling, suggested she rest at least for the first week before she started looking.

"You look as if you need it and feeding up a bit if you

ask me," she smiled. Rose couldn't cope with the kindness before her, and tears began to flow. "Nay, lass, I didn't mean to make you cry." Mrs Longsdon stroked Rose's arm and then turned to put the kettle on.

*

Over another pot of tea, Rose told the housekeeper how she came to be in New York and her life at home. And now she was here; she felt terrified of what lay ahead.

Resting a hand on Rose's hand, the housekeeper smiled.

"You poor child, do as the Master says and rest; no one is rushing you away. And please, no more, Mrs Longsdon, call me Freda."

"Thank you," Rose smiled.

"Sorry, but I'm not sure about that friend of yours." The housekeeper laughed. Rose felt it best to ignore that last remark. Standing to leave, she asked where the children were.

"They're in the classroom, dear. The schoolteacher comes Monday to Friday, nine till two; why don't you go and see the rest of the house and sit in the drawing room."

*

Having thanked Freda, Rose left the kitchen. She found herself standing in the hall. She knew the door to her left led to the drawing room, so she opened the door in front and found herself in the dining room. A large mahogany table with matching chairs seated eight faced the front of the house. The large sash windows that looked out to the pavement and road were draped with dark green curtains to match the carpet. Walking over to the window, she stood awhile, watching the hustle and bustle of the carriages and people rushing around. Then, turning, Rose saw a mahogany sideboard on the far wall and a glass cabinet in the corner of the room.

30

Leaving the dining room, she opened the next door, which was a study, its panelled walls and furniture in dark rich green, a swivel chair stood in front of a desk; the room smelt a little musty with a hint of cigar smoke, and Rose realised it would be Mr Blackwood's study and did not venture in further. The last room was the lounge. It surprised Rose with its calming interior of cream furniture — rose-patterned full-length curtains hung at the French doors overlooking the rear garden. Rose smiled as she remembered the young boy on the ship calling it the backyard.

Suddenly homesick, Rose wiped away a tear as it dropped onto her cheek. She didn't miss her father or brother — but England, with its rolling hills and space. This room had a feminine touch, and Rose wondered if it had been the late Mrs Blackwood's room. She left, not wishing to intrude.

Going back to the drawing-room, which carried the same themed colour of dark green carpet and curtains, Rose smiled to herself. It must be their favourite colour. Sitting down, she thought of Agnes and felt guilty about not waking up and going out with her. But Rose was glad to sit on the sofa. She was tired. Her whole body seemed exhausted from the last few days.

Looking across the far wall, Rose took in the bookshelf filling the entire wall; she wandered over to look. So engrossed as Rose studied the title of Mark Twain, Oscar Wilde, Bram Stoker and her favourite author Sir Arthur Conan Doyle, Rose did not hear the door open behind her.

"Help yourself, Rose," Rose was startled and turned quickly, surprised to see Mr Blackwood smiling.

"I thought you were out all day," Rose queried.

"I just popped back to see if you and your friend settled in. But, unfortunately, I can only stay for coffee which I've asked Mrs Longsdon to bring up, and then I must return. Can you read? Please help yourself to any book."

Rose bristled at the fact he thought she was illiterate. "Mr Blackwood, I am educated. But, just because I'm a country girl, my mother insisted I attend the local Sunday School for lessons," Rose said more sharply than she had intended. Thomas raised both hands in surrender.

"Please forgive me; I did not wish to infer…" Thomas replied. Just then, Mrs Longsdon bustled in with a tray placing it on the table and sensing the tension that had suddenly arisen. She looked at Thomas and then back at Rose, who had become rather pink.

"What have you said? Put both feet in by the looks of things," said his housekeeper.

"I have," replied Thomas. "Please, Rose, do forgive me."

"No, no, I'm sorry I didn't mean to snap," Rose answered as she walked across to the chair by the window.

"Ay, well, try and drink your coffee without falling out," Mrs Longsdon left the room with a tut.

While drinking coffee, Thomas briefly explained his position at Macy's Department store and why he travelled to London to meet his friend Mr Harry Selfridge, who was trying to encourage his boss to open a store there.

"Does he work in New York?" Rose inquired.

"Yes, he's a junior manager at Marshalls Fields Department Store in Chicago. It's similar to Macy's. Just not as fine, well that's my opinion. I'm sure Mr Selfridge would disagree." Thomas smiled. Glancing at his pocket watch, Thomas rose and gave a slight bow. "I must go, but please join me for dinner tonight and your friend, of course." And at that, he was gone.

Later that afternoon, and still no sign of Agnes, Rose heard the clatter of feet running down the stairs; throwing open the drawing-room door, Lucas popped his head around.

"Hello."

"Hello Lucas, are you coming in?" smiled Rose. At that, Lucas entered the room and stood in front of Rose. He was the spitting image of his father.

"Are you going to look after us? We don't have a mummy anymore because she died."

"I know Lucas, and I'm sorry, you must miss her very much." How I would love to look after these children, thought Rose.

"Where is your sister?"

"She is coming. She has gone to get her dolly," Lucas informed her.

A little figure silently slipped in behind Lucas and shyly peeped at Rose. Dropping to her knees, Rose smiled as she held her hand towards Isabella. The child was petite with flowing blond hair and the image of her late mother.

"I don't bite," whispered Rose, who waited for the child to come closer and show Rose her doll, which she called Polly. "That's a pretty name; I wish I'd had one as pretty as this when I was little," suddenly remembering the one her mother had made for her — only for her brother to destroy just for the fun of it. Rose noticed a nasty red mark on her left wrist as Isabella reached out to show her the doll.

"That looks sore, Isabella. How did that happen?" Neither child spoke, and Rose felt she couldn't pursue the matter being new to the house. She hoped Lucas was not bullying his little sister; Rose knew how that felt. Lucas jumped in to tell her about their rocking horse and asked if she wanted to see it. At that, the children took her to the playroom on the first floor. On entering, Rose was amazed to see toys and a train set in one corner with a beautiful large doll house in the other, it's front open, showing miniature furniture inside. The rocking horse stood before the window overlooking the garden. He was magnificent to Rose. He was white with a chestnut mane and tail, almost flowing to the floor. A leather saddle and bridle completed the look.

Lucas ran and jumped on.

"Come on, Issy, jump up," he shouted. Rose helped Isabella up, and resting her hand on her leg, the children rocket the horse frantically, laughing with glee. The rest of the afternoon, Rose spent happily playing with the children.

*

By teatime, leaving the children with Freda to have a drink, Rose returned to her room to freshen up. She must go out tomorrow and find some clothes, shaking out her skirt and hoping she still smelt fresh. The door flew open, and Agnes rushed into the room.

"Agnes, you're back; where have you been all day?"

"Me, I've been downtown, as they call it, looking for work at the theatres. And guess what? I've got a job at the Grand Casino Theatre on Broadway. Oh, Rose, it's beautiful. It has electricity and a roof garden."

"I'm so happy for you, Agnes, but how did you manage that?"

"I was looking around when I noticed a board outside asking for chorus singers; I went in and sang my heart out, and bingo, I start on Monday. Oh, and I can share accommodation with the other girls to leave this house and be free to do my own thing. So there, what do you say of that?"

"You mean you're going? But Agnes, I'll be on my

own. What will I do?" cried Rose.

"Look, I'm sorry, and I know, and we can still be friends, but I've got to do this. It's just what I always wanted. So please be happy for me, Rose; you'll be alright. You will soon find something once you get out there. I saw loads of cards in shop windows asking for help."

"Oh, Agnes, I am happy for you. It's just a shock, that's all, and it's happened so quickly."

It was then that Rose noticed Agnes' change of clothes. "You've got new clothes on, Agnes; where did you get them?"

"Oh, these? The girls at the theatre have a chest full of clothes, so they dug these out for me, and when I go tomorrow, they told me to help myself until I start getting paid. They're so lovely and made me feel welcome. I'm so excited; I can't wait to go. Don't worry, Rose, I'll leave my address, and you can visit, maybe watch the show one night. Bright lights, here I come." Agnes laughed as she danced around the room. Rose felt deflated, knowing she would be losing her friend.

*

That night, Thomas, the children, Rose and Agnes enjoyed a roast chicken with vegetables and jam roly-poly with custard.

"I love custard," Lucas remarked, dribbling custard down his chin. Agnes had regaled them at dinner with tales of her day and the fact that she would leave in the morning. Thomas offered the landau and hoped Agnes would be happy in her new position. Rose couldn't help but notice that he didn't try to dissuade her and seemed relieved to know she was going.

"I must shop tomorrow for new clothes," Rose announced. "I'm so sorry to still be in the clothes I arrived in." Agnes looked at Rose, suddenly realising she had not thought of her friend when picking out her clothes and felt a touch of guilt as she turned to apologise to Rose, Thomas Spoke.

"Allow me to escort you to town, Rose. We shall ride on the Blue Train, and I will take you to Macy's." Before Rose could reply, Agnes looked across at Thomas.

"I've heard of Macy's." Agnes replied, piqued, "It's a big posh shop." Thomas looked across at Agnes.

"As I explained to Rose earlier today, I am one of the company's managing directors; it was the reason for my visit to England."

"Oh, but I couldn't possibly; just a good second-hand clothes shop will be fine," interrupted Rose.

"It's no trouble, Rose, and it won't cost me anything, to ease your mind. I have allowances at Macy's."

"Maybe I better come too then," Agnes laughed. Rose noticed that Thomas did not reply and continued to finish his dinner.

*

Dinner finished, and Rose and Agnes retired to bed.

"I will miss you, Agnes. You will keep in touch. Please promise me," whispered Rose.

"Of course I will. It's just what I want. You know that Rose, you're sad, but please wish me luck."

"I do, Agnes," replied Rose.

"And Rose?"

"Yes."

"I'm sorry I didn't bring you some clothes."

*

The following day after a tearful goodbye, Rose stood at the door watching Agnes give a cheery wave and shout.

"Keep in touch," then she disappeared around the corner in the landau. Rose saw Thomas smiling.

"Don't worry about your friend. I have a feeling she

can take care of herself. So come, let us have our adventure today."

At that, Thomas and Rose set off to catch the Blue Train.

CHAPTER FIVE

Stepping down from the train in New York City, Rose was glad to slip her arm into Thomas'. She had never seen so many people. Walking along the pavement, or as Thomas called it, the sidewalk, she saw street vendors selling shoelaces, some with carts selling hot potatoes, vegetables and many other items. It reminded Rose of market day back home, only more crowded. On street corners, young children were selling newspapers, the postman on bicycles and boot blacker. Rose wasn't sure what a boot blacker was, but Thomas soon explained.

"Will you have your shoes shined while here?" inquired Rose. Thomas turned to answer and saw the twinkle of laughter in Rose's eyes. Then, he laughed and suggested that Mrs Longsdon would be most offended.

"No one could put a shine on my shoes like her," he laughed.

Arriving in Herald Square at 34th Street, Broadway, Thomas stopped outside a vast building. Looking up, Rose saw Macy's Department Store sign.

"How high is it?" Rose enquired.

"Eleven storeys," replied Thomas with a laugh.

"Oh my. I've never seen anything so tall." Rose took Thomas' arm as she leaned back to admire the building. Its expansive windows reflected glare from the sun; the building seemed to disappear into the clouds. Then, guiding her through the double doors, Thomas looked at her as she stood in awe — she had never been in anything so massive before.

A bouquet of fragrances from the perfume counter invaded her senses. As Thomas took her elbow, she passed the glove counter, stopping to pick up a soft leather green pair with a leaf motif. She couldn't help but try them on.

"Have them if you like," Thomas offered, "they suit you."

"Are you sure? They are so lovely," whispered Rose.

"Take two or three pairs," smiled Thomas.

"No, just these; they're so soft, thank you."

Moving through the ground floor past the haberdashery, Rose spotted ribbons of all different colours. I must take one for Isabella. So she thought as they stepped into the elevator, taking them to the first floor. Rose held tightly to Thomas; it was a strange sensation feeling herself travel upwards.

"Your first time in an elevator Rose?" Thomas asked, giving a little chuckle.

"It is. I seem to be doing so many things for the first time since arriving in New York." Rose found herself giggling; it was perhaps more by slight nerves, as she hoped the lift would stop when reaching wherever it was going. Not that she said that to Thomas in case he thought her somewhat naive.

Arriving on the first floor, they entered the ladies' department. Everything a lady should want, from beautiful dresses to coats and hats — including ladies' underwear, was displayed under a glass counter. A tall, elegant lady stepped forward,

"Good morning Mr Blackwood. How may I be of assistance?"

"Good morning, Miss Turnbull. May I introduce you to Miss Watson, a dear friend who has lost her belongings due to fire and needs to restock her wardrobe? Please make sure she has everything she requires."

"Of course, Mr Blackwood, our pleasure, please Miss, would you step this way, and I will ask my senior assistant to assist you." A young girl stepped forward when Miss Turnbull turned and clapped her hands.

Rose turned to smile at Thomas and whispered, "Are

you sure?"

Taking her hand, Thomas smiled, "Enjoy yourself, fill your wardrobe, I insist." Then, as Rose disappeared with the sales assistant, Thomas spoke to Miss Turnbull. "Rose is a dear friend; make sure she has at least four of everything; I will leave her in your most capable hands. I have business upstairs but will return within the hour."

"Of course, Mr Blackwood, leave everything to me."

Rose ran her hands down the fresh new clothes, resting against her skin, making her feel like a new woman. Rose wore a russet skirt, matching jacket, hat and purse. Rose thanked the young assistant for her help.

"Would you like me to dispose of your old clothes, Miss?" the assistant asked.

"No, thank you, please wrap them with the others." Rose stepped out of the cubicle to find Thomas waiting for her.

"Have you finished, Rose?" he asked, smiling.

"Yes. I've had such fun trying all the different clothes on." Rose laughed.

"You look lovely." Then, turning to Miss Turnbull, thanking her and instructing the parcels to be delivered, he took Rose's elbow. "Time for lunch, I think."

They sat at a window table overlooking Sixth Avenue in Macy's upstairs restaurant, enjoying a roast pork dinner with dessert. Rose drank her coffee. She looked over the rim of her cup at Thomas. He is such a fine man, Rose thought. But she couldn't help the niggle that had settled into her stomach. She couldn't understand why he was so kind, and now with all her new clothes, she wondered if she had done the wrong thing. Was it because he expected her to be his mistress? No, I'm certainly not one of those, thought Rose.

At last, unable to stay silent,

"Thomas, may I ask you a question? Please don't be

offended by it." Thomas frowned, had he upset her? Had she not enjoyed her lunch?

"Ask away, Rose, and I promise not to be offended."

"Why have you done this for me? I'm so grateful, but it's just, well, why?"

Because dear Rose, I've fallen in love with you. The first time I saw you, Rose. Your innocent beauty and charm. A smile that lights up your face. You do things to me even, my dear wife. But, no, please forgive me, Rosemary, for I loved you deeply.

Thomas couldn't say any of that. So instead, he looked at Rose with a smile.

"I suppose I'm just a softy for young ladies in distress, and you and your friend were that. I want nothing from you, Rose, only to see you happy and know I've helped you start your new life. Please grant me that. Put it down to my good deed for the year."

"Thank you, Thomas, but I will start to look for work next week, and at least now, I will look respectable."

"I have told you, Rose, there is no rush if and when you find something, remember your room is always there."

*

Later that afternoon, there was much excitement in the Blackwood household upstairs in Rose's bedroom. Isabella, Lucas, and Freda enjoyed a fashion parade as Rose showed them her new outfits and shoes she had acquired that morning. Rose was amazed that everything had been delivered to the house before they arrived home. Isabella was dancing around with a new hat that was too big and covered her eyes. Rose had gone to the toy department to purchase a maroon-coloured train engine for Lucas, who was busy running it around the edge of the carpet. Freda had tied Isabella's hair with a red and silver coloured ribbon, and Freda was delighted with a lace handkerchief with her initials in the corner.

Freda sat on the bed, watching the mayhem around her. She smiled. It was the first time Freda had seen and heard the children truly happy for a long time — Freda had a fair judgement of character, and there was something about Rose that was innocent; perhaps Rose should stay with them to look after the children. They seemed happier since she had arrived. Freda had to admit she was glad when Agnes left. There was a wayward side to her, which usually brought trouble. Maybe she should have a word with Thomas.

CHAPTER SIX

Over the next few days, Rose settled into a happy routine. After arguing and persuasion with Freda, Rose took on the morning dusting, cleaning out the fires and general household duties, leaving Freda to her kitchen. It was the least she could do.

When the children had finished their lessons in the afternoon, she took them to the park. It was named Morningside Park, which Rose felt sounded bright and full of sunshine. She loved the rose gardens, the feeling of space and trees reminding her of home. The lake was glistening under the afternoon sun. The children ran around, glad to be free of the classroom. Freda had given them some bread, and the children enjoyed feeding the ducks. There was just a small cloud hanging over Rose, and that was Isabella each day; she always had a sore red mark on her wrist. She had tentatively asked if Lucas had accidentally hurt her, but Isabella would change the subject quickly and talk about Polly, her doll. Rose had her thoughts but, surely not. Perhaps talk it through with Freda. Rose was sure Freda must have noticed the injury because she had helped bathe the children and then cuddled up with them to read a bedtime story the night before — the wound was apparent.

After returning from their walk — there was a note for Rose sitting on the hall table. Opening it, she discovered it was from Agnes asking her to join her for coffee at the coffee shop next to the theatre on Friday morning. She had lots to tell her. Searching out Freda, she asked if she had notepaper and pen to reply and if it would be alright if she went to see Agnes.

"I'll be back in time for the children when they finish their classes," Rose remarked.

"You don't have to ask me for permission. You enjoy

yourself and say hello to your friend from me."

Rose went upstairs to her room, wrote a quick note, and popped out to post; she felt excited to meet her friend. Rose had to admit she'd missed her. But, with all that and the thought of seeing Agnes again, Rose momentarily forgot about Isabella, something she would always regret later.

*

On Friday morning, Rose went to catch the Blue Train into the city, Thomas had offered the landau, but Rose told him she would enjoy the train's thrill and get used to the busy streets and transport. Telling her to be careful and giving her some housekeeping money, Rose left with a spring in her step. She handed her ticket to the conductor as she boarded the train, who smiled at her and chatted while asking her if she had been in New York long. Rose felt a little hesitant, but he seemed friendly enough and made her laugh, introducing himself as Jack Manus.

"This isn't my real job," he smiled. "It just brings in the coppers."

"Oh, what do you do when not collecting tickets?" Rose asked.

"Me, I'm a boxer at night, best in the district; you should come and watch me one night; you'd enjoy it, babe." Rose thought the word babe sounded strange. After all, she didn't know him. Rose thought back to Jack that she had met all those months ago at home with his promises; how odd she should meet another Jack.

Thanking him with a smile, Rose told him she thought boxing wasn't quite for her. Rose stood as the train arrived at its destination.

"I'll see you on the way back," he laughed, then added, "Maybe I can change your mind." As she stepped down, he took off his cap and, with a flourish, bowed,

44

making her laugh.

Leaving the station and asking for directions, Rose eventually found the theatre café. She neared the door and spotted Agnes sitting in the window, who jumped up, smiling and waving as she entered, throwing their arms around each other and settling into their seats. Agnes ordered tea and cakes, and soon the girls were chatting. Agnes talked, telling Rose about her life at the house she shared with her new friends and her work at the theatre.

"Oh, I can't tell you how great it is; they make you work hard. My feet were so sore for the first few days that I was glad to fall into bed after."

"You're enjoying it, then, Agnes?" Rose smiled.

"Oh, yes, it's just brilliant. I miss you, Rose; let's make this our morning for coffee. You see, it's the only time I have off."

"Well, I can't promise I might get a job, but we'll try."

"Have you found anything yet?"

"No, but I'm going to start looking next week."

"Thought you'd have your feet under the table by now, Rose. Hasn't he asked you to stay? I mean, he's besotted with you."

"Don't be silly, Agnes. He is not, and Thomas has not asked me to stay."

"Thomas is it now?" laughed Agnes.

"Stop it," laughed Rose as she gently tapped her friend's arm. "It would be nice, though. I love the time with the children there. So sweet, and we have such fun." Rose looked thoughtful for a moment before finishing her cake. Then, all too soon, Agnes stood, saying she had to get back for rehearsals.

"Don't forget to meet me here next Friday, babe, ok?" Agnes asked. There was that word again, thought Rose.

"I won't forget; I'll send a note if anything happens."

Leaving the café, Rose wondered whether to go into Macy's again. She had not had the chance to browse last time, and it would be nice to see what else the shop had to offer. Rose had an hour before her train. As she entered the store, the concierge tapped his hat as he opened the door for her. She felt a thrill of excitement; to mingle with the other shoppers was something Rose had never done before, certainly not in a store like this. Her life back home was the butchers, bread shop, and the market on a Friday; she was never allowed to browse. Her father would have called her lazy or worse.

After spending an enjoyable half-hour, reluctantly, it was time to leave if she was to catch her train; she didn't want to be late back for the children as she promised them a trip to the park. Boarding the train, Rose was not surprised to see young Jack. He took out a handkerchief flicking it over the seat in front of her; Rose laughed as she sat down. By the time she arrived at her stop, Jack had tried to ask for her home address so he could call on her and take her for an evening stroll, but Rose was reluctant. So instead, she told him she would surely see him again next week when she revisited her friend. He gave her a hound-dog look, said he would wait until then, and wished her goodbye with a bow.

CHAPTER SEVEN

Arriving at the house, Rose dashed upstairs to change into her day dress and headed for the kitchen, where Freda was busy making an apple pie. The aroma filled her nostrils and made her stomach rumble.

"Enjoyed your morning?" smiled Freda.

"Oh yes, it was good to see Agnes again; her new life suits her. She was energetic and told me about her life at the theatre. I'm pleased for her. I hope nothing goes wrong."

"Why do you think something might go wrong?"

"Nothing, nothing at all. Agnes seems on cloud nine, and it would be terrible if they told her she couldn't stay. I don't know, Freda. It's just me."

"She's unsettled, you lass. That's the problem; you haven't found work yet," she confirmed, "...not that you have to mind." Freda added quickly, not wanting Rose to think she didn't want her.

"I'll go out and find work next week."

"You don't have to. You're fine as you are. You are such a help to me. Should I speak with the Master and see if you can stay on here?"

"No, Freda, if he had wanted me here, he would have said. So please don't say anything. I'm fine. It's just me." Suddenly the sound of feet running along the corridor, throwing open the kitchen door, heralded the children.

*

After lunch, Rose got the children's coats on and set off to the park, Lucas carried a paper bag full of bread to feed the ducks. Isabella was holding her doll. Freda stood watching them from the window, sighing. Thomas was a fool — that young lass was what this house needed. Another thing to worry about was Isabella. Rose mentioned a few nights ago that the marks on her poor wrists were getting worse, but both didn't think that Lucas could do that. He always seemed so caring to his sister. If it got worse, she would mention it to Thomas.

*

While playing with the children in the park, another little girl Isabella's age, joined them, bringing a ball with her.

"Please can we play piggy-in-the-middle?" she asked. Rose smiled as she looked around to see a nanny in a grey uniform sitting on the seat.

She waved and smiled, "I hope you don't mind?" she said. "Only Lillibet is lonely."

"No, of course not," Rose replied, and for the next half hour, the children played happily together. Then, leaving them to throw bread to the ducks, Rose went to sit on the bench and introduced herself to the nanny.

"My name is Maggie, short for Margaret," she laughed, "please call me Maggie. I've seen you before with the children, and I thought it alright for Lillibet to join you this time."

"Of course, she is always welcome," smiled Rose. They soon got chatting while keeping an eye on the children, and Rose found it nice to meet someone different; she learnt that Maggie was twenty-six and worked at the Carmichael's house, the Master being a banker, and his wife Veronica, Lillibet was their only child.

"Are you a friend, as you are not in uniform?" asked Maggie.

"Yes," replied Rose. She felt more comfortable than trying to explain her situation. "I'm looking for work; I've just not started looking properly yet."

"What sort of work?" Maggie asked.

"Oh, a maid's job would be excellent; I've not had much experience but did look after my father and brother and keep the farm going, so I know what's needed."

"They need a maid at the house; our maid left last week to marry, we're short of help. So why don't you speak to the housekeeper Mrs Young, a bit of a battle-axe, but she is fair. It's only round the corner, so you could walk to where you're staying."

"Oh, thank you, I'll do that," answered Rose.

"Tell her you met Maggie, and I recommended you call; I'll mention it when I return. Can't promise mind, but you never know."

Rose thanked her, and they chatted a bit more, Maggie telling her a little about her family and that she worked for Lord and Lady Carmichael.

"Are they connected to royalty?" asked Rose.

"Oh no, well, not that I know of. Lord Carmichael's father owned an estate in Aberdeenshire, Scotland, England, where you come from."

"I come from England but lived on the Moors in Yorkshire, far from Scotland."

"Yes, I don't know a thing about England, but it all sounds nice. When his father died, the Master decided to sell up and come to New York with his new bride Lady Veronica Carmichael. He brought his title because he's a Governor at Wells Fargo and Citibank."

"How exciting to be working for his Lordship." Rose smiled.

"They are good people, and yes, I enjoy being a nanny to Lillibet." Suddenly Maggie's hand flew to her mouth. "Oh, dear, I've gossiped. Please don't tell anyone. I don't normally, what got into me!" frowned Maggie.

"Don't worry, I won't," replied Rose.

"It's time I got my little charge home. It's good to meet you. I hope to see you again." Maggie smiled at Rose.

Going their separate ways at the park gate, Rose

promised she would call around the next day.

"Come about eleven. Housekeeper has her break then."

*

Thomas could not join the family for tea as he had a meeting at work, so Rose ate with Freda and the children in the kitchen. Over dinner, Rose told Freda of Margaret.

"I met her in the park — she's Nanny to Lillibet, who played with the children. Maggie mentioned a vacancy at Carmichael's residence. So I promised to call around 11.a.m. tomorrow. Hopefully, I might be lucky."

"Oh, I know the Carmichael family lost their little boy two years ago to diphtheria. It was a terrible time. They only have the little lass now, a nice family. You don't have to go; I've told you there's no rush." Freda sighed.

"You're all kind, but I must find work."

Suddenly, Isabella began to cry. Rose gathered her into her arms.

"Don't cry, pet," Rose stroked her hair to try and soothe her.

"Please don't go, please don't leave us," Isabella cried even more, "I promise to be good."

"Oh, darling, you are always good, but I must find work. I can't keep relying on your Papa. Comm'n now, bath time, and then I'll read you your favourite story; how's that?" Rose stood, taking Isabella's hand.

Lucas sprang to his feet, bright red. He shouted at Rose, "You're horrid; you've upset Issy!" he ran from the kitchen.

"Oh, Freda, I didn't mean to upset them," Rose said, tears in her eyes.

"Don't worry, they're young and got used to you. They'll soon settle," but Freda didn't think so.

After bathing the children and dressing them in pyjamas and a nighty, Rose and Freda couldn't help but notice Isabella's wrist was sore and getting worse.

"Why don't you talk to the little mite while you read to her?" whispered Freda. "I can't believe it's Lucas. It's not like him, but who else could it be?" Freda was puzzled, but Rose had another thought, remembering her Sunday School teacher forcing two little girls to use their right hand because only the devil wrote left-handed, she had told the class. She had gone home that afternoon and told her mother what had happened, remembering her mother telling her that the teacher was wrong. If that's the case now, Rose was angry.

Sitting on the bed, leaning against the pillow, Isabella snuggled up to Rose; Lucas was still sulking as he ran his train engine along the windowsill and refused to sit with Rose and his sister. Instead, leaving his machine, he sat on the chair, scowling. Rose opened the book to read but then laid it down on the bedspread in a hushed tone. She finally asked Isabella.

"How did you hurt your wrist? Please tell me, sweetheart."

"I can't. It's a secret," Isabella whispered.

"Lucas, do you know how this happened?"

"No, and it's not my fault," he scowled.

"I'm not blaming you, Lucas, but this has to stop; I can only stop it if you tell me, please, I want to help," said Rose.

"No, you don't, you don't care... you're leaving us," shouted Lucas; Isabella began to cry. Rose hugged her gently, stroking the back of her head to soothe her.

"Please, sweetheart, please tell me. I know it's not your brother."

"Don't, Issy, it's a secret," shouted Lucas.

Rose took a deep breath. "Is it your teacher Isabella?"

"If I tell, she said Papa would send me to the madhouse and lock me away forever because I'm the devil." Rose was horrified by what Isabella had told her.

"No, sweetheart, you're not the devil, and no one, not even your Papa, would send you away. What a cruel thing to say to you."

"It's true, and Miss Eleanor says only the devils are left-handed," Lucas said sullenly, who by now was standing at the end of the bed. "She ties Issy's hand to the chair so she can't use it."

"It hurts," cried Isabella.

"Oh, sweetheart, I will not allow that to happen; you will never see that woman again. Also, I will speak to your Papa in the morning. You will stay with Freda in the kitchen when the teacher arrives."

"Don't go, please don't go," cried Isabella — as Lucas ran to Rose, flinging his arms around her neck. After more hugs and reassurance, Rose put some soothing oil on Isabella's wrist and settled the children down; they seemed exhausted after their upset.

Rose was furious as she entered the kitchen and upset with herself for not doing something sooner. Rose felt she would never forgive herself for allowing Isabella to suffer. Then, finding Freda sitting at the table, Rose slumped into the chair.

"You look like you need a cup of tea."

"Oh, Freda, the children have told me how Isabella got her sore wrist." Then, over a cup of tea, Rose told Freda everything.

"My mother was left-handed. God bless her," replied Freda.

"I told Isabella she would never see that teacher again. But what if Thomas insists and tells Miss Eleanor off? I've promised the child."

"More likely, he'll throttle the woman. There'll be murder in this house if we're not careful. We'll tell him in the morning, and you stay with the children. I think I need to be there. Don't want him up for murder — the horrid, horrid woman. I should have said something sooner; he'll be mad at me for not voicing my thoughts. Let's head for our beds; we'll need our strength in the morning."

CHAPTER EIGHT

Thomas' voice resonated through the house, making the cups rattle in their saucers. Little Isabella curled up into Rose's lap, gently crying. Lucas, pale and shaking, stood close. Rose tried to make light of everything, telling them she would take them to the park and buy them ice cream, but she couldn't comfort them. Suddenly, there were many banging doors. Rose heard footsteps running up the stairs, silence for a short time, and then the front door slammed shut. Thomas' voice boomed again, and then suddenly; the kitchen door flew open, Thomas filled the doorway as Freda tried to slip past him.

"Why didn't you tell me earlier? I thought you were looking after the children," Thomas bellowed, making Rose shake.

Lucas ran to his father. "Papa, Papa, stop it!" he shouted, "It's not Rose's fault. It was the teacher. She said you'd send Issy away and wouldn't want her." Isabella slipped from Rose's lap and ran to her father; she cried uncontrollably, gripping him around the waist.

"Please, Papa, don't send Rose away; I want her to stay. Please, please." Thomas hugged his children. He had never seen them in such distress since their late mother's death. He struggled to understand what they were saying. What did they mean Rose was leaving, going where, when? He told them he loved them soothingly and that what had happened was not their fault.

"But you're sending Rose away, please, Papa, please let her stay," cried Isabella.

"I'm not sending Rose anywhere," replied a somewhat puzzled Thomas. After their father's many hugs and cuddles, everyone sat at the kitchen table. Freda made tea; the children had lemonade and biscuits. Rose cuddled

Isabella, with Lucas sat beside her. Rose explained Carmichael's residence position.

Thomas looked across at Rose, his heart heavy as he spoke.

"It's your choice, of course, Rose, but it seems you're needed here; please stay, be nanny to these two. I'll pay a wage, everything above board, but I insist on no uniform, can't stand uniforms."

"What about the Carmichaels?"

"I'll send them a note. I know Carmichaels, they're friends; I will speak to them later. They'll understand. That is, of course, you want to stay, Rose?"

"I would love to."

"Thank God for that. Can we get back to some normality now?" Freda asked.

"What about their lessons?" asked Rose.

"My secretary's nephew is a teacher. The other day, she told me that his student no longer requires his services as the family has sent him to boarding school. He's very nice. I've met him," replied Thomas. His name is Mr David Harold, in his early forties, not married, and a quiet, caring attitude," seeing the panic in Isabella's eyes. Then, holding his arms out, the children went to their father, his voice breaking. He promised them he would never allow anyone to harm them and that little Issy was exceptional, just like her mother, because she was left-handed. And Lucas had been fearless in trying to protect his sister.

"Now, no more tears. I think it's time we all went to the park and had fun, and then we will go to the park café and have lunch; how does that sound?"

"Yes, please!" the children chorused.

"And what about work?" Freda asked.

"It can wait," replied Thomas.

*

Rose collapsed into bed that night. It had been a day. She felt exhausted; they'd had great fun in the park and enjoyed lunch. The children were wholly spoilt, but for once, no one cared. The relief that she would stay at the house made her heart sing. I'm so lucky, she thought. For some reason, she suddenly thought of Jack and smiled. He seemed nice and had made her laugh; would she see him again on Friday? Before she could think of anything else, Rose fell into a deep sleep.

CHAPTER NINE

SIX MONTHS LATER
Agnes

"Corr, my feet are killing me," Agnes moaned, kicking off her shoes and rubbing them after returning to the theatre dressing room. "Suppose that the choreographer shouts AGAIN, LADIES, AGAIN. I will hit him."

"You are moaning again?" laughed her friend Lizzie.

Agnes stuck her tongue out. "Do you think it will be a full house again tonight? I swear they couldn't get one more person in last night. Oh, it's so good to see the theatre full," Agnes replied.

"What you mean is you can't wait to see lover boy." Lizzie laughed. "Are you going to move in and become his woman?"

"You make it sound wrong," Agnes sighed.

"Well, what other way can you put it? Come on, and he's setting you up in a posh flat, sorry, suite — just across the way and telling you, 'You're my girl' — has he asked you to marry him?" Agnes shook her head at Lizzie. "No, didn't think so, and he never will."

"I don't care; I love him and haven't come to America to be a chorus showgirl. Ok, I sound hard, but I will make it big, and he's my ticket."

"I shouldn't let him hear you say that," laughed Lizzie.

"Oh, I love him, not just for what he can do for me. I didn't mean it to sound like that," sighed Agnes. "God, I'm beginning to sound callous, and I'm not honest. I'm not."

"Yeh, right, I believe you," Lizzie giggled. Then, as they left through the side stage door, her man waited.

"Afternoon, ladies."

"Hello Paul, have we kept you waiting?

Unfortunately, rehearsals ran over a bit," swooned Agnes.

Lizzie stood and smiled as she turned to hug Agnes before leaving the two lovebirds; she most definitely was not going to play gooseberry.

"See you later, Agnes," and Lizzie was gone.

Agnes leaned down to kiss him; he returned the gesture with a full-blown kiss, taking her breath away.

"Ready, babe. I've something to show you."

"Oh, yes, I'm all yours," smiled Agnes. Taking her hand, he crossed the road dashing in and out of the traffic and avoiding the horse dung. They stood outside a blue-painted building named Casino Suites. Tom, the concierge smartly dressed in a blue uniform and white gloves, opened the door.

"Afternoon, Tom. I trust everything is ready?" asked Paul.

"All ready, sir. I saw to it myself."

Paul guided Agnes to the elevator, and all too soon, the doors opened into a light, spacious hallway turning left. They headed to the end of the hall; still holding Agnes' hand, Paul threw the door open and stepped into the suite. Agnes gasped; she had seen it before, but not like this.

Paul had spent extravagantly. Above the marble fireplace hung the painting of 'The Card Players' by Paul Cezanne. A crystal chandelier hung, throwing diamonds across the ceiling. Cream drapes full length at the windows looking down 42nd Street. Beyond that, two double oak doors opened into a stunning dining room with a solid oak table for at least twelve high-back chairs and russet seating. An oak sideboard filled the end wall. Another opulent chandelier hung low over the table. Again, the full-length curtains matched the chair covers hung at the double-aspect windows. Finally, two sliding oak doors opened to reveal a main bedroom from the main room; Agnes had never seen such a massive bed. Its red silk bedding and a coverlet flowed to the floor. A cream chaise longue sat at the foot of the bed. Again, red and cream full-length curtains at the windows overlooked the courtyard.

Paul took Agnes into his arms, kissing her passionately.

"This, my darling, is all yours and, of course, mine," he smiled. "Remember. My girl now."

"Oh, Paul, of course, I'm your girl. You know that." Agnes threw her arms around his neck, her hand sliding down to his groin. He stopped her, lifting and kissing her hand before turning away.

"Not now, sweetheart; I've got another job to do. See you in the Roof Garden after the show." A maid returned to the main room and held a tray with two champagne glasses.

"By the way, this is Grazina, our housekeeper; you don't have to lift a finger." Then, after grasping a glass and downing his drink in one, Paul was gone, leaving Agnes to look at Grazina, a short middle-aged woman, her greying hair tied tightly back into a bun, dressed in a grey dress with a white frilled apron.

Agnes smiled at her; "Can I call you Grazina?"

"Of course, Ma'am," she replied. "Would you like another drink?"

"No, thank you, if I drink any more, I'll not be fit to perform later," Agnes laughed.

"I'll be in the kitchen, Ma'am, if you need me." Grazina turned to leave.

"Grazina?"

"Yes, Ma'am,"

"Do you live in?"

"Oh yes, Ma'am, I have a room next door, so I'm not far away if you need me." Leaving Agnes and disappearing through swing doors that must have taken her to the kitchen, which Agnes had not seen so far. Agnes sat on the sofa to gather her thoughts. She felt her heart flutter as she took in her surroundings. The opulence almost overwhelmed her. Never in her wildest dreams would Agnes Clarke become the mistress of such a place. And yes, the mistress was what she was, and Agnes didn't care. Thinking back to her first meeting with Paul after the late show three weeks ago, he had appeared in the girls changing room and, in front of scantily dressed girls, introduced himself as Paul Kelly inviting her to join him for champagne on the roof garden. The roof garden was a place Agnes admired; they had performed there many times.

The sliding roof was beautiful. Agnes had first seen it when it began to close during a show. She was so awed that she had missed her cue — she felt Lizzie's hand in the middle of her back, giving her a mighty shove to join the end of the dance group. Sitting down that night with Paul Kelly was a dream. Other girls looked her way, some admiring, others scowling. Paul Kelly wasn't your typical tall, handsome lover, well, not at five foot two, but he was educated and carried a sophisticated persona with steely blue eyes. He introduced her to his colleagues, whose eyes seemed to travel over her body as if assessing her value. It had made her uncomfortable then, but now they knew she was Paul's girl, and they showed her respect.

He had told her he was a boxer, a damn good boxer. He earned money through bouts. Having gone one night, it was not Agnes' taste. She thought it raw, bloody and brutal. But she told him she didn't like to see him hit, so he didn't retake her. Agnes knew he was also the leader of the Five Points Gang ruling the east side of New York. Agnes turned a blind eye and didn't want to know what that entailed. Since meeting him, Paul had showered her with gifts, gold and silver necklaces, bracelets, and the finest clothes from Macy's, making her feel like a lady for the first time. And now, she was in this suite just for them; it was beautiful.

Paul Kelly was also a jealous man. Agnes had found out early in their relationship when Paul had seen her chatting to a chap who had stopped at the stage door; Paul had flattened him and struck her hard across her face, sending her flying. The next day he was full of remorse.

"You're my girl," he hissed. "I vow never to strike you again." Paul had kissed her hard, drawing blood on her lips. Agnes was careful not to give him a cause. Instead, taking her to a nightclub where champagne flowed and presented her with the gold necklace, she wore now. She had told him about Rose, telling him she couldn't give up their Friday visits.

"Rose is my friend."

"Whatever makes you happy, babe," he had said.

During their Friday morning coffee, Agnes told Rose all about Paul Kelly. Agnes had seen the doubt in her friend's eyes.

"But Agnes, he's making you a kept woman," Rose whispered that day.

"Yeah, I know, babe," she had said. "But I love him, and it's what I want. So please be happy for me, don't judge, hun." She had begged, they hugged, and Rose promised to always be there for her. Their friendship would never wane. Rose had told her about her new beau, Jack Manus, how she had met him, and a regular visitor to the house. Taking her to shows and sometimes walks in the park. Her cheeks had blushed as she spoke of him, and Agnes knew their friendship was blossoming. Rose didn't know that Jack Manus was a member of the

Eastman gang that ran the Lower East Side of New York. Agnes had met him one night at the show at the roof garden. Paul introduced him to her as 'Eat'em Up Jack' and laughed.

"He's with Monk Eastman, mobster of Lower Manhattan we rub along just," hissed Paul. Jack didn't know Agnes, but she knew him, which troubled her. Should she say something? Rose was gentle and somewhat innocent, and Agnes didn't want to see her friend hurt. However, she was annoyed that Jack kept that little secret. Over time, Agnes had learnt that there was tension between the Five Points Gang and Monk Eastman's. Paul had told her that Eastman is known as a 'Monk' short for Monkey, as he reminded his team of an ape — a massive brute of a man.

Not a week passed without a gang member from either group retrieved from the Hudson River. Should she tell? Agnes wasn't sure. She didn't want Rose to think she was trying to spoil things for her. Perhaps Rose would see through him before it's too late.

CHAPTER TEN

The following Friday, Agnes and Rose were in the café drinking coffee, which seemed to be a favourite for Americans, rather than tea. Agnes was full of excitement about her new abode.

"Oh, Rose, you must come and see it. Please say you will. I know Thomas doesn't like me very much, but I want you to see it."

"Why don't I come next Friday instead of here? I'll meet you there, and you can show me around."

Agnes suddenly rummaged in her bag.

"Here, Rose, I nearly forgot I'd got tickets to the family Christmas show in two weeks. There's enough for everyone; bring the kids. They'll love it. It's the one time of the year it opens just for families, and I'm playing the lead role. So promise me you'll come."

"I'll mention it to Thomas when I get back. If it's a family show, there should be no problem. When I see you next Friday, I'll let you know."

"Brilliant, I can't wait... Is that the time? I've got to go." Outside the restaurant, the girls hugged.

"See you Friday, bye babe." At that, Agnes dashed off, and Rose made her way home.

*

Two weeks later and only two days before Christmas, Thomas, Rose, the children, and Freda sat in the front row, enjoying the show. Chorus dancers in red and white costumes wore huge feather plumes on their heads. Acrobats threw coloured balls into the air catching them with ease. A pretty girl in white performed on a unicycle. It was spectacular, and Agnes performed beautifully with such a magnificent voice, Rose thought. Finally, Father Christmas arrived, and all the children had gifts. Afterwards, they joined Paul and Agnes for drinks and food. The children received more Christmas gifts from Agnes and Paul, which Thomas said they must put under the Christmas tree when they return home.

That night, the children had settled into bed, exhausted and happy. Rose, Freda and Thomas sat drinking hot chocolate.

"What a marvellous performance, your friend Agnes can certainly sing!" Freda exclaimed.

"Did you enjoy it, Thomas?" Rose asked.

"Yes, Rose, I enjoyed the evening very much, although I'm not too keen on this Paul Kelly chap. I understand he's a gang member. You will be careful, Rose. I wouldn't want you getting too involved, not that it's any business of mine, only, well, I feel you should be careful," said Thomas. Rose said nothing, and there was a sudden unease in the air.

Freda broke the silence. "Where was that young man of yours? I thought he would have joined us for the evening."

"Oh, he was going to, only something cropped up," replied Rose.

Thomas looked across at Rose. He knew all about Jack Manus. He wouldn't be responsible for his actions if he ever hurt Rose. If only I could persuade Rose that Jack was not her type, but how without sounding petty or trying to spoil her fun. One day he'll slip up, and Thomas knew he would be there for Rose. He just hoped it would be sooner rather than later.

"Well, I'm for my bed," said Freda.

"Me too," smiled Rose, getting up to rinse the cups and saying goodnight to Thomas. The ladies left him to his thoughts.

CHAPTER ELEVEN

A NEW YEAR

Rose woke early on Christmas morning, mainly because Lucas and Isabella jumped up and down on her bed with a gleeful shout.

"It's Christmas, Rose. Please wake up!" Isabella shook her shoulders.

"You little minxes," she laughed, giving them both hugs. "I'm coming; let's get dressed before we go down. Go on, scoot — clothes on."

Thomas and Freda were already in the lounge, standing in front of an enormous Christmas tree, when the door flew open, and two excited children rushed in, closely followed by Rose.

"Papa, Papa!" the children shouted, running to hug him. Returning the hug, Thomas gently ushered them out of the room.

"Breakfast first, I think, and then morning service."

"Oh, Papa, can't we open the presents now?" asked Lucas with a pout.

"No, you know we go to church first," their father replied, smiling.

*

It was a beautiful morning with a sharp frost as Rose and the family left to attend church. Even though the children couldn't wait to open their presents, they enjoyed the early service of carols and greetings from all the parishioners. During the service, Rose thought of her life at home the previous Christmas; it had not been happy. They had attended chapel as usual and then returned home with her mother to exchange gifts. Her father and brother were drinking from a jug of beer on the way back from the chapel. There was no gift from them. Instead, she would help her mother prepare the Christmas dinner of roast chicken killed the day before, vegetables picked by Rose from their garden, finishing with a fruit pudding after filling their stomachs. Her brother and father slept the rest of the afternoon.

Rose had always tried to escape the house for a walk — tempting her mother to join her. Christmas at home for Rose was just like any other day. But not this year. This Christmas was going to be full of fun and laughter. Brought out of her reveries by Thomas, who had gently taken her elbow, Rose smiled.

*

Leaving the church, they offered Christmas greetings to the vicar and others. They returned home, and Freda went to the kitchen to check the goose and start the vegetables before returning to the lounge to join the family and Rose — the children squealing with excitement. The carpet had disappeared beneath wrapping paper and boxes. Isabella received a silver monogrammed mirror, a brush set, a new doll, sweets, and nuts. Freda gave her handkerchiefs embroidered with her initial in the corner. Lucas was already playing with his clockwork soldiers and received model carriages for his train set, including sweets and nuts.

Rose gave Freda a gift of a scarf and gloves in soft cream wool — to much laughter, Freda had brought the same for Rose but in a different colour, purple. Next, Thomas gave Rose a silver bracelet; a tear of delight slipped down her cheek as she put it onto her wrist. Running her finger around it, Rose thought she had never had anything so beautiful. For Freda, Thomas gave her a multi-coloured shawl edged with silk fringing. Finally, Freda and Rose brought Thomas a joint gift of silver ink and a pen set mounted in rosewood for his study. Afterwards, Freda and Rose slipped to the kitchen, leaving Thomas to play with the children. All too soon, the dining table almost groaned under the weight of the food. When it was time for the Christmas pudding, Freda carried it to the table; a blue flame danced around it after Freda had poured brandy over it and then lit it; there were cries of "Oohs" and "Aahs." Lucas and Isabella found a silver dollar each in their portion.

Later after Rose and Freda had washed up and cleared the dishes, the children played in front of a roaring fire. Finally, Thomas, Freda and Rose sat enjoying a coffee.

*

Freda and Rose served cold meat and salad for tea in the early evening, finishing with a Christmas cake slice. Later than usual, the children, happy and exhausted after their day, were fast asleep in bed. Thomas, Rose and Freda sat enjoying a hot cup of chocolate before bedtime.

"What a wonderful day," smiled Rose as she took Freda's hand and gently squeezed it. Thomas smiled.

"For me, too," he said, "Thank you both."

CHAPTER TWELVE

A few days later, Jack called for Rose to ask if she would walk in the park. It was a bright, crisp day, and Rose suggested taking Lucas and Isabella with them as they had been indoors for the last two days.

"Yeah, sure," replied Jack.

But Freda had caught the look of annoyance on his face.

"Why don't you and Jack go alone?" suggested Freda.

Lucas had already heard and was struggling into his boots.

"No, it's fine, Freda; Jack doesn't mind, do you, Jack?"

"No, it's fine. Come on then, let's be off."

Arriving at the park, Lucas and Isabella, glad to be out of the house, ran around in the fallen leaves, kicking them in swirling masses as they let off steam. Jack sulked that Rose had brought the children with her; he wanted her to himself. One thing for sure, he thought, those damn kids can take a bloody running jump when she becomes my girl. Jack had not popped the question, nor was he ever likely to; he just wanted Rose for the same reasons as Paul Kelly had for her friend, Agnes.

"By the way, we've had an invite to a New Year's Eve party at the Casino Royale with your friend Agnes. You will come?" Jack asked, looking at Rose. "Lots of food, champagne, dancing. It will be a great night."

"Oh, Jack, that sounds so exciting. I'd love to come. I've never been to a New Year's Eve party before. It was 'just another night' for us at home." Jack slipped his arm around her shoulder.

"Well, babe, I'll make it the best New Year's Eve party you'll ever have. How's that!"

"There's one thing, Jack, it's Lucas' birthday that day.

He'll be six. We're arranging a birthday party for him in the afternoon," whispered Rose, not wanting Lucas to hear.

Bloody kids, thought Jack. "Well, that's during the afternoon, so you'll be free in the evening. After all, the kids will be in bed by then. I'm not picking you up until eight, so you'll be fine. So come on, say you'll come. Otherwise, I'll stay home alone because I couldn't possibly go without you." Jack smiled at Rose, knowing that was a lie.

CHAPTER THIRTEEN

There was massive excitement in the Blackwood household on New Year's Eve. Lucas opened his birthday presents — Lillibet from the Carmichael family also joined the birthday party tea in the dining room. She had given Lucas a set of coloured marbles. Rose organised party games of musical chairs and hide and seek, which caused many giggles when Isabella forgot she had to stay silent while hiding behind the curtains. Near the end, Freda carried the birthday cake in as everyone sang Happy Birthday, and Lucas blew out his six candles. Lillibet's nanny Maggie, called around six o'clock, taking cake slices for her parents and herself. It had been a lovely afternoon.

*

Rose was dressed and ready by eight, waiting in the kitchen with Freda.

"Oh, I wish I wasn't going now; I should stay here with you and Thomas to wish you Happy New Year!" Rose exclaimed.

"Rubbish Rose, you're young, go and enjoy your evening and have lots of fun. You can tell me all about it in the morning," smiled Freda.

The knock at the kitchen door heralded the arrival of Jack's buddy Stan, looking smart in his brown velvet jacket and white shirt with an open next collar. Freda thought the black trousers and dark brown brogues didn't quite match but smiled.

"Where's Jack" Rose inquired.

"He couldn't come, luv. Jack had a job to do, so you got me instead, don't fret; I'll see you safe the carriage is waiting." He smirked at Rose as he looked her up and down.

Freda felt immediately concerned. Taking Rose's

hand, she whispered,

"Are you sure about this? Do you know this, Stan?"

"Don't fret, Freda. He's a friend of Jack's, so it will be fine, although I would rather have had Jack pick me up." At that, Rose collected her shawl and followed Stan out.

Stan seemed to shift in his seat on the way until his thighs touched Rose's, who shuffled as far as she could to the end of the carriage seat. Thankfully they arrived unscathed at the Casino.

As Rose stepped down from the carriage, she was pleased to see Agnes, who rushed up and hugged her.

"I'm glad you're here; it will be a brilliant night." At that, Agnes hooked arms with Rose, and they entered the Casino Royale and went up to the roof garden where a live band played and drinks were already in full flow.

Standing at the bar, Rose spotted Jack, who was in deep conversation with a giant of a man. He spotted Rose and came towards her.

"High babe, sorry I couldn't collect you; hope Stan looked after you?"

"I thought you would have collected me, Jack." She knew she sounded a little miffed and had not enjoyed the journey with Stan, but she wouldn't tell Jack that.

"Yeah, sorry, babe, I'll make it up to you. Let's have a great night."

At that, Agnes appeared. "Come on, Rose, let me introduce you to Paul's friends." Taking her arm, Agnes took her across the room to a booth where Paul and several of his mates sat. They stood as Agnes and Rose arrived — Paul clicking his fingers to a passing server, demanded champaign. Jack sidled into the end seat, and Rose noticed he seemed uncomfortable running his finger around his collar. She couldn't help but see that Paul and his friends did not acknowledge Jack's presence.

As the evening progressed, Rose began to relax. She

had several dances with the gentlemen at the table, and although Rose felt their eyes wander over her body, they behaved impeccably. First, she danced with Jack, who appeared to have two left feet. Either that or he seemed drunker by the minute, sometimes slouching off to the bar and talking to 'the giant' Rose had called him.

Leaning to whisper in Agnes' ear, Rose asked, "Who is that man? Jack's talking to?" Paul Kelly had overheard and leaned forward.

"Keep away from Eastman, Rose; I should pick someone better than Jack. He's nought but trouble. Go on, Agnes, tell her — I thought she was your best friend."

"What does he mean, Agnes?"

"Oh, Rose, I didn't want to tell you, but Jack is an Eastman Gang member. That's Monk Eastman, the boss who runs Lower East Side. You should be careful; I know things you don't."

"That's not very nice of you, Agnes," Rose felt slightly hurt by her remark.

"Oh babe, I don't want to upset you; I know you've gone out for some time now, but I was going to mention it to you in the New Year. Jack is not who you think he is."

"Well, who is then?" Rose realised she had raised her voice. Although Rose felt braver because of the drink, she knew she'd had too much.

"Look, not here, Rose. Next Friday, let's meet, and I'll tell you about him and the Eastman Gang. Let's not spoil the night." Agnes threw her arms around Rose to diffuse the situation that had arisen. Jack reappeared, grabbing Rose's arm and dragged her onto the dance floor.

*

A buffet was on a long table against the far wall. There was fresh salmon and muscles Rose had never tried before. Agnes laughed when she gave her one, and Rose squinted and spluttered after eating it. Also, platters of fresh ham and chicken with salad, fruit dishes with cream and in the centre of the table, a massive cake decorated with Happy New Year 1898. At one point, Jack had taken Rose, introducing her to Monk Eastman, who had clasped her hands and taken her onto the dance floor; his body odour and beer breath were overpowering. He towered over her — she felt his eyes undressing her.

"So, you're his girl then?" he snarled, "Found a place yet, or are you shacking up in his pit?" Eastman let out a belly of a laugh. Rose was horrified and glad when the music finished rushing over to Agnes.

Paul stood his hands in tight fists as he glared at Eastman. Rose thought a fight would ensue momentarily, but Agnes giggled, kissing Paul's lips, easing the tension. Then, all too soon, the time came; everyone gathered in a circle as 'Auld Lang Syne' was sung, the clocks chimed midnight, a cascade of multi-coloured balloons dropped from the ceiling, and there was a lot of back-slapping and kissing. Jack grabbed Rose, smothering her with a kiss of alcoholic fumes before she knew what was happening. Still, she laughed and joined in; Paul offered a kiss on her cheek, as did his friends. It had been a great evening, one that Rose had never had before.

Then, finally, people started to drift away; Jack stood at the coating booth waiting for Rose to say her goodbyes before heading for the doors out into the cold night. He seemed to stagger and lose his footing slightly as he escorted her to the carriage. Rose knew he had drunk far too much. Jack knocked on the carriage roof as they neared home, stopping it. He paid the driver.

"Jack, why have we stopped here?" Rose was puzzled. It was late — she was tired and ready for home.

"Let's walk the rest of the way," smiled Jack. "I've

hardly had you to myself all night." Rose looked out of the carriage. The streets were dark — hardly anyone was around, and she shivered slightly.

"No, Jack, let's carry on. I'm tired. Just take me home." Rose frowned.

"Come on, where's your adventure... please. It's only ten minutes from the house, just a little walk, please?" grinned Jack.

Reluctantly Rose stepped down, and the carriage drove away, leaving them alone. Jack slung his arm around her shoulders, gently pushing her along.

Rose felt her pulse quicken, this felt wrong, and she was glad of the lights in the shop windows, but they didn't give too much illumination. Rose looked around, hoping to see others, but the street was empty.

"You know you're my girl, don't you, Rose," Jack's voice slurred. "I've decided we'll set up a house together, just you and me, babe; how about it?"

Rose wasn't sure what to say; she certainly wouldn't live in sin.

"Are you proposing, Jack?" Rose asked softly.

"Ay, you what, girl? No, don't be daft. You and I can just set up and live happily ever after. You know that's what you won't, don't you, babe?"

Before she could reply, Jack shoved her against the last shop door. As he drooled over her face like a dog, his revolting breath made her want to gag as he tried to push his tongue into her mouth; she tried in vain to push him off, shocked at what was happening. His hands travelled up her dress, reaching her thighs.

"You know you want this," Jack mumbled, pulling at her knickers. Rose felt frozen to the spot, and her heart beat faster in her chest — she struggled to catch her breath. Then, closing her eyes, she willed Jack to stop. Suddenly her fear made Rose angry, reminding her of her brother the night he came to her bed trying to take her.

"No, no!" she shouted. Jack covered her mouth with his hand. Rose struggled to free herself; why was this happening? Her mind was screaming 'RUN' but to no avail. Rose brought up her knee in one quick movement, striking him in the groin. Jack crumbled before her, tearing the top of her dress as he fell, swearing abusively. Rose didn't wait; she pushed him back against the wall and ran as fast as possible. She did not stop until she reached the house, opened the gate, and ran for the kitchen door.

CHAPTER FOURTEEN

Slamming the door shut, locking and throwing the bolt across, Rose leaned back against it. Tears streamed down her face. The front of her dress hung torn, showing her shift. She opened her eyes to see Freda, but neither spoke. Then, as Freda gathered her thoughts, she rushed over, folding Rose into her arms and leading her to a chair. Grabbing a blanket, she wrapped it around Rose's shoulders. Rose was incapable of speaking and shaking uncontrollably — she sobbed as she leaned into Freda, feeling the warmth and safety of her friend then, as her sobs eased.

Freda quietly asked. "Aye, lass, did he do this to you?" Rose still did not speak; she didn't have to. Freda already knew the answer. Moving away, Freda opened the dresser cupboard door retrieving the bottle of rum leftover from Christmas and pouring a glass; she slipped it into Rose's hand. "Drink this, lass. It will help."

Rose took a sip, "Don't sip it, lass; down it in one," urged Freda. Throwing back the glass, Rose spluttered as the warm liquid slipped down her throat. Then, steadying her nerves and wiping away her tears, Rose told Freda what had happened, surprising herself that she laughed when telling her about kneeing him where it hurt before crying again.

"He'll get a short shift if he shows his face here again." Freda hissed.

*

A short time later, having assured Freda he had gone no further, Rose took herself to bed. She undressed and threw the torn dress into the corner of the room; she never wanted to see that again. She climbed into bed, pulling the bedding up to her chin. Rose cried silently into her pillow.

Freda lay in her bed, shocked at what had happened but somehow not surprised; she never did take to him. He was sly — seen it in his eyes. What should she do? Should she tell Thomas?

*

A few days later, Rose had not left the house. Fortunately, the weather was terrible, with a hard frost and snow, meaning she could play with the children in the playroom. When Rose had a little time to herself and Thomas had left for work, she would disappear into the drawing room, curling up in the wing chair to read.

On the fourth morning, Thomas hadn't gone to work; he found her quietly crying.

Kneeling in front of Rose, he took her hands. "I know what happened, Rose, and don't be cross with Freda. She was right to tell me."

"She shouldn't have," whispered Rose. "I am feeling better. I am. I thought he cared for me. I'm such a fool and naive, I know. I'll get over it. Maybe this weather doesn't help. I can't get out and walk it off. Agnes was right. She tried to warn me, even Paul Kelly tried on New Year's Eve, but I didn't listen." Thomas patted her hand with a reassuring smile. He promised her that Jack would never touch her again.

Rose looked up at Thomas, "You mustn't say anything. I'll not see him anymore if he calls; I'll tell him it's over. It's alright, Thomas, I'll deal with it; I didn't mean to trouble you."

"You never trouble me, Rose, and promise me you will always come to me if you have a problem."

Before Rose could answer, Lucas and Isabella ran into the room, unaware of what had happened.

"Can we build a snowman? Please, can we?"

Quickly wiping her eyes, Rose stood. "Come on then, children, let's have some fun!" With coats, hats and gloves on, everyone went into the garden. Soon, with shouts of excitement, the children built their snowman with Thomas' and Rose's help and proceeded to have a snowball fight. Freda opened the kitchen door shouting that hot chocolate was ready, and a snowball hit her full in the face, making her laugh. She was soon joining in.

Eventually, five exhausted people filed into the kitchen, shedding shoes, coats, hats and gloves. Their shoes left puddles on the kitchen floor. Freda warmed the milk again, and everyone sat around the hot stove, drinking hot chocolate and eating warm cookies that Freda had just baked. Rose felt better than she had since that night, determined it would not spoil her life.

CHAPTER FIFTEEN

The next day as Thomas sat in his office looking up at the ruffian in front of him, he felt slight unease, not that he would ever show it.

"So, she's your bit of fluff? Why am I surprised?" the man sneered.

"My relationship with Miss Watson is none of your concern. Will you do the job or not?" Thomas replied. "I don't want him murdered, just given a lesson." Thomas sat holding the envelope in his outstretched hand towards his visitor.

"It's time the weasel had a thumping. Never can do a job right," the man replied as he went to take the envelope.

Thomas held on to it. "Perhaps your boss should keep his men on a leash," replied Thomas.

"You should watch your tone, mate. Do you want it done or not?" asked the man.

"We've never met, do you understand?" Thomas told him as he released the envelope, which disappeared into his visitor's pocket.

"Yeh, yeh, no problem. Any time mate, you know where to find us. Consider the job done." At that, his visitor left, leaving a stale smell of sweat and tobacco. Thomas stood and opened the window. Sitting again, he leaned back in his chair; and eased the tension in his shoulders.

*

A few days later, Rose began to feel more herself. The bruises on her shoulders where Jack had grabbed her had paled, and her appetite had returned.

It was Tuesday, and the weather had eased, so Rose had taken the children to the park — fortunately, the children had been unaware of Rose's troubles. Upon entering the play area, they saw several children had built a snowman and were now throwing snowballs with their nannies or families. The winter sun made the snow glisten and gave a happy atmosphere in the park. Rose smiled as she met with Margaret, Lillibet's nanny, sitting on the bench to chat while Lillibet threw snowballs and made angels wings in the snow with Lucas and Isabella.

"Have you heard?" Margaret frowned at Rose.

"Heard what. What's happened?"

"We had burglars two nights ago while we slept; it makes me shudder if you please. They took madam's tortoiseshell trinket box her dear grandmama had left her. She is more upset about that than anything else that's missing. The masters doing his nut, the police have not been much good."

"How terrible do they have any idea who did it?" Rose frowned.

"No, whoever it was, they reckon the goods will go on the black market never to be seen again. Poor Madam was so upset that they could have murdered us in our beds. The master blames the cook for not locking the back door, but she's adamant she had."

"Do you think someone let them in?" whispered Rose.

"Cook believes it's the flighty housemaid she is always hanging around the yard when emptying the bins — caught her once kissing some gipsy lout, gave her a real good clip round the ear did cook."

"Was it just your house?" asked Rose.

"No, they hit numbers seven and nine, taken all the small silver, thieving little toerags," replied Margaret.

"I must tell Freda when I get back, although she's always careful at night, and Thomas, the master, always checks."

"Ooh, Thomas, is it, my dear." Margaret laughed.

Rose felt herself blush as she looked down at her lap. "Don't fret, lass. I'll not tell anyone; I must admit he is rather dashing." Margaret laughed.

"Oh well, time to go, kids," called Margaret and Rose. Neither saw the figure lurking near the entrance as they left the park.

*

After dinner that evening and the children snuggled in bed, Rose told Thomas and Freda of the burglaries.

"I have already heard," replied Thomas.

"Aye, lass, the police came while you were out with the little ones, not that I could tell them anything. Still, I'll make extra checks tonight before retiring," Freda said.

"Leave that to me, Freda. Tonight, I'll check doors and windows; we don't want anyone in here while we sleep or any other time," insisted Thomas.

*

As Thomas checked the doors and windows later, he remembered his visitor earlier in the week. He knew they were responsible for several shops in the area but houses; it wasn't their scene. Finally, switching off the kitchen light, Thomas retired to bed.

CHAPTER SIXTEEN

Jack winced as he looked in the mirror, his face swollen, his left eye closed, the right bloodshot, his knuckles scratched and bleeding as he had attempted to fight back with little effect. Taking a breath hurt his ribs. The pain behind his knees was excruciating after they'd struck him with a metal bar. It had all happened the night before as he left the Dog and Gun tavern, turning down the alley to his digs. They had struck from behind, no words spoken until they finished, and then the sneer 'should have treated your woman better' before disappearing into the night. Jack had crawled the rest of the way to his digs, collapsing on his bed, not moving until the following day. Then the pain hit him. Sal, the woman he'd been drinking with in the pub, watched the attack from the corner, followed him home, and was now trying to clean him up.

Jack lashed out, "Piss off, you stupid bitch! Leave me alone."

"Suit yourself," she snarled, slamming the door behind her as she left, taking what money she had found in his pockets while he slept.

Jack spent the next few days lying on his filthy straw mattress, just a single wool blanket to relieve the cold. The stench of stale sweat mingled with dried blood was overpowering; the bucket in the corner of the room was overflowing with excrement and urine. Mice scrambled across the table, nibbling on the dried crust of bread and stale cheese.

As he lay, Jack's anger grew. He'd recognised his attackers, and they'd called themselves mates. How had they found out? That puzzled him; she must have told — but who told Eastman? Rose told that friend of hers. What's her name, Agnes? That's it, who, in turn, told lover boy bloody Kelly. No, maybe Rose had told

Blackwood. Was it him? If he found out it was, they'll be sorry. Someone will answer for his state, God, his ribs hurt. Where's that stupid bitch? She could have brought me a drink back. Jack then remembered he told her to piss off.

Easing himself off the bed, Jack opened his door. He'd get one of the kids from upstairs to fetch him a drink, but, sticking his hands into his pockets, he found them empty. That bloody woman, I'll deal with her later. Slamming the door shut and wincing painfully, Jack collapsed onto his bed again. He wouldn't rise for another week.

*

Over the next few weeks, things settled down in the Blackwood household. The Avenue breathed a sigh of relief as the robbers appeared to have moved on. Rose had put her attack behind her, helping Freda in the kitchen and generally keeping the house tidy, and in the afternoons, Rose would play with the children. They would head to the park if the weather was good, sometimes meeting Margaret, who would regale her with the latest gossip while Lillibet, Lucas and Isabella played. As for Jack, Rose had not seen him since that night, and deep down, she was glad. She had visions of him turning up, looking sad and begging forgiveness. Rose had told Agnes, who offered her a small knife to keep in her bag.

"Slit his throat next time," she had said. Rose had laughed and assured Agnes that there would be no more outings with Jack and would not be slitting anyone's throat. They hugged, and Rose handed back the knife. She didn't want to carry that around.

*

The following day at breakfast, Thomas held a card up.

"I have an invite to a wedding anniversary at the Carmichaels. Will you join me, Rose? It wouldn't be much fun on my own." Thomas smiled at Rose across the table.

"Are you sure? Would the Carmichaels think it strange for me to accompany you?"

"Why should they? You've become one of the family; please say you'll join me."

"I would love it too. When is it?"

"A week on Friday, plenty of time for you to buy a new dress," smiled Thomas.

"Oh, I don't need a new dress; the blue one will be fine."

"Rubbish, I insist; why don't you take Agnes? It's your visit today, isn't it?" asked Thomas.

*

Later that morning, after leaving the children to their classes, Rose joined Agnes at the Casino Royal as Agnes had been doing extra rehearsals.

"Finished, babe, come on, let's be off… time to spend. Ooh, I love getting a new dress," Agnes laughed.

"The new dress is for me, not you," Rose laughed as they made their way to Macy's Department Store. Rose sought advice from Miss Turnbull, in charge of the lady's department. Rose had never forgotten her kindness the first time they had met. Rose and Agnes spent the next hour trying on different dresses and eventually chose a soft peach dress, the top adorned with sequins to the waist. The skirt flowed with more silver sequins around the bottom and a pair of peach slippers to finish. Rose wanted to look good for Thomas — she saw herself blush in the mirror. Her thoughts for Thomas over the months had grown, but she was only the nanny come housekeeper. He would never look at her like that. Sometimes, he smiled at her when he sat across the table, making her heart flutter behind her ribcage.

Agnes suddenly poked her head through the curtain.

"You were daydreaming, sweety. You're all flushed," laughed Agnes.

"No, it's just, well, look at us, Agnes. Who would have thought we would be here trying on these dresses, looking forward to the evening? Oh, Agnes were so lucky," whispered Rose. Agnes placed her arms around her friend's shoulders and momentarily stood looking in the mirror.

"We've done good, girl," whispered Agnes.

Having thanked Miss Turnbull for her assistance Rose and Agnes took the elevator to the dining room and ordered coffee and cake — a perfect finish to their shopping spree.

CHAPTER SEVENTEEN

Thomas and Rose prepared to leave for Carmichael's anniversary dinner evening. Deciding to walk to their residence, which was only a short walk away, Freda stood waiting to lock the door after strict instructions from Thomas, who had ensured the back door was locked and bolted.

"We'll let ourselves in. Not sure what time we'll return," Thomas had said. "No need to open the doors again."

Freda had huffed, "I'm not a senile old fool, yet you know," she had rebuked Thomas. "Will you stop fussing? Just go and enjoy your evening and leave me in peace."

Rose had been upstairs, kissing the children and wishing them goodnight. She was coming down the stairs to see Freda at the door. Kissing Freda with a giggle as Rose heard the conversation between Freda and Thomas. Wrapping her cape around her and linked arms with Thomas as they stepped out.

He squeezed Rose's hand, "You look beautiful tonight; the Carmichaels will love you."

"I'm nervous," whispered Rose.

"You do not need to be," comforted Thomas.

*

Returning to the kitchen, Freda decided to sort out the dresser drawers and cupboards. By the time she had finished, a pile of rubbish had laid at her feet. I'll remove this rubbish and then pop up and check the children. Unlocking the back door and using the wash basket to carry everything out, Freda stepped out to the dustbins, the light from the backdoor giving just enough to see what she was doing. Freda was surprised to see the back gate open. She closed and locked it. Freda thought she heard a noise as she slammed the dustbin lid down.

Looking around saw nothing and went back into the kitchen, closing the back door. Freda was suddenly aware of a shadow to her left — spinning around. She came face to face with Jack.

"Where is she?" he snarled.

Freda scrunched her nose at the stench emanating from him; his clothes were filthy, and it looked like he had slept in them for weeks.

"Where's who?" asked Freda, already knowing he was looking for Rose. "Leave my kitchen now before I shout for the Master."

"Uh, he's not in saw him leave over two hours ago." He had not noticed that Rose had gone with him in his drunken state. "So, where is she upstairs with those snivelling brats? Tell her to come down now," he sneered.

Freda stood rooted to the spot. What a fool. Why did she open the door? She promised Thomas she wouldn't go out and now look. Oh, God, please help, Freda thought. She felt terrified but wasn't going to show him. Freda thought of the children upstairs; he can't go upstairs; she must stop him.

"Rose left with Thomas. If you watched, you would have seen them leave," Freda replied firmly. He mustn't know I am scared, she thought.

"I want to say sorry," wheedled Jack as he moved around the table. Freda felt her hand on the latch. If she was quick, she could dash out and run to her neighbours for help, but Freda thought, I can't leave the children.

"I've told you Rose isn't here; please leave. I won't tell them you've been — no one will be any the wiser," Freda turned the handle, opening the door, but Jack moved too quickly for her and slammed it shut behind her. Moving swiftly around the table, Freda stood near the range, her body shaking, her heart thudding. What should I do? Behind her, she felt for the handle of the bread knife — grabbing it in her hand, she kept it hidden.

Jack continued to sneer.

"A little slap and tickle, nowt else, it's what they all want. All over me earlier in the night she was, and then she started screaming and hitting me, stupid bitch! And who told my boss? That's what I want to know. It was him! God all mighty — wants her for himself, had her between the sheets already, yeh, know his kind! See, it still bloody hurts!" Jack rubbed his left eye, which was still bloodshot and slightly swollen. "It's her fault. She's going to bloody pay," Jack hissed in his drunken, fuddled mind.

All Jack could see was Rose as he lunged at Freda.

She brought the knife around, catching him across the shoulder. His anger rose as he knocked the knife away, pushing her back against the range. His hands circled her throat. Fighting for her life, Freda tried to twist and turn her hands, desperately pulling at his hands. He's too strong. The fumes of alcohol from his mouth engulfed her face. She couldn't take a breath; her eyes hurt, black dots began to appear.

Jack didn't let go.

*

Woken by the loud voices, Lucas stood on the landing peering through the banister rail but couldn't see anything. Why was Freda shouting? Who was that man he could hear? Lucas crept slowly down the stairs, and the noises from the kitchen suddenly stopped. Too frightened to move, he sat crying softly on the bottom step.

*

Sometime later, Thomas and Rose returned home. They stepped through the front door and saw Lucas shivering at the bottom of the stairs. Rose rushed to him.

"Lucas, sweetheart, what are you doing here?"

"They were shouting, the man was shouting, I don't like it. Freda won't come out," cried Lucas.

"Whatever do you mean, Lucas? What is it? What's wrong?" By this time, Thomas had already entered the kitchen. A sudden cry of despair caused Rose to stand and rush toward him.

Thomas raised his hands and stopped her, "No, do not come in! I must get the police now!" he pushed Rose away.

"But, Thomas, what is it? What happened? What's wrong? Tell me!"

"I must get the police, Rose. I must go quickly. Do not enter the kitchen. Stay with Lucas." He ordered.

*

When Thomas had gone, Rose comforted Lucas, but she kept looking at the kitchen door. Rose feared for Freda. Why hadn't she heard her? She must go to her.

"Stay here, darling. I won't be long." Rose gently removed her arm from around Lucas and moved towards the kitchen. As she entered, she saw Freda prone on the floor — blood oozing from her chest. Although Rose rushed forward, she cried in anguish, knowing that Freda was past help. Kneeling beside her, Rose took Freda's hand as the tears fell.

"Oh, Freda, Freda who did this. Why, why?" Rose shook uncontrollably. She heard Lucas crying, calling for her. Rose stood on shaky legs and tried to gather herself. Lucas needed her. She mustn't leave him on his own. Looking down at Freda again, her eyes swimming with tears, Rose returned to Lucas.

"It's alright, darling, don't cry. Help is coming." Rose took Lucas into her arms. They sat together on the bottom step while waiting for Thomas to return.

CHAPTER EIGHTEEN

"Heavenly Father, we commit Freda Longsdon into your safekeeping. Earth to earth, ashes to ashes, dust to dust." As the coffin lowered gently, a small gathering watched under a heavy-laden sky — with a hard frost and snow flurries. Rose didn't hear the final words from the Minister — she clung to Thomas' arm, tears blinding her as she picked up a sod of earth. Rose shivered and threw it onto the coffin.

"Oh, Freda, why?" she heard herself ask again.

Agnes tried to comfort her friend back at the house as she gave her a sweet cup of tea. "Drink this. You look frozen."

The Carmichael's nanny Margaret was looking after Lucas and Isabella. Their cook had sent her senior assistant to help, and she had made an excellent spread for those wishing to call after the funeral. Rose sat hunched — her heart heavy. She reached out to take Agnes' hand. Then, looking across at Thomas, who stood tense as he spoke to neighbours while they expressed their sadness.

"It's my fault," whispered Rose.

"How can it be your fault?" Agnes looked frowning.

"I know who did it; how do I tell Thomas he'll throw me out, that's for sure." Rose cried.

"You're talking rubbish, babes. You're just upset and angry, the police will catch him," said Agnes.

"But I know," Rose muttered. Agnes took her friend's hand and quietly led her from the room.

Sitting on Rose's bed, Agnes tried to comfort her again.

"Ok, Rose, what is it? What are you trying to tell me."

"It's him,"

"Who?" asked Agnes, but with a sinking feeling, she

already had an idea.

"That first night after it happened. I couldn't sleep. I went down to the kitchen and made myself a hot chocolate drink. That's when I spotted it. I knew. It was on the floor in the corner by the dresser. I just knew it was Jack's." Rose went to her dressing table, opened her jewellery box and took a chain. Laying it in her hand, she went across to Agnes.

"What is it?"

"A watch chain; I know it's Jack. He never went anywhere without it, even in his work clothes."

"But, babe, it's just a watch chain," replied Agnes.

"No, it's Jack. I'd know it anywhere. It's different with its twist in the link and that bit of silver running through. He was here. He murdered poor Freda. Oh, Agnes, what am I going to do? It's my fault."

"It's not your fault; how many times do I have to tell you!" Agnes replied a little frustratedly.

"But you don't understand that he would never have come to this house if we hadn't been friends. How am I going to tell Thomas?" Rose felt the tears as they rolled down her face.

"Tell Thomas what?" Neither Rose nor Agnes had heard Thomas arrive; he stood at the door looking at them. Then, moving over to Rose, kneeling, he took her hand. "Tell me what, Rose?" he whispered. Rose cried uncontrollably until, with a hiccupping voice, she told Thomas.

"I'll go in the morning; I'm so sorry."

"You will go nowhere. Agnes is right; it is not your fault. Neither of us knew he would do this. And anyway don't you dare leave the children; do you want to break their hearts even more? No, Rose, we stay together and comfort each other," replied Thomas. My god, Rose, don't you dare leave me; whatever would I do without you? I love you, don't you know that? But Thomas never said those words as he helped Rose from the bed and led her from the room, with Agnes following to join their visitors.

*

After an eternity, their visitors left with words of comfort still ringing in Rose's head. She was glad when night fell. After comforting and kissing the children good night, she disappeared to her room. Having undressed, Rose climbed into bed, burying her head into the pillow. She sobbed at the loss of her friend.

At the Royale suite, Agnes also cried that night in bed, encircled in Paul Kelly's arms. Kelly kissed her gently, soothing her as she told him of her conversation with Rose.

"Poor Freda, I remember that first time I met her. She never looked down at us. On the contrary, Freda kindly fed and helped us that first night. I know she thought I was common and a tart, but she loved Rose; she became like her mother, and Jack killed her. How could he? Do something, darling; he mustn't get away with it. Chop his bloody head off, feed his balls to the dogs; I don't care. The police won't find him, but you can." Laying exhausted in her lover's arms, Agnes eventually fell asleep.

Paul Kelly looked out at the dark sky through the bedroom window. He sighed. No one upsets my girlfriend. Tomorrow I'll call the team. Jack Manus will wish he'd never been born.

*

The following day, Thomas looked at Eastman's henchman standing in front of the desk in his office.

"Find the culprit and deal with him; I don't care how," Thomas spoke vehemently.

The man chuckled, "Ha, already know, guv, haven't

you guessed by now, only one man could do that."

"Who?" enquired Thomas.

"Bloody hell, mate, thought I was thick! Jack bloody Manus!"

"How do you know?"

"Word on the street travels quicker than a farting pigeon," he laughed.

"Well, sort it before I find him first," snarled Thomas. The henchman looked at Thomas, dropping his head slightly and frowning, his voice suddenly just above a whisper.

"I'm sorry for your loss. I knew Freda. She was a proper lady. Jack won't have a head when I've finished with him."

"You knew Freda?" Thomas asked, looking surprised.

"Yeh, we grew up together in the Bronx. I have much to thank Freda's parents; they were decent folks, took me in and brought me up. Freda and I have always kept in touch."

"That explains why I saw you at the funeral," replied Thomas.

"Yeh, well, don't take that as me being soft. Ok, mate?" At that, the henchman left, leaving that stale aroma behind.

*

Jack sat shivering under Poughkeepsie bridge's abutments. Having sobered up from that night, he knew he could not return to his digs. Cold, his stomach rumbling, Jack had not eaten for several days, the rattle of the trains overhead nearly driving him insane — feeling too frightened to be seen. He knew that Eastman's men would by now be looking for him. Worse, the thought of Paul Kelly's men. Stupid bitch, he thought, why did she have to stick her nose in? He hadn't meant to kill her but knew he had lost control that night. It's all your fault.

Rose, thought Jack, unable to admit his guilt. The other thing that puzzled Jack taking the fob watch from his pocket, was the loss of his watch chain. Had he dropped it in the kitchen? And if so, had Rose found it, would she know it was his? Jack thought back to the day of his grandfather's death. He'd looked down into the coffin and saw him dressed in his Sunday best with his Waltham fob watch and chain in his waistcoat pocket. What good was it to him stone-cold dead, but Jack thought it would look good on him. He smiled as the coffin lid lowered. No one noticed it was missing. Now all Jack had was the watch. He knew he must have lost the chain in the struggle with her, and the police would have it — Rose would have told them it belonged to him.

*

Jack ventured out of hiding some days later, hunger gnawing at his stomach. He knew the soup kitchen at the back of Trinity Church on Wall Street would be handing out hot soup and bread. It was dark. Jack kept to the shadows. He had to grab the food and hi-tail it back before anyone noticed.

CHAPTER NINETEEN

On Sunday morning, ten days after that horrific event, Rose and Thomas were sitting drinking coffee, grateful to the Carmichaels for allowing their senior cook to stay until a replacement for Freda was found. Just the thought made Rose cry. Isabella and Lucas played upstairs; she would take them to the park after lunch. At times, meals had been awkward for the children.

Only this morning, Lucas had refused his porridge, crying. He told his father that Freda had made it better and wanted Freda to return. Thomas took Lucas into his arms and gently explained that Freda had gone to heaven. Isabella cried and asked if they could go to heaven and see her. Rose had comforted her, and now when saying their prayers at bedtime, they included sending love to Freda. Rose hoped it would help the children, but it wasn't easy to understand that Freda would never return.

Lucas suffered from nightmares, his bed wet in the mornings. Rose changed his sheets without a word, hoping Lucas would heal while young. Then, a knock at the door made them both look up.

"Excuse me, Mr Blackwood, but two police officers to see you," said the cook.

Thomas stood. "Thank you, cook." Going out into the hall.

Rose heard voices, and Thomas returned to the lounge with the officers. Rose looked up with tearful eyes. "Rose, my dear, this is Inspector Steers and Captain Byrnes."

"I'm sorry to trouble you," Inspector Steers replied, "but we need to discuss the events of that night."

"Can I offer you both coffee?" Rose asked.

"Thank you, miss. That would be very kind," replied Inspector Steers. Rose left the room, and Thomas invited the officers to sit.

"Forgive me, Inspector Steers, but we've already gone over this. I find it extremely distressing to repeat myself." Thomas stood, his hand resting on the mantle.

"I appreciate that, Mr Blackwood, but I am sure you agree we are doing our best to catch the culprit," the Inspector looked at Thomas, frowning.

"Culprit, Inspector? You mean murderer, surely." Rose returned with a tray of coffee and biscuits, placing them on the side table.

"I'll see how the children are doing; I promised to read them a story," said Rose.

"It would be appreciated, miss, if you could stay." Inspector Steers smiled. Rose was taking a handkerchief from her pocket, wiping away a tear. Then sitting, the Inspector took the coffee from Rose before she took a seat, leaving his captain to speak.

"If I may, Miss, what is your position in the house?" Captain Byrnes enquired.

"I am the housekeeper and nanny to Isabella and Lucas," Rose replied.

"Erm, I see." Captain Byrnes stared at Rose as a smirk passed his lips.

"I don't like your tone, Captain!" Thomas replied sharply.

"Forgive me, Sir; I only ascertained the young girl's position in the house."

"Miss Watson. The lady's name is Miss Rose Watson, and position in this house, as you put it, I can assure you, is honourable." Thomas replied sharply.

"Of course, Mr Blackwood, I had no wish to infer anything else," replied Captain Byrnes. Rose was unable to control the tears escaping and running down her cheeks. Her hands shook as she rested them on her lap.

"Forgive me, Miss Watson; please accept my

apologies."

Thomas, who by now was becoming agitated, moved to comfort Rose. Inspector Steers coughed as he replaced his cup and saucer on the table.

"Perhaps, Captain, we could get to the point. My apologies for my officer's rather crass start. Please allow me," the Inspector stood as he turned to Rose. "Miss Watson, this is challenging, but do you know anyone who may wish to harm Mrs Longsdon."

"If we knew Inspector, we would have said by now," Thomas replied curtly.

"It's alright, Thom… er, Mr Blackwood, I must tell them of Jack," interrupted Rose.

"Jack, Miss?" enquired the Inspector.

"His name is Jack Manus. We were friends for quite a while until, well, until he decided not to be a gentleman one night, and I told him I no longer wished to see him."

"And what may I ask happened that night," the Inspector asked.

"Well, he…" Rose stuttered.

"I think, Inspector, it is obvious of his disgraceful behaviour towards Rose that night — without further detail," said Thomas.

"I would prefer to hear from the lady herself." The Inspector smiled at Rose, who wiped a tear and whispered.

"We were returning from the New Year's Eve party. Jack grabbed me, pushing me into a doorway. I managed to shake him off and run home. Need I say more, Inspector?" After a cough, the Inspector looked at Rose.

"That still does not explain why you think this Jack Manus is guilty of attacking Mrs Longsdon." Rose stood and moved towards the door.

"I have something to show you." Rose left, returning quickly. Her fingers clasped around the watch chain she held out to the Inspector. "The next morning, I rose early, unable to sleep. While making myself a drink in the kitchen, I saw this in the corner next to the dresser. It's Jack's. It belongs to his watch. Poor Freda must have grabbed it, trying to defend herself." Rose cried, collapsing into the chair.

Thomas' voice rose slightly. "I think, Inspector, you have all the information you require. Miss Watson needs rest. Just do your job and apprehend this villain before I do."

"I would be obliged, Sir, that you leave the apprehending to us. Our men are searching, and now that I am aware of Jack Manus — my men will find him shortly. But, in the meantime, please do not take matters into your own hands," replied Inspector Steers.

"Of course, forgive my outburst, Inspector. You must understand I am angry and distressed at the loss of Freda. She was not just our cook but also a very dear friend."

"And you both believe that Jack Manus returned to seek revenge?" Inspector Steers asked.

"Who else could it have been? We can only assume that he watched the house that night, noticing we had left for the Carmichaels, as you already know, and attacked Freda," replied Thomas. "I told her to keep the doors locked, but Freda opened the back door for some reason, and that's how he got in."

"But why? To kill poor Freda?" cried Rose. "His anger was with me, not Freda."

"Enough, officers; we can tell you no more than you already know." At that, Thomas led the officers out into the hall. Sitting on the bottom stair sat Lucas and Isabella looking up, their eyes full of tears. Thomas gathered them into his arms.

"What are you doing down here?"

"We were looking for Rose. She said she would come

and read to us." The door to the lounge opened, and Rose swiftly moved to take Lucas' and Isabella's hands.

"I'm sorry, darlings, I'm here now. Let's go upstairs, and you can choose your story."

"Why are you crying, Rose? Did the policemen make you cry?" asked Lucas. He turned and glared at the two officers standing in the hallway. "You leave Rose alone," he shouted.

"Hush now," Rose gathered them into her arms and gently guided them upstairs.

"Well then, good day Mr Blackwood and apologies for any upset caused; we are only trying to do our job."

"Of course, Inspector, It's just… We are all finding it very difficult," said Thomas, shaking their hands as he showed them the door.

Walking away from the house, Captain Byrnes guffawed. "Uh, housemaid and nanny, who are they kidding."

"Our concern, Captain, is in the death of Mrs Longsdon, not the goings-on in that house," replied Inspector Steers.

"Just saying, Sir, just saying," snorted Byrnes.

"There is an alibi for that evening, it checks out, I assume?" Inspector Steers looked at Byrnes.

Byrnes sneered. "The Chief and his good wife were present at Carmichaels. He tells me that the beauty on Blackwood's arm caused a stir within his groin."

Inspector Steers laughed. "She does that alright." Then, ignoring his Captain's words, Steers thought aloud. "Jack Manus, I know that name. He's one of Eastman's stooges, and I have a feeling he'll be floating in the Hudson River before my officers find him."

"Do we leave it at that, Sir?' asked Captain Byrnes.

"Let me put it another way, I, for one, have no intentions of stepping on Eastman's toes. I want to keep my head for a little longer." Then, climbing into the waiting carriage, the Inspector tapped the roof with his cane.

*

After breakfast the following day, Thomas and Rose sat at the table with a fresh pot of coffee. The children had returned to the nursery for lessons with their tutor Mr Harold who arrived over six months ago. Although older, he was tall with receding hair and soft brown eyes. He had a penchant for colourful waistcoats, which the children thought were fun. On arrival, he showed calm and understanding of Isabella and Lucas' upset, allowing the children to like him. Thomas and Rose were glad the children had taken to him.

Just then, Cook knocked on the dining room door to clear away the table.

"Begging your pardon Mr Blackwood but I must inform you that the Carmichaels will require my services due to her Ladyships Birthday party at the end of the month."

"Oh yes, we have an invite, Rose. Perhaps it would give you something to look forward to after…" Thomas looked across the table at Rose and smiled.

"I don't know." Rose stuttered.

"Don't think about it now, nearer the time. Perhaps it might do us both good." Thomas replied.

Cook coughed lightly. "Have you found anyone to replace me yet?"

"Oh, forgive me, Cook. I will sort something out as quickly as possible. We are most grateful for all your help these last weeks. You have been invaluable to us."

"If I may, Sir, my sister Ivy has been the cook for Lord and Lady Downley at Springton Manor for over twenty years. She is an excellent cook, adores children, and urgently seeks another position."

"Why is that Cook? I mustn't step on the Lordship's toes," replied Thomas.

"As you know, Sir. His Lordship is retiring from Government shortly and moving to their country estate. It already has a resident cook, they are willing to take Ivy with them, but you don't need two cooks. The old saying Sir, too many cooks spoil the broth. And my sister is keen to stay in the area because of her family. She's very homely, Sir, and I'm sure you would like her."

"Thank you, Cook, forgive me, but I've never known your name since you arrived. May I ask your name?"

"It's Janet, Sir, but I prefer Cook; I'm a stickler for boundaries."

"Thank you again, Janet, err, Cook," Thomas smiled. "I will contact Lord Downley today. Perhaps you could warn your sister. After all, she may not wish to join us," Thomas replied.

"My sister would be happy to participate in the household." At that, Cook cleared away the table disappearing back to the kitchen.

"Perhaps it's just what we need, and she sounds lovely, especially if she likes children." Rose sighed. "Janet has been so good, but she's very strict and never allows me into the kitchen to get a cup of tea and chat as Freda did." Rose giggled, then suddenly turned to tears. "Oh, Thomas, it will never be the same without Freda; I miss her so much."

Thomas stood, encircling Rose into his arms.

CHAPTER TWENTY

A dirty, unkempt figure shuffled along the pavement, keeping close to the squalid tenements of the Lower East Side. Jack was cold and hungry. A cough rattled his chest. His third venture out from Poughkeepsie Bridge's abutment hunting for food, hoping he wasn't too late. Nearly midnight, but the soup kitchens sometimes stayed open late. Twenty minutes later, having warmed and filled his stomach with soup, bread, and a slice of fruit cake, Jack shuffled back towards his hiding place. I've got to get out of New York, he thought.

Leaving the tenements behind, he crossed over the waste ground towards Poughkeepsie Bridge, pulling his dirty coat tighter to keep the biting wind from his body. A hand suddenly rested on his shoulder.

"Boss wants a word with you. Swampo, tell the boss we've found him. He knows where to meet us." Jack froze. It was too late. They had found him. His heart pounding, Jack was propelled through back streets past the last tenements, dragged over waste ground across the railway tracks toward the factories.

"Get off me. Leave me alone!" Jack struggled, but he was too weak and, with a sinking feeling, knew Kelly's men were taking him to the meat slaughterhouse.

*

Carcasses hung from hooks, the stone floor awash with blood soaked Jack's trousers as they dragged him towards a smaller room. The stench of rotting flesh assailed his senses, making him heave; his meal from earlier rose into his mouth. Jack swallowed it back down. Standing behind a table stood Paul Kelly.

Struck across the back of his knees, Jack crumbled to the floor.

"Please, Mr Kelly, I didn't mean to do it," Jack

begged.

"Shut your mouth, you pathetic little shit."

"It was an accident. I didn't mean to strangle Freda." Jack's voice was high with panic.

Kelly nodded to his henchman, who placed a mincing machine on the table.

"No one, do you hear me? No one, least of all a piece of shit like you, upsets my girl or her friends, murdering one of their own without consequences!" sneered Paul Kelly.

"Please, please, Mr Kelly. It was an accident, please; I didn't mean it. I'll leave New York. You'll never see me again."

"He's right there, Boss," laughed the men.

"Please, Mr Kelly, please, don't do this! Please!"

Hauled to his feet and grabbed around his neck, Jack felt his left hand pulled down towards the mincing machine. The excruciating pain made Jack scream. Moments later, his left ear sliced from his head and tossed to the Bullmastiff.

"Here, Ike, supper," laughed the henchman as he threw the ear to the dog, which grabbed it and ran. Suddenly Jack felt lifted off his feet by two strong arms, only to be impaled on a dangling meat hook. A heavy fist to his stomach left him gasping in pain. Jack's heart pounded. He knew his words meant nothing. The pain of being impaled through his back was indescribable; Jack felt sweat and blood run down his body, before pooling in a sticky puddle on the floor. He was sure he would faint — another punch to his middle made him cry out again. Paul Kelly grabbed him by his shirt, looking into Jack's eyes.

"My girl wants your balls. Can't disappoint." Paul Kelly hissed.

"No, please!" Jack gasped.

"Finish him and send what's left back to Eastman." Paul Kelly spoke to his men as he turned and left the building. The screams of Jack Manus rang in his ears. As Kelly walked towards his carriage, Otto, Swampo's Jack Russell, ran past him with two bloodied meat pieces in his mouth. Paul Kelly smiled. He had carried out Agnes's wishes.

*

With the first few slivers of dawn arriving, a horse-drawn carriage sped through the Lower East side and turned into Essex Street, the breath from the horses snorting dissipated in the early morning mist. The carriage door swung open as the carriage approached Silver Dollar Smith Saloon. A sack tossed — it landed in front of the saloon doors, the home of Monk Eastman. The horse-drawn carriage then quickly gathered speed and disappeared into the mist.

CHAPTER TWENTY-ONE

Rose woke early one morning in March. Spring sunshine broke through the curtains filling her room with light. The winter months had seemed long and dark; so much had happened since Christmas. She drew back the curtains. A light snow flurry had settled on the lawn, making it sparkle like jewels on a carpet. A cat had left a trail of pawprints as it'd meandered through the garden. The trees shed the snow from their leaves in the gentle breeze. Rose sighed. She felt — she wasn't sure what she felt. Rose loved her home, the children and, of course, Thomas. But was this to be her life? She missed her chats with Freda, oh, dear Freda. Rose had regarded Freda as the mother she had lost as a child. Ivy, the new cook, had settled in about a month ago and was warm and friendly. The children had already helped with baking, and Lucas said his morning porridge was almost as good as Freda's. Lucas' nightmares were less, and his bed had been dry the last week.

Thankfully Ivy seemed to bring a little normality back to the house. Last night, while Thomas was out — and with the children in bed, Rose had taken herself down to the kitchen for a cup of hot chocolate and sat at the oak table while chatting to Ivy, just as she had done with Freda. Oh, Freda, Rose wiped away a tear.

She was scolding herself as she turned and headed for the bathroom. Why couldn't she shake off this melancholy feeling? After breakfast and while the children have their lessons, I'll go to Macy's and browse; perhaps Agnes is free, and we could meet for coffee. So, with that thought, Rose gathered up Lucas and Isabella, who had run into her room and headed for breakfast.

*

Stepping off the blue train, Rose went straight for the

Casino Royal to find Agnes busy with rehearsals and unable to join her for coffee. After a quick hug and telling Agnes not to worry, Rose made her way to Macy's. Just as she neared the door, a carriage drew up, and Lady Carmichael stepped down.

"Rose, my dear, how lovely to see you. Are you shopping too, or just come for coffee?" Lady Carmichael smiled.

"I just thought I would browse and maybe take something back for Lucas and Isabella,"

"If you don't mind me saying, you're looking a little down, my dear. Please join me for coffee."

"Oh, I wouldn't want to intrude."

"Nonsense, my dear, I won't hear of it." She placed her hand on Rose's elbow and guided her into Macy's.

*

Sitting at a window in the coffee shop, Rose looked down onto Herald Square, watching the people hustling about, others strolling, and horse-drawn carriages pulling up in front of the main door. She watched ladies alight in their finery and stepped through Macy's doors. Finally, Rose turned her head, sighed deeply, and looked straight into Lady Carmichael's face, which smiled back at her.

"My dear," she whispered. "What troubles you? Can I help?"

"Oh, no, I'm so sorry. Please do forgive me, Lady Carmichael."

"Please call me Veronica."

"Thank you, Veronica, it's just me. Oh, I'm just feeling. Oh, dear. I don't know what it is. I can't explain my feelings. I am sorry you must think me very silly," replied Rose.

"Not at all; you need a hobby or interest to help fill your days. We've all been there, my dear." Veronica reached across, taking Rose's hand. "But we haven't all suffered as you have these last few weeks. No wonder you're feeling low." A tear slipped down Rose's face before she could stop it. "Oh my no, you mustn't let it get you down," whispered Veronica. Rose took a handkerchief from her pocket, wiping away her tears, hoping no one had noticed. "I know just the thing, my dear. I'm having afternoon tea on Thursday at home with the ladies from the YWCA."

"Whatever is that?" asked Rose.

"The Young Women's Christian Association," Veronica smiled.

"What does it do?"

"Ah, we work closely with the Red Cross and State of Board Charities. We helped young ladies like yourself and your friend when you arrived in New York. Except we missed you, but then, of course, you caught the eye of Thomas, who came to your rescue."

"I didn't deliberately see Thomas — if anyone did, it was Agnes, not that she was forward in any way. We just happened to become friends while onboard ship." Rose felt she should befriend Agnes.

"Now, my dear, me and my big mouth, I didn't mean it to come out like that." Veronica waved her hand in the air. "All I'm saying is if you hadn't known Thomas, what would you have done when you left Ellis Island, where would you have gone, and who would you have trusted? That's what I meant, dear."

"True, it doesn't bear thinking about," replied Rose.

"Well, we ladies are there to help these young women who arrive. Look, Rose, come on Thursday and meet my ladies if you like what we do and feel you want to get involved; we certainly need all the help we can get. How about it?" smiled Veronica. "What have you got to lose."

Rose smiled. "Maybe it will help me."

"Good, now, my dear, can I offer you a lift home?"

As they rode back in the carriage, they talked about Ivy, their new cook and how she had settled in — the children even liked her food, to which they both laughed.

"I miss Freda so much," whispered Rose.

"Yes," replied Veronica sympathetically. "She had been a family member for many years, even helping with the delivery of the children."

"How did Mrs Blackwood die?" asked Rose.

"He never told you, my dear?"

"No," Rose frowned.

"She died about a month after giving birth to Isabella, a blood infection, the doctor said. Poor Rosemary had been ill since its inception, but no one knew the problem. She quietly slipped away during the night. Poor Thomas was devastated."

"There's a portrait of Mrs Blackwood on the stairs; she was beautiful," said Rose.

"Oh, yes, I remember Thomas having it for their first wedding Anniversary. Perhaps when you marry, he'll have it taken down; after all, my dear, you don't want to be looking at dear Rosemary every day." Veronica smiled at Rose.

"Marry?" spluttered Rose. "I'm just the housekeeper and nanny."

"Don't you love him, dear? Only I couldn't help but notice at my birthday party Thomas couldn't take his eyes off you, or other times when you have been to the house — he loves you." Veronica's eyes twinkled as she looked at Rose.

Rose felt her cheeks blush. "No, Veronica, you are wrong," stuttered Rose.

"Oh my dear, now I've embarrassed you, I'm sorry, but it's clear for anyone to see he's like a gooey-eyed puppy. You feel the same, my dear. Am I wrong?"

asked Veronica.

"What a gooey-eyed puppy?" Rose laughed, as did Veronica.

"No, you know I didn't mean that." Veronica laughed again.

"Oh look, we've arrived," noticed Rose, anxious to change the subject and climb out of the carriage.

"Don't mind me. I love a bit of romance." Veronica replied as Rose stepped down from the carriage.

"See you on Thursday and bring the children. They can play with Lillibet, and Margaret will look after them. Bye, dear." Veronica waved. Rose was relieved to leave the carriage, she felt flustered and hot. Was it so obvious, thought Rose? Oh god, please don't let Veronica tell Thomas, she thought.

CHAPTER TWENTY-TWO

Rose walked with Lucas and Isabella to the Carmichaels a few days later. Margaret waited with Lillibet in the hall, excited to have her friends play.

"Thank you, Margaret. Are you sure you don't mind looking after them?" asked Rose.

"Bless them. The more, the merrier," laughed Margaret, who was already climbing the stairs after the children.

"Rose, my dear, you're here." Veronica had heard them arrive and had come into the hall. Rose handed her coat and hat to the maid before following Veronica into the lounge, finding several ladies enjoying afternoon tea. They smiled as she entered, and after introducing everyone, not that Rose would remember all their names, she sat next to a rather buxom lady.

"I'm Tilly," she smiled. "It's so lovely to have a new face join us; I'm sure you will enjoy our little soirée." Tilly laughed. Rose thanked the maid, who offered her tea as Veronica clapped her hands.

"Ladies, we must discuss plans for next Tuesday, if we may."

An hour later, Rose had learned a lot about their work, willingly offered to help and was surprised that Veronica's husband had donated money to purchase the building called Hull House, contributing to the running of Toynbee Hall and the Quaker Pennington House.

During the meeting, Rose learnt that the properties would house ladies arriving in New York independently. They found work at the Textile or the Teddy Bear Factory and domestic work in many large houses and estates outside New York. Those from farms were happy to be sent to farmers and ranchers. The society also arranged visits after the first month to ensure all was well; they would then call unexpectedly twice or thrice a year. Rose was shocked to learn they worked tirelessly, preventing unscrupulous men from enticing vulnerable young women. They would tell them it was to entertain their gentlemen friends and live a life of luxury. They were nothing more than brothels. Sadly, some slipped through the net.

That night at dinner, Rose told Thomas about her meeting with Veronica, and she would like to help.

"Of course, Rose, but please do be careful. You, of all people, know what it's like on Ellis Island. Just stay close to Veronica." Thomas frowned. He hoped Rose wasn't becoming restless. Thomas knew how she had struggled since losing Freda but couldn't bear to lose her. Perhaps it was time, he thought. What if she said no? What if I frighten her away? I couldn't handle that. Thomas sighed and walked over to the mantle, taking up his pipe and lighting it. Rose mistook the action and worried that Thomas disagreed.

"I won't neglect the children, Thomas, if that's what you're worried about," a little sharper than she had intended. "But I need to do more to be involved in helping those less fortunate. Agnes and I were lucky, but others won't be. Please, Thomas, you do understand."

"Of course, Rose, you misunderstand me. I, well, I want you to be careful." Thomas poured another glass of wine, passing one to Rose. "Come, let's not argue. I think it's an excellent idea. I'm all for it if you think it will interest you." Thomas smiled as he clinked his glass with hers. Rose smiled. Was he just a little condescending? She hoped not and would prove this was not a fad to Thomas.

*

Rose met with Agnes the following Friday at the Casino Café, enjoying coffee and cake. Rose told Agnes about her meeting with Veronica.

"Ooh, Veronica, what happened to Lady Carmichael?" Agnes laughed.

"Agnes, stop it. You are making fun of me. She asked me to call her Veronica and made me feel welcome in the circle. It's nice. I need this, Agnes, surely?" Pleaded Rose as she looked Agnes in the face.

"Stop being so serious; what's wrong, babe? Talk to me."

"I don't know, Agnes; I just don't know. I feel restless since Freda died, and I don't know why."

"Stop blaming yourself," replied Agnes, taking Rose's hand.

"I'm not."

"Yes, you are, and you can stop it right now. Do you hear, babe? It was not your fault. Will I not repeat myself? I'll get Paul to sort you out."

"Don't you dare?" Rose found herself giggling. "Oh, Agnes, I always feel better seeing you."

"Well. I think these charity ideas are just what you need. Tell me all about it next week. Right, I need another slice of cake." Agnes called the waitress over, ordering fresh coffee and cake.

*

Meanwhile, Lady Carmichael had arrived at Macy's department store to enjoy her morning coffee. Walking through the store to the lift, she saw Thomas talking to a store manager. She wandered around browsing until he had finished and accidentally bumped into him as he turned to take the escalator.

"Veronica, my dear, forgive me, how clumsy of me." He reached forward, kissing her hand.

"Flattery will get you everywhere, you rogue." Veronica smiled. "Have you time to join me for coffee? Please say you have. There's nothing worse than morning coffee without company." Thomas took his pocket watch out to check the time.

"Of course, Veronica dear, I don't have a meeting until twelve." At that, she slipped her arm through his.

The conversation over coffee was convivial. Veronica explained their meeting on Tuesday about Ellis Island and how she felt it would help Rose take up a cause.

"I do hope you agree with me, Thomas?"

"Rose talked about it over dinner that night, and I think it would be good. First, however, you will take care of her?"

"But of course, Thomas. Speaking of Rose, my dear Thomas, may I be so bold as to ask your intentions towards that young lady," smiled Veronica.

Thomas fidgeted with his napkin. "I think that's for me to decide, Veronica." A little sharply.

"Oh, don't get all defensive with me. How long have we been friends? I'm only asking. After all, you must know that people gossip, especially a young and beautiful lady who resides in your home under the pretence of nanny and housemaid."

"Veronica, it is not 'under pretence' as you put it, Rose is lovely with the children, and they love her. And yes, she does look after the housekeeping. So, where's the harm?"

"Oh, Thomas, stop it. You know what I mean." Veronica reached across, laying her hand on Thomas. "Do you love her?" Veronica stared into Thomas' eyes. "Well, you do. I know you do. What's the problem? Don't you love her enough, is that it?" After a deep sigh, Thomas looked at Veronica.

"I've loved her from the moment I first saw her — my love has grown stronger over this last year."

"Thomas, dear Rosemary, God rest her soul. I know she would not want you to be lonely. She has been gone for four years. It's time to settle down. Think of the children; Rose adores them as they do her."

"I fear she may reject me; there's ten years difference. I couldn't bear to ask for her hand, only for Rose to refuse. How would we survive? Go on, tell me that, my dear Veronica." Thomas looked across the table, a deep frown on his face.

"Why are men so blind they cannot see what is in front of their eyes? Rose loves you. Stop being scared. If you genuinely love her, then make her honourable and happy. Please don't end up like me, dear Thomas. You would marry for true love, not a marriage of convenience like mine. Why do you think I involve myself with charities? It helps fill my days."

"Is Philip that bad?" Thomas frowned.

"Oh, no, he's good, just not the man I truly love. You know that. But I have learnt to accept my life. Maybe one day I will be free." Veronica sighed. "He's disappointed I'm unable to produce an heir. Perhaps if I had, he might be different. But there we are."

"I'm sorry to hear that. I thought perhaps things had improved these last few years. You both seem happy when we attend your dinners."

"Looks are deceiving, my dear Thomas. But enough of me, we transgress. What are you going to do about Rose?"

"I must think before you bully me more," both laughed. "Now, Veronica dear, seeing you've put my world to rights, I must bid you the good day. I have a finance meeting in the board room in ten minutes. Isidor Straus will be present. I mustn't be late." Thomas stood, taking Veronica's hand with a slight bow and left the coffee shop.

Veronica watched him go. Marry her, you fool, or I shall have something more to say, she thought. Ooh, a wedding. I must look for a new outfit and hat.

CHAPTER TWENTY-THREE

Sunday morning, it dawned bright. After church and lunch, Rose readied the children for their walk to the park. Arriving in the hall, Rose was surprised to see Thomas with a hat, coat, and smile.

"Papa," cried the children. "Are you coming to play with us?"

"I am. It's such a lovely day. I thought I would join you all." Rose felt her heart flutter as they left the house, her arm through his and holding the children's hand. They looked just like a happy family enjoying an afternoon stroll.

*

The park was in its early spring glory. The daffodils covered the lawns like a blanket; iris and snowdrops encircled the base of the trees. The sun shone. Rose breathed in the fresh air and sighed.

"Look," said Thomas, "there's a bench free. So let's sit Rose while the children play."

"Stay away from the pond," called Rose to the children. They waved and laughed, running off to join other children playing.

Thomas removed his hat and watched Lucas and Isabella running around and laughing. He glanced at Rose; what if she says no? Thomas coughed. "Rose, are you still happy with us?"

Rose turned to look at Thomas.

"Why do you ask that? But of course I'm happy."

Thomas looked Rose in the eye. "It's just these last few weeks; you seem distant, distracted. I'm worried that maybe you thought of moving on. Not that I want you to, of course. And it would break the children's hearts." Rose sat a moment at a loss to understand what Thomas was saying.

"Do you want me to go? Is that it? Is this why you've joined us today?" Rose felt sick in her stomach, her heart hammering in her chest. Oh no, he wants me to leave. She tasted the salty tear falling silently down her cheek.

"Oh god, Rose, I'm making a mess of this; I don't want you to go. What I'm trying to say is I, erm." Thomas fiddled with his hat, twiddling it around his fingers. "Well, what I want to say, Rose, is — I've admired you since the first moment we met, and since then, my love for you has grown. I hope you feel the same. But, if you do, would you do me the honour of becoming my wife?" Rose sat transfixed, looking Thomas in the face, her tears turning to joy. He loves me, she thought. At that moment, Isabella ran up with daffodils in her hand.

"Look, Rose, I've brought you some flowers," she thrust them towards Rose, unaware of the conversation she had just had with her father.

Taking the flowers from Isabella, Rose smiled as she turned to Thomas. "Yes, yes," she replied. "I love you dearly." Thomas scooped Rose and Isabella into his arms. Then, releasing them, he looked at Isabella and Lucas, who had joined them, wondering why Rose was crying.

"Lucas, Isabella, I've just asked Rose to be my wife."

"Does that mean Rose can be our mama?" asked Lucas.

"Would you like that?" asked Rose. The children looked at each other and then threw their arms around Rose.

"Yes, please, please be our mama forever!" they chorused. All four huddled together; those passing would have wondered what had just happened to make a small group of people so happy.

*

Six months later, the organ played the 'Bridal Chorus' on

a beautiful autumn morning — as music-filled Trinity Church. Assembled guests watched Rose walk down the aisle, escorted by Lord Philip Carmichael. Rose wore a long, ivory silk and lace wedding dress and carried a bouquet of roses, orchids and orange blossoms. Isabella in pink chiffon and Lucas in blue walked behind as bridesmaid and pageboy. Thomas turned to watch her, and his heart overflowed with love. Then, to the sound of 'Ode to Joy, ' the bells rang out as Thomas and Rose, now Mr and Mrs Blackwood, walked out into the autumn sunshine. Guests followed, showering the newlyweds with paper confetti. Then, the horse-drawn carriage festooned with streamers and cans tied to the back took the happy couple as they made their way to the reception at Casino Royal, arranged by Paul Kelly as a wedding gift, where celebrations went well into the night.

CHAPTER TWENTY-FOUR

A NEW MILLENNIUM

Standing on Trinity Church steps, a thousand-strong choir sang out 1899 and welcomed in the New Century. At midnight, fireworks shot up into the night sky, followed by an electric light display from several buildings; thousands stood in awe of the show. Rose, Thomas, the children, including Ivy, the Carmichaels, Margaret and Lillibet cheered on. Tinhorns given to all young boys blew wild and loud. People cheered and hugged each other, including total strangers; it was a time that people hoped the new millennium would bring a bright new future.

*

After the outdoor event, the Carmichaels invited everyone back to celebrate the New Year. The children drank warm milk, hoping it would calm them before bed.

"Happy New Year, one and all." Philip raised his glass and chorused. Thomas, Rose, and Ivy reciprocated.

"Did you see the fireworks, Papa? They were so amazing." Lucas said, still hopping from foot to foot. "Can we stay up all night and say hello to the new morning?" he asked excitedly.

"No, young man," laughed Thomas and Rose. "I think you've had enough excitement for one day." Isabella, now beginning to wilt, snuggled on Rose's lap.

"I didn't like the bangs," she whispered as she finished her drink and soon fell asleep.

Margaret, the nanny, was quickly taking Lillibet to bed. The milk had helped to soothe her, and she snuggled into her nanny.

"Night, Night, Mama, Papa. Bye, bye," she yawned. Veronica bent down and hugged her.

"Forgive me, everyone, but I'll help put this little one to bed," Veronica and her nanny left with Lillibet. Thomas, Rose and Ivy stood.

"Time for us to go. It's been a wonderful evening and lovely to finish with goodwill." Thomas scooped Isabella into his arms from Rose, wishing Philip and Veronica goodnight as they headed home. All too soon, the children were wrapped up in bed. Thomas and Rose also retired.

"Sweet dreams, my darling," whispered Thomas as he nuzzled into Rose's neck.

*

Two days after the event, Rose was up early. Lucas and Isabella were already in the kitchen with Ivy enjoying their breakfast. Isabella, now five and Lucas, seven, had settled down and loved Rose as their mama. Thanks to Veronica and Rose's firm friendship, the children shared Lillibet's nanny, Margaret. Rose was determined to spend as much time with the children, especially at bedtime. Thomas had wanted to get a full-time nanny. Still, Rose was adamant. Finally, Thomas gave up the fight. However, he did insist on a full-time maid leaving Rose free to assist with the charities.

That morning Thomas had already left early. Thomas had explained a few days earlier to Rose about a potential merger with a financial group in New York that he hoped would go well. Rose knew she might not see him until late that night.

Having had breakfast with the children, Rose kissed them before ensuring they had settled with their tutor. Rose was on her way in the carriage heading for Toynbee Hall to meet with the governor's board at ten o'clock. A lot had happened since her marriage to Thomas nearly two years ago. Veronica Carmichael had persuaded Rose to become secretary for the YWCA. Rose, at last, had found a calling. However, those on the State Board of Charities soon discovered Rose was no pushover.

Once or twice a week, she joined the YWCA ladies at Ellis Island docks awaiting the arrival of new migrants. Stunned by the poverty surrounding her, Rose soon stepped up, determined to help young girls with only the clothes they stood in, believing the tale of New York pavements painted in gold. It took the young girls hours, sometimes less, to realise this was not the case. Many were glad to find refuge and work at the factories or farms within two weeks. Sadly, some accused Rose and her friends of being condescending and snobbish.

"Stick your ideas up where the sun doesn't shine," they had screamed. It didn't take long for them to learn otherwise. Sadly, some disappeared forever, but others turned up half-starved at Toynbee Hall or the other houses. The ladies took them in with no reproach, just a willingness to help and guide them to find safety and work.

While at the docks on one such occasion, when Rose was busy helping two young women whose officials had just cleared, she heard a voice; a tingle of dread ran down her spine, making her shiver even though the heat was unbearable. Turning her head slightly, she saw him. What in god's name was he doing here, Rose thought. Abel, her brother, stood no more than fifty yards away, his arm slung around the shoulders of a frightened young girl. She tried to smooth his temper as he shouted.

"How much bloody longer you idiots keeping us here? We've our fortune to make. Shift your bloody selves." Abel shouted — still as ignorant and arrogant, thought Rose. Carefully looking around, she was surprised not to see her father. Perhaps Abel had run like her.

"Excuse me, but have you gone off helping us?" enquired one of the women looking at her, sighing.

"I'm sorry, I thought I recognised someone, but I was mistaken." Rose smiled at them. "Now, ladies, come with me, and let's get you settled in."

That night Rose told Thomas about spotting her brother.

"I hope he doesn't find me."

"He won't; New York's a prominent place. It sounds like he'll end up in the rough tenement areas. So, I shouldn't worry, my dear. But if he does, you tell me straight away." Thomas leaned over, taking Rose's hand. "Promise me, my dear," he said quietly.

"I will," Rose smiled as she looked into Thomas' eyes. "Love you," she whispered. Thomas looked longingly at Rose.

"It's late, my dear, shall we." At that, both stood and headed for the stairs.

*

On Friday morning, Rose met Agnes. Nothing came between their Friday coffee morning. They caught up on gossip and Agnes' latest performances. Six months earlier, Agnes married Paul Kelly in a private ceremony at the Casino Royal that Thomas and Rose had attended. The other performers put on a show in the lounge, hundreds of balloons cascading onto them as they began their first dance. It was such a wonderful evening, and much to Rose's surprise, Thomas and Paul chatted away like friends.

While having their coffee and cake, Rose told Agnes about seeing Abel.

"It was such a shock, Agnes."

"But he didn't see you?" Agnes enquired.

"No, thank goodness. I hope Abel doesn't seek me out. What am I going to do if he does?"

"I don't think there's any chance. It's a big town, babe. He'll properly end up in the buildings on the east side of the tenements. He's not going to find you."

"That's what Thomas said last night."

"No, don't you worry. And if by some fluke he does well, tell me, and I'll get Paul to sort him out." Agnes laughed.

"No, don't tell Paul he's done nothing yet. And you are right. It's a big world out there," Rose sighed.

*

Meanwhile, at Macy's offices, Thomas discussed the same person with Ely — one of Eastman's men. Thomas and Ely held an uneasy truce since Jack Manus. Ely had known dear Freda for years and felt her loss.

"I want him kept an eye on," Thomas told him.

"Since when did I become a bleeding babysitter?" Ely muttered.

"You know what I mean, any trouble, any sign he's getting close to Rose. But then, you know what to do," replied Thomas.

"I'm beginning to think you're worse than my boss," Ely chuckled.

"Never," replied Thomas.

"You know he still thinks you had something to do with the killing of Jack Manus, well, you or Kelly. He's not forgotten," Ely laughed. Both men looked at each other; neither commented, just a twitch of a smile.

"Anyway, back to business. I'll find this Abel fellow and keep an eye on him. It can't be that difficult to find blond hair blue-eyed English boy. He'll stand out like an alley rat." Chuckling, Ely turned and left, leaving that aroma of his behind.

CHAPTER TWENTY-FIVE

It had been a hell of a crossing. After two weeks of throwing up, the stupid little bitch did nothing but complain. Abel was relieved to see land. His drinking mates back home had told him about the land of the free, its pavements lined with gold. Yeh, thought Abel. I'll make my fortune, return home, and wave it under their snivelling noses.

"Are we docking soon? I hate this boat," Julie whined from the bunker bed.

"Ah, shut your face." Abel groaned at her.

Abel had booked steerage, sharing a room with forty others, so he wasn't wasting his money on travel. But the journey had been horrendous. It had been dark, overcrowded, unsanitary and foul-smelling, and most of their time had been on deck, occasionally even sleeping there. He wished he had never brought Julie with him, but the silly wench had gotten herself up the spout, and she begged and begged to go with him. She knew her dad would kill her — or worse, him, now he was lumbered with her. Perhaps once they'd landed, he could hopefully lose her.

They had to spend the night in the detention block before being checked by doctors and released. As he lay on his bed that night, Rose came into his mind. Had she come to New York? His mate's brother at Liverpool dock was sure he'd seen her boarding the ship for New York. Abel had ridden like hell to stop her, but it was too late; the gangplank was already up. Of course, his sister could have landed on one of the other islands. Would he find her? Abel shook his head. Nah, no chance, he thought.

Early the following day, while waiting to be released, his arm dangling around Julie's shoulder, others told him he'd get accommodation if married, so he thought he would use her a bit longer. Abel saw several women appearing to help those who had arrived singularly. Some charity or other nosy wenches he thought. Nought but do-gooders who need them. He nearly pushed Julie towards them to get rid of her; only he required her to get accommodation. Eventually, some toad of a twit with a clipboard handed them a slip and told them to head for Jackson Street East side — a voucher for food for the first three days.

"Where the hell's this place then?" Abel shouted at the official.

"Follow the others. They're heading in the same direction," the angry official replied, who had had enough of people like Abel by now.

Arriving at the tenement building on Jackson Street was a four-storey, brick-built house. Walking up the steps from the sidewalk, Abel pushed the broken door open, the smell hit them so hard it nearly threw them back down the steps.

"Abel, we can't stay here," Julie cringed.

"I said shut your face or find something yourself. I'm sick of your whining." Leaving her to follow, Abel entered the long hall to find a staircase.

"Oy you, you got a docket. Can't stay here without a docket." A giant man with his dirty braces strained over a shirt just as dirty, stood blocking out the light from the door, his body odour making Abel and Julie gag. Abel handed him the docket.

"It's from the docks. They told us to come here; you've got a room for us?"

"A room, oh ay got a room all right top of the stairs third door along." Licking his lips, he drooled at Julie. "My rooms in the basement if you want some company anytime," he sneered.

"You'll have to pay me," laughed Abel.

"Abel, no, don't," cried Julie.

"Well, stop your snivelling, or I just might." Abel disappeared up the stair to the top landing, reached the third door pushing it open. The stench was just as putrid; there was no window; it was a middle room. Laying on mattresses along the far wall, he spotted two old fellas and four children, their clothes dirty and torn, with noses full of snot and crying. Nearest to the door lay two empty mattresses. Abel dumped his bag on them.

"Abel, please, we can't stay here. It's it's..."

"What did I tell you? You got somewhere better?" Abel sneered. Julie sat on the damp mattress, thinking a beating from her father would have been better than this.

The door opened, and another four women walked in, looking at Abel and Julie. They nodded.

"Just arrived, have you?" their Irish brogue almost singsong.

"Yeh, what's it to you?" Abel glared.

"I'm Julie. Pleased to meet you." She smiled, and the women who had spoken smiled back.

"You can help get the meal if you like," Julie jumped up, glad to be away from Abel.

"I'm Neave, by the way, and this little one..." she ruffled the top of the child's flea-ridden hair. "Is Mauve? She's mine." Gesturing to the other women, she introduced her sister Gwen and her two boys. Rian and Aiden. "I hope you settle in. It's not much, but it's a roof over our heads. Make yourself as comfy as possible, and if you need anything, don't be afraid to ask, okay?" Neave smiled.

"Thank you," replied Julie.

CHAPTER TWENTY-SIX

A week later, at their Charity Board meeting, Rose informed her colleagues of a Briarcliffe Farm Manor letter requesting urgent farmhands — an invitation to The Charity Board Ladies to visit and view arrangements.

"We do have many farming ladies on the last arrival. It could be the answer to our problems. But, unfortunately, we can only send so many out to the farming communities." Veronica replied.

"On our behalf, I have already replied, and we have an invite to visit on Thursday," informed Rose.

"They seem anxious for help. Why don't Rose and I visit?" Veronica turned to Rose.

"That would be fine," the ladies chorused.

"Any other discussions, ladies?" Veronica smiled.

"Excuse me, but I'm a little concerned about information from a cowhand who called yesterday concerning the treatment of two young girls we sent to Whispering Willow Range," said Tilly.

"Why, whatever is wrong?" asked Rose and Veronica together.

"The cowhand spoke to my husband yesterday, asking him to tell me the committee should visit unexpectedly. He didn't give details. But my husband knows him well, assuring me the cowhand was concerned and please not to tell he had informed us. It's not far from Briarcliffe Farm, I believe. Could you perhaps call? I don't like to think any of our ladies are in trouble. The owner seemed so nice and friendly when we first visited. I would go, but I have dinner to arrange. My husband is bringing business gentlemen that evening." Tilly informed them.

"That's fine, Tilly. We'll call after our visit to Briarcliffe." Veronica confirmed.

"It all sounds a little bizarre." Rose exchanged a

worrying look.

*

Thursday morning, Veronica and Rose set off to visit Briarcliffe Farm Manor. They had left early to avoid the midday heat, hoping to arrive in time for lunch, confirmed by telegram on Wednesday.

"I'm looking forward to our visit," she was never tired of seeing the open plains. They stretched for miles, the ever-changing colours of fields reminding Rose of home, not that she missed home. It was the changing seasons. One minute the moors were tranquil only to change in an instance a fierce wind, rain and sleet, almost frightening as it tried to suck the strength out of anyone caught in it. Rose had hidden in her bed as a child, afraid the howling beast would rip the cottage away with them in it.

"Rose, did you hear me?" Veronica turned, smiling.

"Sorry, I was miles away. What did you say?"

"I thought we'd strip off and run wild when we arrive." Veronica giggled.

"No, you did not." Rose thumped Veronica on the arm.

"Well, I could have if you'd listened," Veronica laughed.

"Oh Veronica, for some reason, I suddenly thought of home, not the home itself. The moors on a day like this could be just as beautiful if not more so."

"Do you miss England?" asked Veronica.

"No, not now; the unknown probably made me feel homesick when I arrived. But no, I would never wish to return." Rose looked at Veronica.

"What about you? Do you miss Scotland?"

"Yes." Veronica sighed. "I miss its rugged beauty, its lochs and mountains, the changing seasons all in one day, but, more importantly, because of my love, my only love, my first love, is still there."

128

"Don't. I shall cry," said Rose lifting her hand and softly touching her lips. "Why did you not marry him?" Veronica was quiet, and Rose thought maybe she had overstepped the mark. "I'm sorry, Veronica, forgive me. I did not wish to pry."

"No, no, it's not you. When I think of Robert, I cry with anger at my Father. Poor Robert had no money. Well, what groomsmen do," smiled Veronica.

"The groomsman? Do tell." Rose smiled.

"Not a lot to tell. Robert and I had grown up together. We played as children and even shared the schoolroom, so Robert would eventually learn to read and write to take over from his father. As we grew, our childhood friendship turned into young lovers. It was no whim. We truly loved each other I was happy to live in one of the ground's cottages. But alas, both fathers' soon put a stop to it. Father sent me to my aunt's estate in Inverness, and Philip arrived on the scene.

"Don't get me wrong; Philip is a good husband. But I don't love him."

"Does Philip know?" Rose found herself whispering.

"Oh yes, dear, but I came with money and a title Philip desperately needed. So, he went with the title, which means a lot, especially here. I inherited everything because we had only been married a year before my father's sudden heart attack and death while hunting. So, Philip sold up the estate, and we moved out here so that his banking career could flourish."

"May I ask, would you ever return? Rose glanced at Veronica.

"In an instance, but I'll have to wait until Philip falls off his horse, not likely because he hates riding." Veronica laughed as she whipped the reins encouraging the horses on. They continued their way in silence. Rose was amazed at the revelation she had just heard. Poor

Veronica, she thought.

"Oh, that reminds me. Our nanny tells me she heard there's measles in the area. Many children have it. We must be careful. It can make children so poorly," informed Veronica.

"I remember our whole Sunday school went down with it as a child, and children died. It was terrible," Rose sighed.

"Well, we don't want that do we," frowned Veronica.

*

About an hour later, they arrived at Briarcliffe Manor farm. Again, they were both struck by the size, all thoughts of their conversation about measles forgotten.

The farm was moderate in size, but the land stretched as far as the eye could see. Warmly welcomed by Mr and Mrs Briarcliffe, hence the farm's name.

"What a wonderful homestead." Veronica smiled at Mr Briarcliffe and introduced Rose as they stepped onto the porch.

"Gee mam, it sure is," replied Mr Briarcliffe. "Please call me Tyron, Ty if you like. Come on, meet the wife. Minnie? Minnie? Where are you, woman? Visitors have arrived."

"No need to shout, dear; I heard the first time." A petite woman appeared against her husband's giant frame, her pinny still on. She welcomed Veronica and Rose warmly.

"Excuse his boom; Tyron is as loud as the Simmental Cattle." Minnie laughed. "Come, you must be tired after your journey lunch is ready."

Having freshened up after their journey, Minnie showed them into the dining room, with a large enough table to seat twelve. Looking around, they saw massive horns adorned the walls and rugs scattered across the floor. As they sat, two maids appeared, and all too soon, they were eating. The table is filled with enough food to feed the five thousand, thought Rose.

Having enjoyed a lunch of succulent beef and all the trimmings, Rose felt almost incapable of standing. Declining the Bourbon offered by Tyron and thanking Minnie for such a wonderful spread, they ventured out. Tyron helped them into the landau to drive them around the estate.

Veronica and Rose were amazed at the facilities offered for the following two hours. Normande and Simmental Cattle, including Jersey, much to Rose's surprise.

"Good for cream them," Tyron explained, "don't beat my Jim Beam Bourbon," he guffawed loudly.

Heading back to the farm, he showed them chickens that ran free, ducks, and pigs in their hundreds.

"I hope you can find me a pig farmer. I lost the last chap. Silly bugger ran off to find gold. He'll learn." He then showed them the vegetable garden; it wasn't a garden. It was four acres. "Vegs are ready for picking." Tyron explained, "Just not enough hands can't have them going to waste. That's why I called you. We desperately need pickers." Tyron thrust his hand out towards the crop.

"May I ask." smiled Veronica.

"Why shucks, ask away. That's why you're here." Tyron laughed.

"I was curious to know where all this produce goes."

"Mostly, we serve beef and vegetable markets from here to the Canadian Border. I hope to get over that eventually. I believe the worlds to conquer, that's what they say." Tyron turned and smiled at Rose and Veronica. "With ladies like you finding me good honest workers, that dream will happen. I'll take care of the lasses that come. You have no fear of that. And you are welcome to check anytime, day or night. Comm'n follow me. I'll show you where the workers sleep."

At last, they walked towards two sizeable solid wood barns, one of which Tyron slid back the enormous green door. Stepping in, Veronica and Rose gasped. It was dry and warm. Bunk beds were down both sides, with clean sheets, pillows, and warm blankets for colder nights. A stove stood at the far end of the barn, lit during winter.

"I hope this is ok with you ladies, but we don't have room in the house. It's warm and dry here, and our other hands are happy with the other barns for the men. Minnie feeds them well. Good breakfast to start the day, midday lunch, and a good hearty meal at night. It's their space to do what they like, within reason. The Mrs and I won't have any shenanigans, and if they're going to join us for church on Sundays, we leave at eight. Come on then, back to the ranch time for tea and cake. I know you ladies like that sort of thing. Me, I'm a quick glass of Jim Beam."

Veronica and Rose were astounded as they walked into the dining room to see the table again laid with sandwiches, cakes, tea, or coffee.

"Oh, my word, we are still full after lunch." Veronica almost groaned.

"Nonsense, you must have a sandwich and a slice of cake," Minnie smiled.

"It will soon disappear at teatime," boomed Tyron.

An hour later, Veronica and Rose departed after discussing the arrival of twelve ladies by Saturday. They were all keen farmers and desperate for work, unsure whether they worked with pigs but would inquire on their return.

"We'll enquire for a young pig farmer — if we don't have one of our ladies interested in pigs that is," Veronica told Tyron. Thanking their hosts, they knew their young ladies were safe.

Just as Veronica and Rose were about to set off, Veronica turned to Tyron.

"I'm not quite sure of my bearings. Could you direct me on the path to Whispering Willow Farm?" she smiled, and Tyron frowned.

"Whispering Willow Farm, ladies, I wouldn't recommend it. Don't get me wrong. I'm not worried about losing helpers. It just, well, it's not the place."

"But we already have two young girls working there. Two of our committee ladies left them about a month or so ago." Veronica looked concerned at Tyron.

"You surprise me, ladies, a farm with no women, only the young lasses?"

"What do you mean no women?" Veronica frowned. "He introduced his wife to Tilly and her helper while they were there."

"A wife? No, he never married. I shouldn't think anyone would marry into that family." Then, finally, Minnie arrived on the porch.

"Is something amiss?" she asked.

"Minnie, I was just telling the ladies about Whispering Willow Farm," Tyron explained to his wife.

"Oh, my dears, you don't want to go there. It's not safe." Minnie said, a worried look forming on her brow.

"I was just explaining we have two young girls there. The committee left them at least two months ago." Veronica explained to Minnie.

"He told them he was married," Tyron told his wife.

"Goodness no, Danver never married. His sister Floss escaped him years ago." Minnie said.

"Oh, my goodness," muttered Rose alarmed.

"We have information to visit the farm from a concerned local cowhand," explained Veronica.

"You hang on, ladies. I think one of my men, no make

that two, should accompany you. If those lassies need help, you're going to need them."

"If there's a problem, bring those lasses back here," insisted Minnie. "And be careful, ladies."

CHAPTER TWENTY-SEVEN

It took them nearly an hour to arrive at Whispering Willow Range Farm. Jessie and Tom, the two cowmen, had driven the carriage leaving Veronica and Rose sitting in the back, wondering what faced them upon arrival.

"Don't see any vaqueros," mumbled Tom.

"Excuse me?" smiled Rose.

"Cowhands, Ma'am, ranch seems a little quiet to me."

"They had a field full of longhorn when the ladies were last here to leave the girls. I remember Tilly telling me." Veronica spoke, looking concerned.

"They've never had longhorn, only horses," replied Jessie.

"Oh, but that field was full of them when Tilly and I came first. I, I don't understand. Oh dear, whatever have we done, the girls? What about the two young girls we left with them? Oh, this is so worrying!" Veronica jumped down as soon as the carriage pulled up outside the homestead. Then, running up the veranda steps, she knocked heavily on the door.

"Hello, Mr Danver. Are you there? Hello?" After several knocks, it was clear there was no one home.

"You ladies stay here. We'll look around," the men set off toward the barns.

"Oh, Rose, those girls are only eighteen. I'm so worried." Veronica sighed as she looked across the open plain.

"Perhaps they've gone to market; they could be back soon," replied Rose, more by hope than anything else. A shout from the barn caused Rose and Veronica to jump. Tom waved his hand, and they set off to join him.

"What have you found?" they chorused.

"I think your girls were using this barn; look, clothes and bedding tucked away in the corner. Going over to examine the clothes, Veronica looked up at Rose.

"But the girls were to stay in the house. They had a loft room. The woman showed it to Tilly and me on our first visit and again when Tilly brought them. It was a large, carpeted room with two beds. It looked very cosy. I don't understand why they are sleeping out here." Tom laid a hand on Veronica's arm.

"Sorry, Ma'am, but I think you've been lied to." Veronica felt a lump rise in her throat, letting out a sob as they left the barn.

Veronica looked wildly around. Concern edged on her face. "Whatever has happened, we must find the girls. We are responsible for them."

"Why is there no one here?" asked Rose. "If it's a working farm, then where is everyone?" Rose turned to look at Tom.

"They could be down in the town. There's no horse market, or we would be there. There'll be in a bar if I know them." Tom replied.

"That's all very well, but where are the girls? Why aren't they here?" Rose said again.

A movement at the end of the field caught Jessie's eye. Striding off, he soon broke into a run. Veronica, Rose, and Tom followed, wondering what he had seen. They came across a terrified girl hiding in the ditch, her clothes in tatters. She was half-starved. Veronica recognised her immediately.

"Janice!" Veronica cried. "Whatever has happened? It's alright. Don't be afraid. We're here now."

"You left us," Janice cried. "Why, why leave us with them?" She was almost hysterical. Rose bent down, scooping her up into her arms, and soothed her. Then, gently pulling her up, they returned to the farm. As they approached the barn, Janice screamed and backed away.

"It's alright, Janice. Let's climb into the carriage."

After getting Janice settled, she calmed slightly and had a drink of water.

"You left us!" she cried again.

"Oh, you poor child, I would never have done that if I'd known, I promise you. I'm so sorry." Veronica almost cried.

Taking her hands, Rose spoke softly to her. "Janice, where is your friend?"

"Dead!" she screamed, "They killed her!"

"What do you mean they killed her?" whispered Rose as the bile rose in her throat.

"I think we've found her," Tom mumbled, "There's a mound just under the tree near the stream."

"Oh no, no, please don't say that." Veronica cried in alarm.

"They killed her," Janice repeated.

"How girl?" asked Tom.

"Please, Janice, you must tell us," Rose gently encouraged.

"It was four nights ago they took Helen to the house full of men. They were drunk. I heard her screaming. I was so frightened that I ran and hid. The next morning, I watched as they carried her out and buried her under the tree. They came searching for me, but I managed to hide. They'll be back. They've only gone to town; they'll return with more men. Please, please take me away!" Janice collapsed into Rose as she cried uncontrollably.

"You ladies stay here; Tom and I will get the other lass. We can't leave her here, she needs a proper burial." Half an hour later, with the remains of her friend wrapped firmly in blankets, they left Whispering Willow Farm, heading back to Briarcliffe.

During the journey, Janice told them of their harrowing experience.

"When you left us, we had tea, and everything seemed

fine. And then the men arrived. We thought they were farmers. The woman we thought was Mr Danver's wife laughed at us, told us we would have to earn our keep, and then left. That night we slept in the barn. They locked us in; we couldn't escape. And then, it started. They grabbed Helen, took her into the house, and they, they."

"It's alright; you don't have to explain." Veronica held the girl in her arms. Veronica was shocked and annoyed that she was responsible for leaving these poor girls in their care. The Danvers had lied to her and Tilly, and they had believed them.

Their journey back to Briarcliffe took longer than usual; Veronica comforted Janice as she cried. Upon arrival, Minnie immediately took the distraught Janice into her arms and to the kitchen, a young lad sent for the doctor. Rose and Veronica were glad of the whiskey to help recover from the shock. Tyron advised Rose and Veronica to leave the girl with them.

"Don't worry about the other poor girl. We'll make sure she has a proper burial. We have a family plot on the grounds. We'll ask the preacher to attend."

"What about the owner Mr Danver?" asked Rose.

"You leave that with me. We'll get the sheriff there. They won't get away with it."

By now, it was late in the afternoon. Having seen Janice again and ensuring she was safe with Minnie, they thanked Tyron and left Briarcliffe to head home while it was still light.

*

Lying in Thomas' arms that night, Rose cried for the girl she hadn't known. But she made a promise that this would never happen again. Instead, she would make it her mission to double-check the working conditions before leaving innocent girls on farms, factories or houses again.

Exhaustion took Rose, and she fell into a deep sleep. She dreamed of someone stroking her cheek. But, instead, she heard a soft voice whispering, Mama. Mama. The calling dragged her from her slumber. Rose is suddenly aware that Isabella is standing by her bed.

"Sweetheart, what is it?" whispered Rose.

"My throat hurts," Isabella cried. Then, Rose felt her forehead, gathering Isabella up and taking her back to her room.

"You're hot, darling. It's just a chill. We'll have you well again soon." Rose gave her a few water sips, climbed into bed with Isabella to provide comfort, and fell asleep.

CHAPTER TWENTY-EIGHT

Rose woke late the following day. Isabella stirred and whimpered.

"Sweetheart, do you still feel poorly?" Rose laid her hand on Isabella's forehead, which was hot.

"Mama," she cried softly.

"Stay in bed, sweety, and I'll get you a drink." Hugging her before leaving, Rose turned to pull up the bedclothes, noticing a rash around Isabella's neck. Rose lifted her nighty, her body covered in spots. Then, leaving the room quietly, she headed downstairs to find Thomas having breakfast in the dining room.

"Oh, Thomas Isabella is poorly. I think she may have measles."

"Are you sure, Rose?"

"I think so; I've seen the rash before at school. We all got it; all the children, including myself, were poorly for weeks," She remembered the death of five young girls, quickly discarding the thought from her mind.

*

Later that morning, the doctor arrived and examined Isabella. He soon confirmed measles advising Rose to keep her warm and encouraging her to drink as much as possible. Downstairs he spoke to Thomas and Rose.

"I'm afraid it's very contagious. Lucas will have it as well. I must warn you both that it can become severe."

"What are you saying?" Thomas spoke sharply to the doctor. The doctor raised his hand as if to fend off.

"I would be derelict of my duty not to warn you. Sadly, there have been many cases since the New Year Celebrations."

"Have children died?" whispered Rose.

"Sadly, yes." The doctor replied.

"Is there anything more we can do?" asked Thomas.

"Very little, I'm afraid. Just keep your daughter warm and get her to drink plenty of fluids. I will call again in a couple of days unless she worsens — then do not hesitate to contact me immediately. I bid you a good day as I have several other young patients to see." Raising his hat as he left.

Rose sent a note to Veronica, informing and excusing herself from the arranged committee meeting, concerning the disturbing day they had had.

That evening Lucas became poorly. He cried, wanting hugs from Rose. She lay on the bed, comforting Lucas, leaving Thomas to cuddle his daughter. The following day, the news reached them that Lillibet also had measles.

Over the next few days, Rose had very little sleep. Isabella seemed to get worse, and on the fourth day, Thomas summoned the doctor. After examining her, he turned to Rose and Thomas.

"She is very poorly. There is little else I can do. It would be best if you kept her warm with plenty of fluids. Also, I am concerned about her throat. It is very swollen." The doctor frowned.

"There must be more we can do?" Thomas asked as he agitatedly pushed a hand through his hair.

"You are doing all you can, Mr Blackwood, I assure you. I am pleased to see Lucas is a little better today. That is something." The doctor replied.

Rose stayed with Isabella, cuddling her to offer comfort. Ivy, their cook, tapped lightly on the bedroom door that afternoon. She entered quietly and walked over to the bed.

"Rose dear, I've made an old drink remedy my mother used to make when we were ill. Let her drink it. It can't do any harm," she said tenderly.

"What's in it?" asked Rose, taking the cup to her nose

and sniffing. "It smells nice." Lifting Isabella's head, she encouraged her to drink.

"It's boiled Burdock root with nettles and elderflower. I've brought a jug with me. Give it to her every ten minutes; hopefully, it will soothe her throat, helping her swallow." As Ivy left the room, she told her Agnes had called, but she did not want to disturb her. So instead, she said Agnes 'sends her love' and 'will call another day again.' Ivy also offered to look in on Lucas.

"Thank you, Ivy." Tell Lucas I will come soon.

*

The following morning there was news from Veronica and Philip. Lillibet was dangerously ill. Fearing she would not survive, Veronica begged Rose to call. After lunch, Thomas said he would stay while Rose dashed along to see Veronica.

Arriving at the Carmichaels, the maid met Rose at the door. Her eyes were red from crying.

"Please come in. Lord and Ladyship are upstairs, and you must go straight up." Rose felt her heart quicken as she climbed the stairs. Margaret, the nanny, was on the landing.

"Oh, Miss Rose," she cried, "the poor little mite." Pushing the bedroom door open, the room in darkness due to the curtains being closed — it took a moment for Rose's eyes to adjust. But Rose did not need to ask. She saw Veronica sitting in the rocker, cradled in her arms. Lillibet, the rocker, stopped as Rose knelt and wrapped Veronica and Lillibet into her arms. The grief overwhelmed all. Philip was standing in the doorway, unsure of how to cope. While Rose comforted Veronica, her mind was back home with her children; she should be there but could not abandon her friend. Finally, Rose knew Philip was standing behind her, leaning back on her heels and looking up.

"Oh, Philip, I'm so sorry," Rose croaked. She rose and moved away, allowing Philip to encase his family. She left them to grieve. Margaret was still on the landing. They hugged before Rose descended the stairs, opened the front door, and rushed back to her home.

*

She entered her home and pleaded, "Please, God, keep them safe."

Collapsing into Thomas' arms, Rose cried. "Lillibet is gone. It's so, so sad, poor Veronica and Philip." Thomas hugged her close. "Thomas, what if?" Rose started to say.

"Hush, my darling, we must be strong. Do not think that." Thomas whispered, the thought already crowding his mind.

During the next few days, Rose never left the children's side. Instead, she moved Lucas in with Isabella to be there for both. Ivy continued to give her herbal medicine to both children. Thomas only visited the store in the mornings and then went home for the rest of the day, helping and encouraging Rose to rest, but to no avail — she would not leave the children. Relaxing in the chair next to the bed when she could.

On the sixth night, Isabella was at her worse. She was hot, delirious, and too weak to drink; Rose and Thomas were beside themselves as they feared the worst. Throughout the night, Thomas and Rose remained with Isabella. Lucas, already much better, was asleep on a mattress on the floor. Rose leaned against the pillows cradling Isabella as she mumbled and thrashed around. Thomas sat in the chair and cradled her little hand in his. Rose prayed; she prayed harder than she had ever done. Rose thought of Lillibet, and the tears would not stop.

"Please, sweetheart," Rose whispered, "please stay with us." Oh God, please take me instead. Ivy knocked and quietly opened the door. She had brought another jug of her herbal medicine.

"She won't swallow it," cried Rose.

"Let me; the child senses your distress." Ivy dipped the corner of her clean handkerchief into the liquid and squeezed it into Isabella's mouth, making her cough and splutter.

*

Rose woke to a thin streak of sunshine through the bedroom curtains; dust motes floated around the room. Rose felt stiff and disorientated; the room was quiet. The mattress Lucas had slept on was empty. The chair beside the bed also. Rose frowned, wondering where Thomas and Lucas were. Then, lying for a moment, she realised she must have slept. Afraid to turn her head, Isabella was too quiet, and with tears running down her face, Rose forced herself to look. Two bright blue eyes were staring back.

"I'm hungry, Mama," Isabella whispered.

"Oh, my darling, you're awake," Rose cried, pulling Isabella into her arms; she hugged her, never wanting to let go.

"Why are you crying, Mama?"

"Because I'm so happy you're feeling better," Rose replied, laughing and crying simultaneously.

The bedroom door opened, and Thomas looked in.

"You're awake, my love."

"Oh, Thomas Isabella is better. Our daughter is well." Rose cried. He moved quickly across the room; sitting on the bed, he hugged them both.

"Her temperature dropped early this morning. You were both asleep. I didn't want to wake you," Just then, Lucas ran in, jumping on the bed. He hugged mama too.

"Issy better, Mama?" Lucas almost shouted.

"Yes, darling, she is," Rose laughed.

"Me too; I've been downstairs and had a bowl of

porridge with lots of honey; it was good. Do you want some Issy? Are you feeling better?"

"I'm hungry, Mama," whispered Isabella.

"Then, porridge, you shall have my sweet," replied Thomas and Rose.

CHAPTER TWENTY-NINE

Meanwhile, Abel was drinking bourbon in the saloon, moaning to anyone listening.

"Bloody hell, weeping and wailing, sick to death of hearing it." Two of Eastman's men eyed him suspiciously. They are big rough giants, but when kids die, even they felt sad.

"Your kids mate?" one of Eastman's men asks.

"Nah, I don't have kids. This bloody measles lark… three kids dead where I'm staying —mother's weeping and wailing enough to get any man down." Just then, a youth sidled up, buying Abel another drink.

"Cheers, mate," Abel leered at him.

"Just arrived, have you?" asked the youth.

"Aye, I come from England. Come to make my fortune." Abel laughed.

"We all say that — there isn't any, though."

"Any what?" Abel slurred slightly.

"Money, gold, whatever you're looking for, not for us. Names Marty, what's yours?"

"Abel, pleased to meet you."

"Abel as in bloody bible Abel?"

"Yeh, what's wrong with that?"

"Nothing, just asking," smirked Marty. A snigger went around the bar. "Things aren't good where you're staying, I hear," Marty enquired.

"Say that again!" muttered Abel.

"Why don't you come back with me to meet the gang." Marty smiled.

"Yeh, why not? I've got a girl with me. But, on second thoughts, all she does is whine she can stay with the misery." Abel staggered after Marty as they left the saloon.

Eastman's man Ely watched as Marty left with Abel.

"We need to talk to the boss." Ely winked at his mate.

Abel followed Marty down the fourth and seventh avenues before Marty pushed open the door of Hell's Kitchen Saloon. It took Abel a moment for his eyes to adjust to the gloom. The floor was sticky underfoot. Small dark tables scattered around with the odd chair. Again, the stale smell of cigarette smoke stung the eyes. Marty introduced Abel to the barman.

"This here is Mallet Murphy."

"Who's your new pal?" Murphy leaning on the bar counter raises an eyebrow at the stranger.

"Be nice, Murphy; I thought Abel would like to join us."

"You mean Abel as in…"

"Yeh, yeh, Abel in the bloody bible."

"Why do you call him Mallet?" asked Abel.

"Here, Mallet, show him the reason." From below the counter, Murphy produced a heavy-duty kitchen mallet.

"Just in case you don't behave," he sneered.

"Give him a drink Mallet; make him welcome." Mallet slid a glass of brown liquid over the grimy counter. Able was unsure what he was drinking, but it quenched his thirst. After drinking several glasses of it, he swayed on his feet; only the bar kept him from falling over. A while later, Abel was involved in a card game, losing what little money he had.

"Comm'n mate, let's get back to the digs. So you can sleep it off." Marty laughed as he threw his arm under Abel's — they stumbled on wobbly legs out of the bar.

*

Waking up sometime later, Abel had no idea whether it was night or morning. His clothes felt wet, having slept on damp rags, the smell of rotting food and body odour assailed his nose. His head thumped. God, he thought his digs were terrible, but this, wherever this was, was even worse. Then, realising he was in a cellar, he reached the door in the far corner and stepped out into the alleyway, colliding with Marty.

"Just been to the John; it's down the bottom, mate," Marty laughed.

"Where the hell am I?" stuttered Abel. "Have you seen it in there? It's a dump; bloody hell thought my digs were bad, but that!"

"Yeh, what's wrong with it? If it doesn't suit you, then get lost. You were happy to crash out last night. Oh no, you can't go. You owe my mate Biff money."

"What, what money?" The banging in Abel's head stopped him from thinking.

"Card game mate, last night you lost three games. Said you'd pay him today when you got your money from the digs, remember?"

"No, I don't, and anyway, you took my money last night." Abel pulled his trouser pockets inside out.

"Your girls got money; that's what you said. Let's get it now, Comm'n. You said you lived three blocks away." Marty grabbed Abel's arm and strode off, leaving the alley. "Which way, mate?"

"Jackson Street East side," mumbled Abel.

Arriving at his digs, Abel and Marty stepped over a drunk sleeping on the bottom step, and through the open door. At the top of the stairs, Abel pushed open another door; the smell of death was overpowering.

"Bloody hell," remarked Marty, "you complain about our place?"

Neave sat crouched on her lap, wrapped in a threadbare blanket in the far corner. She cradled a small child who would never see another day. Beside her, another little body lay buried beneath more rags.

"Where's Julie?" Abel demanded.

The woman looked up, her bloodshot eyes full of

grief. "She's out," she whispered. "Gone for help. Please, Abel, please help us." Neave implored. Ignoring her, Abel turned to the corner he shared with Julie, rummaging amongst her clothes to find her purse, emptied the contents, and then strolled from the room, slamming the door behind him.

"Bloody hell, mate, I thought I was hard, but…"

"Yeh, what? I'm sick to death of her wailing. Kids are better off if you ask me!"

Marty didn't speak — Abel missed the look he gave him.

*

Later that night, Abel stood on the corner of Bayer Street Lower East side, watching the man step down from the carriage; only one reason for visiting this part of town. The Lady Gophers opened their door for the night. Rich pickings are afoot, and Abel had no choice but to partake, having given what money he had to Marty's friend Biff, he still owed him — Biff Ellison demanded payment in total, one way or another. Abel had quickly learnt he was one of the gang leaders and thought nothing of slitting a throat. Instead, Abel would wait for the gentleman to reappear from his night of entertainment and strike. Marty had told him this was the best time as they would be intoxicated and relaxed, making them easy pickings even after paying the Gopher Girls.

Things did not go as planned. Knocking the man to the ground and attempting to riffle his pockets, Abel gave no thought to the carriage driver, who struck Abel across his left shoulder, making him scream in pain. Then, turning on the driver, Abel brought his knife upwards, burying it into the stomach. The man collapsed back, and having grabbed the gentleman's watch and money, Abel ran down Bayer Street into Marty around the corner, who shouted, "RUN."

"Bloody hell, should have seen him — a right maniac you are." Laughed Marty as he told the tale to his mates later that night as they stood in Hell's Kitchen Saloon swigging beer. Several of the Lady Gophers' arms are around the men. Battle Axe Annie, a tall masculine woman, sidled up to Abel. Her hair was a rich copper, and her piercing green eyes bore through anyone questioning her. She wore a brown leather skirt, her small axe hanging from a wide belt around her waist, a matching jacket and creamed coloured blouse with a black circular hat.

"Need comfort for the shoulder, sweetheart?" she whispered. Abel laughed, cheered on by alcohol and his newfound mates, feeling he suddenly belonged. He remembered the adrenaline rush as he thrust the knife deep into the flesh of the carriage driver and the startled look on the man's face — his bloody shoulder hurt where the driver had struck him. Yeah, well, the driver wouldn't do that again. He'd taught him a lesson. Marty, Biff, and others clapped him on the back.

"Welcome to the Gopher Gang," they chorused. Then, after watching for a while, a figure quietly left the saloon, disappearing into the night.

CHAPTER THIRTY

SPRING

Sitting on a bench in Morningside Park, Rose tipped her face up to enjoy the warm rays of the spring sun. The daffodils and crocuses carpeted the ground with colour. The leaves on the trees are beginning to bud. Rose breathed in deeply and sighed. The last few morns and evenings, Rose had felt a little bilious since lunch with the committee ladies a week ago, leaving her looking pale. Even Thomas had commented on it at breakfast that morning, especially as she could only manage a slice of toast. Rose hoped it would pass soon.

Leaving the children with their tutor, she returned to visit Veronica. It had been almost a month since the children recovered from measles. But not Lillibet. Dear Lillibet, so small, so sweet; Isabella and Lucas had cried when told she was in the arms of the angels. Rose wiped away a tear as she thought of the funeral. Even the sky had rained that day.

Isabella had not entirely escaped from the disease, leaving her deaf in her right ear and only recently, their tutor informed them that she appeared to require reading glasses — he'd noticed Isabella squinting when reading and writing. After taking Isabella to the American Optical Company shop, Isabella now wore round silver spectacles with a tortoiseshell flip-top case to carry them in. Rose smiled, remembering Isabella returning home and running up to her Papa, asking if he thought she was pretty with her new glasses. Thomas, of course, told her the glasses did not change her beauty, only enhanced it. Rose's thoughts drifted back to Veronica. The loss of Lillibet has left her empty. She'd seemed unable to accept comfort from Philip, who spent more and more time at his club.

Thomas also persuaded Rose to take on Margaret, the nanny, because Isabella and Lucas knew her well. Rose knew he was right. She needed to spend more time at the charities while Veronica grieved. However, the ships still arrived, and new migrants descended on Ellis Island, needing help.

Veronica had confided in Rose that morning that she had written to her first love, Robert pouring out her grief.

"If he replies, if Robert still loves me, I think I shall return." Veronica had cried. Rose felt shocked, letting her know she loved her and would miss her dreadfully if she decided to return to England. Rose did not like to ask how Philip would react.

"Veronica dear, don't do anything suddenly; please give yourself time. I understand your grief, but returning to England is a huge step."

"Oh, my dear Lillibet," whispered Veronica. Rose hugged her.

Rose couldn't help but worry about the charities; how would they cope without her? Perhaps I could persuade Veronica to join me at the next meeting. It will help to get her out and spark her interest again. I can only try, thought Rose. She couldn't bear the thought of losing her dear friend. Sighing, Rose knew it was a selfish thought, but she couldn't help it.

*

Returning home, Rose entered the kitchen to find Ivy, the cook, busy preparing lunch.

"Hello dear, how was your friend today?"

"About the same, Ivy. I'm so worried. Veronica's so lost in grief that I'm unsure what to do," Rose sighed.

"It's only been a month. Her Ladyship must feel bereft without Lillibet. I can understand her loss. My younger sister Mattie lost four little ones during the last pandemic of scarlet fever." Ivy told Rose.

"How terrible, Ivy, I had no idea!" Rose was shocked.

"Yes, well, that's life, my dear. She still has three others, all thriving now. Bless them. Before I forget, there's a note for you on the hall table. It came just after you left this morning."

"Thank you, Ivy. I'll go and see what it is." Rose left the kitchen, collecting the envelope as she headed into the drawing room; recognising Agnes' handwriting, Rose sat to read her note.

*

Rose sat in the Casino Royal Theatre the following day, waiting for Agnes to finish rehearsals that afternoon. Her note was somewhat cryptic, asking her friend to come, as it couldn't wait until Friday.

"CUT! Thirty-minute break, everyone. Thirty minutes!" The dance choreographer shouted.

"About time. My feet are killing me." Agnes moaned to her friend Tilly. "I'm off to see my friend Rose for coffee. See you later." At that, Agnes dashed out of the rehearsal rooms and headed for the coffee shop.

"Rose, you came," called Agnes as she threw her arms around her. "Come on, a coffee. I'm parched." At that, Agnes dragged Rose to the roof garden.

Sitting with her friend, Rose looked across at Agnes.

"Comm'n then, your note was rather strange. What's so important?" Rose smiled.

"Oh, Rose, I've tried to be careful, but I don't know what to do. I haven't even told Paul yet."

"Sorry, but told Paul what? Agnes, dear, you're making no sense. Whatever is the matter?" Agnes looked at Rose above the rim of her cup, her eyebrow-raising slightly; a slight hint of a smile crossed her face. Both girls looked at each other for a moment before the penny dropped.

"Oh, Agnes, you're not?"

"Shush, don't tell the whole damn world."

"But Agnes, that's fantastic news...Isn't it?"

"I don't know. I'm unsure how Paul will take it, what about my singing, my career. But, oh, don't sit there looking at me like that. I like my life as it is, thank you very much." Agnes sighed.

"You must tell Paul immediately. I'm sure he'll be overjoyed,"

"We're not all like you, Rose; maybe I don't want to be a mother. I'd been so careful not to get caught, and now. Oh bloody hell, Rose." A tear trickled down Agnes' face, something Rose rarely saw. Rose handed her handkerchief to Agnes.

"You must tell Paul tonight, don't leave it. It will only get more problematic if you do." Rose saw a frown emerge on Agnes' face. For the first time, Rose saw vulnerability in Agnes which surprised her. Rose reached across, laying her hand on Agnes'.

"Are you afraid to tell him? Will he, you know, will he be mad? Agnes dear, are you afraid to tell him?" Then, removing her hand from Rose, Agnes smacked her friend's hand.

"God no, what do you think he's like? He's not a monster, well, not to me anyway," laughed Agnes.

"I think you'll be surprised. I think Paul will worship you even more. Go on, Agnes. Tell him tonight and let me know by morning. Promise?" Rose smiled at her friend. Taking a deep sigh, Agnes got up and hugged Rose.

"I promise. I should have known you'd look at the romantic side." Agnes laughed. "Can I be a mother, though? That's the question, babe?"

CHAPTER THIRTY-ONE

Battle Axe Annie turned her head on the pillow, looking at the figure beside her. Lying flat on his back, snoring, Abel had seemed pleased with his efforts to woo Annie. Her room was an apartment on the ground floor of a Tenement building shared with five others. It consisted of one bedroom, a sitting room with curtains and a floral carpet. A little luxury that Annie thought she deserved. It had a small kitchen with a wood cooking range, and, most importantly, it came with an indoor closet. Annie had paid cash in full and owned the apartment outright. The five other flats were the same except for the indoor toilet. An outdoor privy stood in the yard. Only the favoured were allowed to share her room and on her terms. She was known as Battle Axe Annie and was the leader of the Lady Gophers.

Some say she's more brutal than all the Gopher men put together. A small, handled axe with dried blood encasing the blade lay at the side of her bed. Annie swung it quickly and easily, splitting any head open of those who upset her. Annie had no desire for love from any man. They are just a means to an end. She knew Abel thought he'd won her over.

"Dream on, Loverboy," Annie smirked as she looked at Abel. They used each other for her needs and Abel for her room's comfort. But one false move and Abel's head would ache. Annie pushed him hard.

"Comm'n your lazy sod, move; you're not staying here all day."

Annie swung her legs off the bed and threw on her silk dressing gown given by a grateful client. Lighting a cigarette, she leaned against the mottled window, looking down into the square, watching barefoot kids scrambling around in the gutter, rifling the rubbish that lay about for any morsels of food. Even in her room, she could feel the tension in the air. The Gopher Gang and The Hudson Dusters had clashed violently, leaving three dead and many injured in the last weeks. Still, Annie knew the big one was coming. She was ready; no one encroached on her patch without consequences. The boys were due to meet that afternoon. Biff, their leader, was raring for a fight.

Just then, Abel disturbed her thoughts.

"Any food, Babe?"

"Sod off and get it yourself," she growled without turning from the window. Abel meandered over to her, placing his arms around her waist. Swinging away from him, she crossed the room, picking up her axe. Then, standing, she glared at Abel.

"I told you to sod off. I've things to do."

"Yeh, yeh ok babes, I'm going," Abel muttered, sidling past Annie and leaving the room; he ran down the outside steps disappearing into Lower East side. God, she's a bloody nutter, that woman, thought Abel. Still, she wasn't bad between the sheets, but he'll have to move on soon. All this gang war stuff was frightening the hell out of him. Abel wasn't sure how he'd got mixed up with the Gopher Gang and Biff. Bloody Biff, he's another nutter. Abel smiled, remembering the robberies recently, not afraid to use the knife, the excitement inside him was thrilling when in control, listening to the pitiful plea for help. His father learnt that quickly, the old bugger did nothing but moan, moan, moan, from morning till night. Finally, he'd had enough and stuck the knife in, burying him on the moors, then doing the distraught son bit, telling anyone who would listen that his father hadn't returned from collecting peat. Eventually, everyone assumed he'd stumbled down an old pit mine. Abel couldn't wait to sell the farm and get on the next boat to

America.

Abel grinned, remembering Rose's lover, Joe, Jack, whatever his name was, waiting at the Old Cross for her. When I turned up, the look on his face was just brilliant. He's another one cluttering the old, mined shaft, laughing to himself as he turned into Seventh Avenue, the aroma from the pie shop reminded him that he hadn't eaten since yesterday, and his stomach rumbled.

Devouring the pie as he sat on a low wall, gravy running down his chin, Abel took in the squaller, the kids in thin, dirty clothes, most with no shoes. He remembered the tavern back home where he had boasted of getting rich and returning to England to rub it into his mate's faces. They had laughed at him. They would laugh at him if they saw him now, knowing he'd found no pot of gold, no land of the free, just deprivation everywhere he turned. It wasn't what he thought it would be. He had to get away and find work, anything but this. Maybe try and find that sister of his. Who knows, she could be living a life of luxury. Yeh, that's what I'll do. See, my bloody sister, thought Abel with a smile.

*

That night, Abel stood with Marty, Biff, and the gang in Battle Row Saloon. They had been there since late afternoon, and although the beer had flowed, their mood was strangely sombre; the lads were itching for a fight. Cudgels, knuckle dusters, knives and guns bulged in their coat pockets. Marty had handed Abel a Six Shot Derringer, which he had hidden. A shiver of excitement flowed through Abel — even though he wanted to be anywhere but the saloon. Then, finally, the doors swung open, and Battle Axe Annie and the Gopher girls swaggered in.

"We've just seen the Hudson Dusters gathering on the corner of Hudson River Docks," Annie informed those present.

"What all of them?" asked Biff.

"Yeh, the gang's Goo Goo Knox, Rubber Shaw, and Bum Rodgers are all there. We counted at least two hundred. We girls are ready, aren't we girls?" shouted Annie.

A roar filled the saloon, and the girls stamped their feet — many carrying meat cleavers, others with cudgels and knives.

"What are we all waiting for?" a shout went up near the door.

"Comm'n lads, let's make this a night they wished they hadn't started," Marty shouted. The saloon emptied, and the Gopher Gang spilt out onto the sidewalk.

*

Biff stood in front of his men — in his hand, a Colt 1849. From side alleyways, others joined them. The Five Points, Eastman, and the smaller gangs. The Whyos gang, are seemingly ready for a fight. Across the wasteland, The Hudson Dusters stood armed and ready. It was beginning to look like a wild west shootout. Blood would run that night.

A single shot broke the standoff as the gangs faced each other across the open wasteland. A shout went up; hundreds of men and women charged.

Abel propelled forward with the crush of men lifting his Berringer and releasing a volley of shots; the thrill of the kill surging through his body. Screaming and shouting filled the air; bullets flew, and meat cleavers swung. Abel fell backwards against a wall finding himself unable to breathe as blood filled his lungs.

*

Later that night, as the dust settled after the battle, the wasteland was awash with blood from the men and women as they lay dead or dying. Children and women were picking over the bodies. The law could do nothing except arrange the removal of the deceased to the morgue — the police knew it was useless asking for witnesses. No one ever saw or heard a thing. The battle was over in less than twenty minutes. Who won? Only those who survived. Those that did survive hid in the cellars or back to their traipsing ground. It had been one of the bloodiest nights of Gang warfare, and it would not be the last.

Slumped in a chair in the Battle Row Saloon, Annie grimaced and cursed while Mallet Murphy stitched up the deep cut on her left shoulder. Her axe was leant against the chair, still dripping with the blood of the night's attack.

"How many girls have I lost?" sneered Annie.

"Four, sorry Annie," mumbled Murphy.

"Bloody hell. Still, it was a good fight. I'm proud of them all. Watch what you're doing with that bloody needle!" Many others, including Marty, leant against the bar, more to support their legs which could not keep them standing, downing glasses of beer, all with cuts and swollen eyes. They raised their glasses and toasted those lost.

"Here, what happened to the bible Abel? Did he cop it?" asked Murphy.

"Yeh, last I saw him, he was coughing up blood good and proper. Bible Abel was becoming a right pain in the butt mind. He never did stop moaning. Good riddance. Still, he fought well. I'll give him that." Marty replied. The men raise their classes again.

"To Bible Abel," they all cheered.

Sometime later, Annie eased herself off the chair. Then, picking up her axe, she slowly left the saloon. "I'm off to my bed," she announced to no one. Shortly after, the bar emptied, and weary bodies shuffled back to their abode.

CHAPTER THIRTY-TWO

Two weeks had passed since the bloody gang war on the waste ground of Hudson River docks. Further minor skirmishes had broken out since, leaving another two dead. Word spread quickly through the other city gangs, one of whom informed Thomas Blackwood of Abel's death. Leaving Thomas with the difficulty of telling Rose, Thomas was sure Rose was in a delicate situation and had no wish to distress her with the news. But they had promised each other never to keep secrets.

I'll wait until the weekend, he thought.

*

In Jackson Street, Julie, who had arrived in America with Abel, sat outside on the bottom of the tenement building steps. A few moments ago, the Landlord had thrown Julie out because she could not pay her rent for the room she had shared with Neave and her sister, who'd both lost their children in the measles pandemic. Julie had tried to offer comfort, but she could do little. Sitting now with her meagre belongings, Julie wiped away a tear.

What a fool I was to believe Abel! He said they would make their fortune in America. Abel had wooed her back home, promised her marriage, and taken over the family farm. Instead, he discovered she was carrying his child. Terrified her father would beat her for bringing disgrace and the family disowning her, she turned to Abel, hoping they would marry and offer her a home. Instead, he sold the farm and got tickets for America. Julie had run and left with him. Within days of the journey, she knew it had been a terrible mistake causing the loss of her baby, leaving her with horrible stomach cramps and sea sickness.

She had no money and nowhere to live. For the first

time in her life, Julie was homeless and frightened. The landlord appeared on the top step leering at her at that moment.

"I told you there's a bed downstairs for some comfort." Julie shuddered at the thought as she picked up her belongings and started to walk away.

*

Hours later, her body aching, Julie returned to Ellis Island. The harbour was heaving with people. There were two ships moored. She noticed people already beginning to board one. Mingling with the crowds, she discovered that one vessel had just arrived, the other bound for England. Julie pondered whether she could sneak onboard. What if they found me? Would they lock me up? Looking across to the arrivals building, Julie noticed the ladies she had seen when arriving. They appeared to be organising the new arrivals. Would they help her? She had nothing to lose. Walking over, Julie found herself standing behind a tall, elegant lady with flowing hair, the colour of the corn reminding her of the cornfields at home.

"Excuse me, excuse me." Julie repeated. The lady turned and smiled.

"Can I help you? Are you looking for accommodation?"

"No, please, I want to go home; please, can you help me?" Rose smiled down at the girl dressed in a plain blue dress and jacket — at her feet, a tattered carpetbag and what appeared to be a pillowcase full of clothes.

"Have you just arrived, have the officials confirmed you're not fit to stay?" Rose asked.

"No, nothing like that; I've been here a while now." Then, before Julie could stop herself, she burst into tears. "I came with my friend, but he's dead, and I've no money. I don't know what to do," she sobbed.

"You poor girl, come with me." Rose picked up one of her bags and walked toward a small building. As she went, she looked back to one of the ladies, calling, "Tilly dear, hold the fort. I need to help this young girl. I won't be long." Tilly smiled, waving Rose away.

Sitting on a wooden chair in what appeared to be a medical building, Julie looked around, waiting for Rose to reappear. Several people sat opposite her and complained that they could not join their families and continue their way. Some had a familiar cough that Julie had heard at home. Her grandfather had died two years earlier from consumption.

"I'm sorry."

Julie listened to the nurse say to the young man,

The nurse continued. "We can't allow you to stay. You must return home on the next ship." The nurse informed him.

"But, please, I've nothing to return to," a coughing fit took his breath.

"I'm sorry, but it's the law. You cannot stay. Now wait there, and I'll get someone to escort you back to the Terminal Building." The nurse patted him on the shoulder. "I must attend to others," she told him, leaving the young man alone. The nurse then turned her attention to an elderly lady who appeared very frail. Julie didn't think she would make a return trip.

Rose returned with tea and sandwiches; Julie looked up, thanking her.

"What's your name?" asked Rose.

"Julie, Julie Bradley, I come from England."

"When did you arrive?" Rose queried.

"About six months ago. I came with my boyfriend; he promised to marry me when we arrived. I carried his child. I lost it during the crossing," Julie wiped away a tear.

"I'm so sorry to hear that. Have you anyone to stay with?"

"No, we had a room in Jackson Street, but my boyfriend didn't come back one day, and then I learnt Abel got himself killed during a gang war. So his mate Marty came to tell me."

The name Abel made Rose stiffen slightly, and her heart flutter. Could it be? She thought. Julie hadn't noticed Rose's frown and carried on.

"I want to go home; I wish I'd never come, but I've no money. Abel returned to the room one day while I was out and took all my money. He left me with nothing. The landlord threw me out unless I slept with him. He was awful, and I couldn't do that; I just couldn't. Please help me. Can you help me? I want to go home," Julie became quite distraught.

"Calm yourself. We'll solve the problem," Rose felt sorry for the girl.

"My dad will kill me, but rather that than stay here."

Rose smiled at her.

"I don't think your father would do that. They would be very concerned about you, not knowing what happened to you. As for going home, if you don't want to stay, I'll have a word with the authorities and see if you can board the ship waiting to return. They will have to treat you as one of the passengers who just arrived. You'll have to be medically unfit to stay. Have another cup of tea, and I'll return in a few minutes."

"Thank you," Julie smiled at Rose.

Julie drank another cup of tea and was glad of a sandwich and a slice of cake offered to her by one of the helpers. While having it, she watched the young man sitting opposite her glance furtively around, realising no one was watching him. He gathered his bag and quietly slipped out of the room; as he passed Julie, he raised his finger to his lips, mouthing.

"Shh." Suppose he was desperate to stay; who was Julie to stop him? Julie just smiled as she watched him leave. A few minutes later, the nurse returned, looking quizzically at the empty seat. Turning to Julie, she asked,

"Have you seen the young man sitting here, Miss?" Julie smiled and shrugged. The nurse tutted and walked away. Sometime later, Rose returned, gently touching Julie on the arm, who had closed her eyes for just a few moments to find sleep had taken her.

"I'm so sorry; I'm just so tired." Julie yawned.

"No need to apologise. I do understand."

Rose looked at the young girl. "May I ask how old you are?"

"Why won't they let me go home if I'm not old enough?" Julie looked anxiously at Rose.

"Of course not, don't distress yourself. I was just wondering, you look so young." Rose laid a hand on Julie's arm.

"I'm seventeen," Julie replied.

"I was nearly your age when I first arrived," smiled Rose. She was trying to put the young girl at ease. Rose sat down on the chair next to Julie.

"You'll be pleased to hear I've managed to find your passage on the ship that leaves tonight. Of course, it's only Steerage, but at least it will get you home."

"Oh, thank you, I'm so grateful."

"Do you have far to go when it docks in Liverpool?" asked Rose.

"Yorkshire, I come from a small village called Castleton. It's on the moors, a bit barren but nice in the summer," smiled Julie.

Rose didn't say anything, but she knew it well. What a small world we live in, she thought.

"And your boyfriend, Abel, was he from there?" asked

164

Rose. Already thinking she knew the answer but needed clarification.

"In the next village, Abel lived with his father on a farm, but his dad died. Abel couldn't wait to sell it, which paid for the tickets to come here. He promised to marry me, then I found out I was pregnant. I miscarried shortly after setting sail. I think it was the seasickness. I thought he was kind and loved me, but he didn't; it was just a ruse to get me into bed with him. I feel like such a fool. I feared my dad would beat me, so I came with him. He abandoned me as soon as we got here. He joined some stupid gang, and now he's dead. I went to the morgue to see him, but I had to run because they told me I would have to bury him, but I had no money. I felt horrible, but what else could I do."

Julie felt the tears run down her cheek. Rose leaned forward and hugged her, whispering.

"Don't worry; I'm sure things will turn out alright."

"Yes, well, that's alright for you to say you're not homeless and destitute." Julie snapped. Then suddenly, slapping her hand over her mouth. "Oh god, I'm so sorry. I didn't mean that. You've been so kind. I don't know what came over me; please forgive me. I'm just so desperate and frightened. I'm sorry." Julie looked up into the kind eyes of Rose.

"I was like you once," Rose told her. "Running away from a hard life, a brutal father and a brother, which is another story."

"You're not from here then?" asked Julie.

"No, like you, I came over as a migrant. It was frightening, and I felt lonely too. I was lucky to make a friend called Agnes during the crossing. We've been friends ever since. And then I met a wonderful man. We've been married nearly three years and have two lovely children."

"Blimey, I hope you don't mind me saying, but you've only been married for three years and have two kids." Julie smiled.

"My husband was already a widow. I'm stepmother to them, but I feel they're mine." Rose smiled.

"Looks like you're having another," Julie laughed. Rose laid a hand on her tummy and smiled.

"How could you tell? It's early days yet," Rose smiled.

"You looked like my mum when she had a bairn; her face always glowed like yours now." Julie giggled. "Oh, I miss my mum and brothers and sisters. I can't wait to get home."

"Well, your wish has come true, and you leave tonight. Now come with me, and I'll get your papers and see you onboard."

*

About an hour later, Julie and Rose stood at the bottom of the gangplank. Julie held a medical certificate stating her refusal to America due to a heart murmur in her hand.

"A heart murmur?" giggled Julie. "At seventeen?"

"Never mind, the physician is a friend. It was the only way to get your returned voyage," replied Rose.

"I know, and I'm grateful. I'm going home, thank you." Julie threw her arms around Rose.

"Look after yourself," Rose slipped a small purse into Julie's hand.

"No, I can't. You've done enough already." Julie pushed the purse back towards Rose.

"It's enough for your train home. So take care of it, and I've put the address of the Immigration House. Please let me know you've arrived safely."

"I will, I promise." At that, Julie walked up the gangplank of RMS Campania. Rose waved and smiled, realising she was boarding the same ship that had brought her to America. Rose felt no sadness watching this young woman on her voyage back to England. No, Rose thought my life is here. Turning and walking back to the Immigration Station, Rose thought of Veronica. Could this same ship take my friend away? Please, God, I hope not, dear Veronica; I would feel lost without her. Veronica had not heard from her love Robert, but Rose knew it took time for mail to travel.

Rose went in search of Tilly.

"Did you get her sorted, my dear?" asked Tilly.

"Yes, the poor girl arrived with a young man who abandoned her and left her penniless. Still, she is on her way home now," replied Rose. Tilly smiled and gently touched her arm. Saying no more, the ladies carried on with their duties.

*

Rose sat with Thomas in their drawing room after dinner that night; Lucas and Isabella tucked up in bed. Rose told Thomas of her day and meeting with Julie, helping her board for the return journey on the same ship, the Campania that had brought Rose and Agnes.

"Do you miss England, my darling?" asked Thomas.

"No, Thomas dear, I have you and the children. What more could I ask for." Rose smiled as she snuggled against Thomas. "But there is something that troubles me, Thomas." Rose looked up into Thomas' face seeing him frown. "Julie told me about Abel. I believe she meant my brother. If so, then he's dead. Caught up in some gang battle."

Thomas sighed, hugging Rose closer to him.

"It's true, my darling. You've heard me speak of Ely?"

"Yes. Freda's friend. Oh, dear Freda," Rose whispered.

Thomas continued. "It was Ely who informed me a couple of days ago. So I thought I would tell you this weekend when we are home for the day. I wasn't sure how upset you would feel, and I didn't want to leave you alone all day. So I hope you'll forgive me for not telling you sooner."

"Of course, Thomas, dear. Did Ely tell you how it happened?" asked Rose.

"It was a gang war, my dear. Forgive me if I won't detail too much, only that your brother died quickly."

"I should feel sad, but I don't. We were never close. Julie also tells me my father died. Abel sold the farm and came to America, searching for his fortune like many. Poor Abel, to be taken so soon after arrival."

They sat quietly for a while as they finished their coffee. Rose looked across at Thomas. She felt herself smile.

"Thomas dear, there's something I must tell you." Thomas raised an eyebrow. "Well, erm, I'm with child," Rose giggled nervously. Thomas took her into his arms.

"Oh, my darling, I thought you were. Your mornings haven't been too good. I am so happy; we must tell the children in the morning. It's late now, my dear. Shall we retire? You must have plenty of rest." Thomas smiled as he stood.

"Not too much rest, my darling." Rose giggled.

*

Over the next few months, Rose bloomed as she went about her daily life, which had settled into a routine. Despite grieving, Veronica returned to work, helping the ladies with the charities.

CHAPTER THIRTY-THREE

On a snowy night, two weeks before Christmas, Tobias Thomas Blackwood arrived screaming into the world. Rose, propped up by pillows, smiled exhaustedly. It had been a long labour.

While the midwife fussed around her, Rose looked down into her son's eyes. They were startlingly blue, and he was perfect with that head of blonde hair. Isabella and Lucas had rushed into the bedroom with Margaret, their nanny. The children stood gazing at their little brother.

"Can I help you bathe him, Mama?" whispered Isabella.

"Can he play snowballs with us soon?" Lucas asked earnestly.

Rose laughed. "Of course you can, my darling," Rose said as she cuddled Isabella into her. "But, Lucas, my dear, I think he's a little too young yet to play snowballs. He'll love it when he's a little older."

"He can play with my train set. Then, I'll make him station porter," said Lucas excitedly.

Thomas, who had been standing behind the children, laughed.

"Comm'n you two time to leave your Mama to rest; you can see them again in the morning."

"Oh, but Papa were not tired," they said, yawning.

"Kiss your Mama goodnight and your little brother." Both children wrapped their arms around Rose and gently kissed their brother on the forehead, leaving the room with their father and nanny.

*

Across town, in the Casino Suites, Agnes was also popped up against a mountain of pillows. In her arms was a beautiful little girl. Paul Kelly sat on the bed, pure joy on his face.

"A daughter, I have a daughter, you clever girl," he leaned in to kiss Agnes.

"Do you still love me?" Agnes whispered as she looked into Paul's eyes.

"Do you need to ask?" A sudden scowl upon his face. "You've just given me the most beautiful gift."

"I'm sorry, don't be cross. It's just me." Agnes smiled.

"Don't ever ask me that again." Paul's face lightened, and he gently took his daughter into his arms; he stood looking at her. "I've always wanted a daughter, and you, my precious, will be called Lilly-Rose Kelly." He whispered, "I will love and protect you and your mother as long as there's breath in my body." Agnes smiled. She liked the names, even though she had not chosen them. Just then, Paul looked at Agnes.

"Darling, forgive me, but I always said if I ever have a little girl, I shall call her Lilly-Rose."

"They're beautiful names, I couldn't have chosen better," smiled Agnes. Paul leaned down, kissing Agnes gently on the mouth; he quietly said.

"Never doubt I love you." It was a picture of pure joy as Paul sat on the bed, his arm around Agnes, cradling Lilly-Rose in his other. Agnes closed her eyes and wished they could stay like that forever.

*

The following day Veronica called around at the Blackwood household. She sat in the chair at the side of Rose, cuddling baby Tobias.

"Oh, he's so lovely, Rose. You and Thomas must be delighted. I'm so pleased everything went well."

"You will be his godmother, won't you, Veronica?"

"It would be an honour Rose — thank you for asking me." Rose did not include her husband, Philip. Veronica was still living in the same house but separately. They had grown apart, unable to reconcile after losing their dear child Lillibet. Having received no word from Robert, assuming he no longer wished to be a part of her life, she had thrown herself back into the charities with Rose, who had been relieved to have her back in the organisation, and, most importantly, she had not lost her friend. Veronica had helped and guided Rose through her pregnancy.

"The purchase of my apartment has gone through," Veronica told her. "I am so looking forward to being on my own."

"When do you move?"

"The beginning of the New Year, it will be a fresh start for us. Phillip has spoken to his lawyers, who have quietly drawn up the divorce papers. We will be signing them at the end of December. Philip has been good and has made life easier for me."

"Will you miss him, Veronica?"

"Oh, I'll see him occasionally. We haven't fallen out; we just never fell in love. He needs to be free to find someone who will love him. There's no animosity between us. I'm glad he freed us both, and to hell what anyone says." Veronica laughed, disturbing Tobias as he snuffled in her arms. "I think he needs his Mama." At that, Veronica returned Tobias to Rose.

Standing, she bent and kissed them both, promising to return the next day.

*

After feeding Tobias and gently placing him in his cot, Ivy arrived with a tray of thick homemade soup and bread.

"I think I'll get up after lunch, Ivy. I'm getting bored of lounging in bed," Rose said.

"You make the most of it, my love; you need plenty of rest. Don't want the Master shouting at us now, do we," Ivy laughed. Just then, the nanny arrived with Isabella and Lucas.

"The children wanted to see you before lunch," Margaret smiled.

"Shall we all eat together?" laughed Rose. So Ivy went to bring their lunch upstairs as a treat to share with their Mama.

*

Christmas arrived with immense joy and excitement in the Blackwood household. Baby Lilly-Rose, Veronica, Agnes, and Paul Kelly came for Christmas dinner. Ivy and Margaret joined the family and guests, pulling Christmas crackers and wearing silly hats; it was a joyous time.

On New Year's Eve, Rose, Thomas, and family, including Margaret, Veronica and Ivy, were invited to the show held at the Casino Royal Theatre. This time, Agnes sat as a guest, enjoying the show. Grazina, Kelly's housekeeper offered to look after baby Tobias and Lilly-Rose.

CHAPTER THIRTY-FOUR

The month of January 1900 was heavy with snow. Unable to get out, Rose had missed her friend Agnes. Veronica had moved into her new apartment at Morningside Avenue, South Harlem. She had purchased apartment three on the first floor, a recently built property of five spacious apartments. It consisted of two bedrooms, a sitting room, a large window overlooking the rear garden, an ornamental pond, and rose bushes that would bloom from Spring onwards. The view from her lounge window at the front looked across to Morningside Parkland, giving an open outlook. Veronica had called twice during the week at the Blackwood household, as her abode was only ten minutes away, giving Tobias lots of cuddles and bringing small gifts for Lucas and Isabella. Philip sold their previous home, not wishing to stay after their split and moved into an apartment near the bank. Veronica had employed a housekeeper who called in daily. Her only regret was that she had heard nothing from dear Robert. Not knowing whether he was alive and well or had moved on and married, frustrated Veronica. If only he would write her a few lines to let her know. Veronica had spoken with Rose and admitted it was fruitless to return to Scotland and perhaps cause Robert problems if he'd settled with a family.

*

The cold weather took hold over the next few weeks. Mr Harold, the children's tutor, could not get in, so Rose and nanny Margaret kept the children busy. Rose continued with their reading and spelling, and Isabella learnt to sew with the nanny's help. At the same time, Lucas played with his train set. Both children helped with baby Tobias at bath time.

As the sun came out one weekend, the children

dressed warmly, played in the garden and built a snowman adorned with twigs for the arms, an old scarf of their papa's and a carrot for his nose, taken from the kitchen table. At the same time, Ivy was busy stirring a pot.

Tobias was a contented baby, sleeping well; Rose only woke once to feed him during the night. Thomas had sent a note to Paul and Agnes ascertaining their health and baby Lilly's. A reply returned to Macy's. Agnes had sent the letter to Thomas for Rose, telling her how sweet and contented Lilly-Rose was. Much to Agnes' surprise, 'Paul adores her and spends as much time with Lilly-Rose as he can.' She told Rose that she still had not returned to the theatre and that all was well and hoped to be out once spring arrived. 'How can one tiny being of love change everything?' Agnes had added.

*

March arrived with the roar of a lion; the wind howled, and the snow turned to rain. The snow had melted within a few days, leaving the roads and sidewalks slushy. By the second weekend, the wind dropped, the rain went, and the sun appeared.

Rose and Margaret, the nanny, walked into Morningside Park on a glorious spring morning. Tobias wrapped warmly in his perambulator. Lucas and Isabella ran around, glad to be free of the house. The daffodils waved their heads in the soft breeze; Rose and Margaret sat awhile, enjoying the freedom.

"I must return to the charity board next week," Rose said. "The ships will be coming in. The women will need help."

"Don't fret over the little Master. He'll be fine." Margaret smiled as she pulled his blanket up just a little more.

"I know," replied Rose. "It's just the thought of

leaving him."

"All mothers feel the same, but you won't be away long." Margaret smiled.

Just then, Veronica arrived and they all spent an enjoyable two hours in the park together, playing piggy-in-the-middle with Lucas and Isabella. Squeals of laughter as Veronica kept missing the ball.

Back home, Veronica stayed for tea, the two women arranging to meet at Toynbee Hall the following Monday morning. Thomas arrived home, and Veronica excused herself. He offered to walk her home, which she said wasn't necessary, but Thomas insisted.

CHAPTER THIRTY-FIVE

Mid-April and Ellis Island once again heaved with the arrival of two ships. The RMS Lucania arrived first from Liverpool, carrying hundreds of migrants from Ireland to escape the poverty sweeping their country. Some were also from Liverpool, hoping for a new life — the second coming early afternoon SS Furnessia from Glasgow. The charities' ladies knew their main concern was with the first ship, as the next one was a second-class passenger ship. Most passengers were returning from visiting relatives in the United Kingdom or on business trips. If anyone travelling alone required assistance, they would ask in the main hall.

*

Two hours after disembarking from SS Furnessia, Robert McGibbon still felt as if he was at sea. His legs were not relatively stable, and he felt himself swaying ever so slightly. Standing in the Immigration building, he enjoyed the tea and cake the volunteers offered him. Then, seeing an official with a clipboard, Robert touched him on his shoulder.

"Excuse me?" Looking at the smartly dressed young man, the official realised he was not from the RMS Lucania.

"Just arrived on the Furnessia, Sir?" the official asked.

"Yes, I'm sorry to trouble you, but could you tell me how to get to Lower Manhattan? Morningside Square, to be precise."

"Ah, you're a good hour from here, Sir. I suggest you get a carriage, the safest way to travel. It will take you directly." Robert thanked him. "Follow me, Sir, and I'll show you the carriage rank."

The official called a porter to store Robert's luggage on the trolley; they headed to the main outer door.

Before too long, Robert found himself seated in an open-top carriage. Robert stared around him; being a countryman, he had never seen so many people. With the hustle and bustle of the harbour and the shouts of workers unloading from a cargo ship, Robert wanted to cover his ears. His father would laugh if he saw him. Get a grip, man, he would have shouted. Robert found himself smiling.

As they drove out of the harbour gates, Robert passed four carriages and watched as girls no older than his two nieces back home, who had just celebrated their sixteenth birthdays, climbed into them. Two ladies standing by the carriage doors ticked off their names on a clipboard. Then, from the building opposite, a lady stepped out with three other young girls, and for a moment, Robert gasped. His heart quickened. He looked again, but the lady in question had disappeared. His carriage continued quickly, leaving Robert unable to see past the harbour entrance. Robert's heart slowed as he sat back in his seat, frowning. It couldn't have been. God, I'm so anxious to see her. Perhaps I should have written before setting off, he thought. Oh well, I'm here now. I want it to be a surprise.

Leaning back, Robert turned his face upwards and enjoyed the sun's warmth. His journey from Glasgow, England, had been long and arduous, and although his accommodation was comfortable and the food excellent, he was not a fan of the sea. The first few days, Robert had struggled to keep his meals down. Although he laughed as he thought of his legs wobbling when he walked down the gangplank, they still did three hours later. Finally, brought out of his thoughts, Robert sat upright, suddenly aware of gunfire in the distance.

"What is that?" he shouted to the driver.

"Nothing to worry about, Sir, just some idiots arguing. Your first time in New York, is it?" the driver asked, slapping the reins on the horse's back, causing them to break into a quick trot.

"Yes," Robert raised his voice above the noise.

Robert's mind wandered back over his last year. Shocked after receiving the letter from Veronica, Robert was determined to drop everything and rush to her side. Unfortunately, not possible due to his mother's poor health.

In January, England mourned the death of Queen Victoria. At Robert's home, his father ran the stables and prepared the hunters for his customers and the squire. Robert had just registered with The Jockey Club, deciding to turn his skills to racehorses, the thrill of attending races watching the apprehension of jockeys as they mounted, heading out to the start and, of course, the win. So far, his most significant achievement was the 63rd Grand National in March this year, held at Aintree near Liverpool. It was touch and go that day whether it would run. Eventually, the horses set off in a howling snowstorm. The syndicate's horse Drumcree was pushed into second by Gruden. Although disappointed, no one could disagree that it would be a race to remember because of the conditions and that the winner won by chance. His trainer admitted he had packed butter into the horse's hooves to prevent snow from clogging; it appeared to work. Their horse Drumcree had won several races, still bringing a reasonable price for a second. All the time, Robert had thought, I must write to Veronica.

Relaxing in the carriage, Robert smiled. Finally, at last, he was here. He couldn't wait to tell Veronica all his news. His letter of introduction to the New York Jockey Club was safely in his wallet. Robert's biggest hope was to be part of the winning team at the Kentucky Derby in May of the following year. He looked forward to meeting with the McDowells, already a thoroughbred racehorse owner. Robert sighed suddenly, feeling sadness as he thought back to waving goodbye to his father nearly three weeks ago as he boarded SS Furnessia in Glasgow.

"Don't desert us too long, my dear boy," his father had shouted.

Now Robert felt a pang of guilt. Would he ever return home again? Perhaps one day for a visit, Robert hoped it would be with Veronica as his dear wife. So, dear Veronica, he thought, so near my darling.

The carriage crossed Poughkeepsie bridge, and Robert was suddenly aware of shouting looking over to his left. A gang of men looked intent on killing each other. Not like this back home, thought Robert.

"Don't worry, Sir," shouted the carriage driver. "Be passed in a minute, a little light entertainment for you," he laughed. A shot rang out. The carriage driver slumped in his seat, the reins dropping loose. Within seconds Robert was up, climbing into the seat next to the driver gripping the reins in his hands; he desperately tried to control the frightened horses. As they slowed, Robert breathed a sigh of relief. Bringing the horses to a stop, turning his attention to the driver, Robert was relieved to hear him moan.

"Hang on, and I'll get us some help." Another shot rang out.

CHAPTER THIRTY-SIX

The following afternoon Thomas looked up from his desk at Macy's. A frown crossed his forehead. In front of him was the familiar figure of Ely.

"Why are you giving me these things?"

"I thought her ladyship would like them," Ely replied.

"What happened?" asked Thomas.

"My mates and Hudson Dusters decided to have a minor kerfuffle."

"They're never minor," replied Thomas. Ely smiled.

"Ay, well, it was for my men. The young fellow was in the wrong place at the wrong time; he caught a loose bullet. I checked him over but could do nothing — bullet in one side out the other."

"Keep the gory details to yourself," Thomas sighed.

"Went through his pockets and found his wallet and the Carmichaels old address, a photograph of her ladyship, so thought the best thing to do is bring his belongings to you. Otherwise, it would all have disappeared in seconds. Instead, they've taken him to the city morgue. Sorry to bring sad news, but there it is." Ely told him. Thomas rose from his seat, extending a hand and thanking Ely.

"I'll call on her ladyship this evening. Thank you for bringing his things to me," Ely acknowledged the hand and left, leaving his familiar aroma behind. As Ely walked down Fifth Avenue, he was annoyed that the young wastrel ducked just as he fired. He felt sad for the young man whose life was lost.

That evening Thomas told Rose of Ely's visit; shedding a tear, Rose felt sad for Veronica, who had waited all this time for Robert only to have him snatched from her grasp so cruelly. The following morning Thomas and Rose visited Veronica. Rose held her hand as Thomas retold Ely's story.

"I've asked them at the city morgue to hold Robert so you can visit if you wish," Thomas replied. Veronica sat numbed.

"Why is life so cruel, Rose? All this time, I thought he would never come and now..."

"I am so sorry, Veronica," whispered Rose. "Would you like me to come with you if you see him?"

"No, my dear, it's not for you, but Thomas, I would be grateful for your support."

"Of course, Veronica, we shall go in the morning."

"I must ensure he has a proper burial and write to his parents. But, oh, it will devastate them. They're bound to blame me."

"What happened was out of your control, Veronica dear. It would help if you did not blame yourself." Thomas stepped forward, taking Veronica's hands into his, hoping to comfort her.

*

At the end of the week, the sun shone down on the small gathering of people at Morningside Cemetery. Veronica stood motionless, watching Robert's coffin lowered gently. After prayers, Veronica, Thomas, and Rose stood awhile until Thomas took both ladies' arms and gently led them away. Then, a small gathering of friends, including Paul Kelly and Agnes, returned to Veronica's. Little could be said. Unbeknown to anyone, Paul Kelly had come under the pretence of accompanying Agnes. His man Ely had informed him of the unfortunate stray bullet, his only way to offer his condolences.

The following day Veronica arrived in Rose's sitting room.

"Are you sure you feel up to this?" asked Rose, "I can take Tilly with me to meet the next ship."

"No, thank you, Rose, but I must carry on. If I don't, I

shall crawl into a corner, never to emerge again." Veronica stepped forward, Rose took her into her arms, and there they stood. "Oh, Rose, he came to me. He still loved me, and a damned stray bullet robbed me of him. Life is so unfair. I've lost dear Lillibet, and now Robert, I shall go insane if I don't work."

"I won't allow that to happen." Rose smiled gently. "We'll get through this together."

"I sat down last night and wrote to his parents. I hope they forgive me for taking him from them, but they need to know," said Veronica sadly.

"They will understand, I am sure; they knew of his love for you. Nothing could have stopped him from coming. No one was to know what would happen. But, come, Veronica, we must leave for Ellis Island, or the ship will be in before we arrive."

Rose and Veronica left to gather their hats and coats, climb into the carriage, and head for the docks. Rose suddenly shivered as she thought of Robert a week after climbing into the carriage, never making it to his beloved Veronica. Rose turned to look at her friend, taking her hand. Then, aware of what each thought, they settled back in the carriage for the journey.

CHAPTER THIRTY-SEVEN

Spring turned to summer, and life became a routine for Rose, Veronica and Agnes. Isabella had just enjoyed her fifth birthday. Thomas, Rose and the nanny had taken the children for a week's holiday in the Catskill Mountains. Going by railroad was a thrill for Lucas. While there, they walked, enjoyed the cleaner air, and visited Kaaterskill Falls. It was good to refresh the mind to improve health, especially for Lucas and Isabella, who still had problems from the measles pandemic. Isabella tired easily.

Baby Tobias appeared to love the clear blue sky and trees around him, kicking his little legs, laughing and giggling all day. A swing fastened to the tree never seemed still. Squeals of laughter resonated down the valley. Lucas had gone out on the rowing boat with his father and caught salmon earlier in the day. With delight, the children watched their papa and mama prepare and cook it on a barbecue to eat outside on the cabin's porch. For a few days, life seemed free and accessible to everyone.

One evening on the porch of their cabin, Rose rocked gently on the rocker. The children had settled for the night. Thomas appeared with a glass of wine in each hand. They sat together in comfortable silence, enjoying each other's company and watching the sunset disappear below the mountains until stars lit the sky.

"What a wonderful week we've had," smiled Rose as she took Thomas' hand.

"Indeed, my dear, we must do it yearly," replied Thomas. "By the way, before our holiday, I talked to Harry Selfridge, he's keen to holiday in England again. He has his mind set on building a store in London. According to Harry, the ladies of London have very few department stores to cater for their needs."

"Oh Thomas, are you to go with him? I don't wish to sound mean, but the thought of you leaving us for so long," Rose gently squeezed his hand.

"Calm yourself, my dear, as if I would leave my family. No, Harry is asking for my advice and, perhaps knowing him, some financial gain. Macy's Department Store will wait until we have seen all the information before embarking on an extravagance. I must say, though, it does sound somewhat intriguing." Thomas chuckled. "Harry has the grand idea of calling it 'Selfridges' the chaps quite the confident retailer." Thomas yawned, standing, offering his hand to Rose "time to retire, my darling."

*

A week after returning from their holiday, Rose, Veronica, and the ladies were back at Ellis Island. After settling several young ladies needing help, Veronica strolled through the immigration arrivals checking they had missed no one when a tall, elegant gentleman raised his hat and smiled at her.

"Ah, excuse me, but could you help? I'm looking for my niece arriving on the SS Pretoria from Hamburg. I've asked several of the Immigration officers here, but no one seems to have found her. I am somewhat concerned."

"Have you tried the registration office; perhaps she's waiting there," Veronica replied, somewhat taken aback by the handsome gentlemen standing before her.

"Forgive me; my name is Captain Friedlander; my niece's name is Katrien; she is seventeen and a little mischievous, shall we say." Veronica laughed at the twinkle in his eye as he told her of Katrien.

"Let me take you to registration and see if we can locate your niece." Veronica, followed by Captain Friedlander, arrived at the office to find that no one was waiting to be collected.

"Do you know what she is wearing, or perhaps you could describe her? It might help to find her?"

After describing his niece as tall for her age, "she gets it from me…her height, I mean," the captain chuckled. "You cannot miss her with her hair of russet colour and green eyes. I told her to wait for me at the reception centre, but I looked everywhere and wasn't late arriving either. I wonder if she didn't make the boat, perhaps still stuck in Hamburg."

"Oh no," replied Veronica with a smile. "I think I remember your niece. At this very moment, she is travelling on the carriage to Toynbee Hall, a place for young ladies arriving independently."

"But she knew I was coming; what do you mean travelling to Toynbee Hall, and what is Toynbee Hall, may I ask?" Captain Friedlander became somewhat agitated.

"Please, Captain, do not stress yourself; my name is Lady Carmichael. I'm a director of the Young Women's Christian Association. I assure you your niece is relatively safe. However, she did appear to be on her own and did not comment that her uncle would be arriving."

"Yes, well, as I said, she is somewhat mischievous.'" Captain Friedlander replied.

I could call her something else, thought Veronica, but said nothing. "Please come with me, and I'll introduce you to Rose. We'll go there immediately." Then, returning to the carriage, Veronica introduced the captain to Rose. "It appears, my dear, we scooped up a young lady we shouldn't have. I've asked the captain to join us." Veronica laughed. Rose lifted an eyebrow towards Veronica and smiled as they excepted the captain's hand, stepping into the carriage.

CHAPTER THIRTY-EIGHT

"KATRIEN!"

The voice boomed across the room, making those present stop what they were doing; two young girls dropped their cups of tea. All heads turned to see a tall man striding across the room. Eyes fixed on the young flaxen-haired girl laughing with her tales of her journey from Hamburg only a moment earlier. Uncle Willem shouted at the young girl as she ran across the room, throwing her arms around the man.

"You found me, uncle. I've had such an exciting time with these people; they've been so kind."

"Please stop your incessant talk and tell me why you did not wait child, as I instructed?"

"Oh, uncle, you're cross. I'm sorry." Katrien dropped her eyes, in a look of remorse.

"You do realise, Katrien, that I was concerned for your safety, and I've had to trouble these two ladies." Veronica stepped up and touched the captain's arm.

"We've found your niece; all is well. Please don't stress yourself," hoping to defuse the situation. "I think it calls for another cup of tea and sandwiches. Come, let's all sit," smiled Veronica.

After enjoying refreshments and listening to Katrien's tales from her journey, including suffering seasickness and throwing up over a duchess on her way to join her cousin in Kentucky, Captain Friedlander stood to leave.

"Thank you, ladies, for caring for my niece. Perhaps I could persuade you both to join us for dinner tonight. We're staying at the Waldorf Astoria Hotel."

"Thank you, Captain, but there's no need," replied Rose and Veronica.

"I insist, please. It's the least I can offer." After a bit of further persuasion, Veronica accepted. Rose declined graciously, explaining she had children and would be dining with her husband.

Sitting in the carriage travelling home, Veronica giggled. "That young madam is going to be a handful. I hope her uncle is ready for her."

"Oh, I think he's in for quite a shock with that one," laughed Rose.

"I wish you were joining us this evening, Rose," Veronica frowned.

"Nonsense, I'm not playing gooseberry."

"Don't be silly, Rose; it's just a thank you." Veronica flapped her hand at Rose.

"He is rather handsome, though, don't you think?" replied Rose with a glint of mischief in her eyes.

"Stop it; I shall tell Thomas his dear wife has been flirting." At that, they both collapsed into fits of laughter.

*

Veronica stepped down from her carriage at seven o'clock that evening, entering the Waldorf Astoria Hotel on Fifth Avenue. Captain Friedlander greeted her in the lobby.

"Lady Carmichael, I'm so pleased you joined us."

"Veronica, please."

"Veronica, it is, and please call me Willem." Taking Veronica's elbow, he escorted her to a chair.

"Shall we wait for my niece in the Foyer? Katrien won't belong. Ah, here she is now." Veronica saw Katrien wearing a soft, baby pink satin and lace gown with a high neckline and little puff sleeves. Pink satin slippers complement the outfit. Katrien's flaxen hair swept back from her face with a pearl grip, the rest flowing freely down her back. What a beauty, she thought. Katrien hugged Veronica with young enthusiasm.

"I'm so glad you're here," she laughed, gently

scooping her arm through Veronica's.

"Shall we?" Willem escorted the ladies through the foyer, past the grand fireplace of marble, adorned by three statues of the Italian Renaissance, passing the grand staircase and the Empire Room housing the elevators and into the dining room. The Maitre'd showed them to their table. Veronica glanced around. She had always wanted to come to the Waldorf, but Philip had always favoured the Hotel Astor in Times Square. The dining room was elegant, with panelling and columns carved of marble from Northern Russia, its carpeted flooring with matching drapes. The Chippendale furniture finished the look. Veronica found herself sighing gently, wondering what Philip would have thought.

During dinner of oysters, Rockefeller roasts beef and trimmings, with coffee to finish, Veronica learnt of the sad demise of Katrien's parents and Willem's brother from cholera three years earlier.

"Oh, my dear, how awful for you." Veronica laid her hand on Katrien, noticing a tear slip down her face. Veronica gently wiped it away with her lace handkerchief. Katrien smiled.

"It still makes me feel sad," whispered Katrien.

"So, have you both only just arrived here in New York?" asked Veronica.

"No, no, I've lived here for five years now. Katrien stayed with her dear Grandmama until her death two months ago," Willem said.

"I stayed with a friend while Uncle Willem organised a passage for me to join him here," Katrien explained. "Uncle Willem deals in diamonds, don't you, uncle."

"I do indeed. I advise Tiffany's. They've recently branched out into high-class jewellery."

"How exciting I love Tiffany glass. I have several lamps at home but no tiffany jewellery," Veronica smiled.

"We are moving to our new home on Fifth Avenue at the weekend; it will be lovely to unpack fully," Katrien chatted.

"May I ask why you're residing at the Waldorf if you've lived here for five years?" asked Veronica. "Oh, please, don't think me rude by asking."

"Not at all." Willem raised a hand. "A bachelor's apartment is no good for my niece to join me. So, I have purchased a house and updated it. We hope to move in at the end of the week — a big change for us. But, of course, I have already employed a cook, housekeeper, and maid for Katrien. After all, one must take one's guardianship seriously." Willem laughed. "You must come and visit us when we're both settled."

"Oh, please say you'll come." Katrien smiled.

Veronica looked at Willem, smiling, "Well, if your uncle doesn't mind, perhaps I could take you to Macy's and visit my dear friend Rose who you met at Ellis Island."

"Ooh, yes, please, could we shop while there?" Katrien asked excitedly.

"Of course, it would be fun," replied Veronica.

"Excellent idea. I wondered what Katrien would do while I'm at business," said Willem with a smile.

"If I may be bold, what if your husband will mind you spending time with my niece?"

"Oh, Philip and I are divorced. It was all very amicable. It just wasn't meant to be. I've kept my title as it helps with the business." Veronica saw the frown on Willem's face. "Oh, dear, now I've shocked you."

"Not at all. We are in America, and one must adjust to the American way of life," replied Willem.

"There were other mitigating circumstances I cannot go into," whispered Veronica.

"Please, Veronica, do not stress yourself. I…"

"Uncle Willem had a lady friend for two years, but she got fed up with waiting for him to say the married word. Is that not true, Uncle?"

"Yes, thank you, Katrien," smiled Willem, his eyes twinkling. Katrien had broken the awkwardness, and laughter erupted.

*

Returning home after her evening, Veronica sat in bed enjoying her supper drink and thought over her night with the Friedlander family. It had been delightful. She would tell Rose about it in the morning when she visited. Then, turning her head, Veronica looked at the photograph of her dear Robert picking it up; she kissed it.

"I will always miss you, my love, but life goes on whatever happens. I hope you'll be happy for me." Kissing the photograph again, she replaced it on her bedside table; switching off the light, Veronica snuggled down, and all too soon, sleep took her.

CHAPTER THIRTY-NINE

"Mama, mama, please, please, can we go?" chorused Isabella and Lucas as they hopped from foot to foot, in the dining room just after breakfast.

"Papa, please," pleaded Lucas. Thomas threw his head back and laughed. On the first page of his morning paper was a photograph of elephants and camels, with clowns and various other exhibits. The headline read, "Join Barnum and Baileys Greatest Show on Earth Parade — Sunday, September 15th, 1900 - Come One and All."

"It will be very smelly," replied their papa.

"Please, mama, tell papa we can go. It will be such fun." The children chorused.

Rose frowned. "What a shame we have two ships coming into Ellis Island this Sunday. They've been stuck at sea for two weeks due to bad weather. Veronica, me, and the ladies will have to be there. Those poor people they'll be in a dreadful state, no doubt. Perhaps Thomas, you could take the children to the Parade and take the nanny with you. I'm sure Isabella and Lucas will have lots of fun."

"Thank you, Mama," said the children excitedly. "Please, papa, please," they begged. Thomas laughed as he threw his arms up in the air.

"Very well, my dear, if I really must," replied Thomas.

"Is that a yes, Papa?" cried Lucas.

"Can we ride the elephants?" asked Isabella.

"Most certainly not." Thomas laughed. "Your mother will never forgive me if I bring you home in pieces. Now shoo, and let me finish my paper in a little peace, and then we'll have a walk in the park." Then, turning, the children ran to the nanny who had just appeared at the door.

"Nanny, we're going to see the circus parade," the

children chattered away as they disappeared upstairs to play in the nursery.

*

Early fall in Morningside Park had become Rose's favourite time. Lucas and Isabella loved running around, kicking the leaves or throwing them into the air to let them fall like confetti over their heads. Thomas and Rose apologised to the groundskeepers, who looked slightly miffed after raking them up to put into the wheelbarrow.

Trees with yellow-orange and russet leaves gently fell in the breeze. Nanny pushed Tobias in his perambulator, now sleeping after his feed. Arm in arm with Thomas, Rose strolled past the fountains and waterfalls as they cascaded at the eastern end. The perfume from the rose beds assailed their noses. They stopped to admire Lafayette and Washington's recently installed bronze statue. Rose sighed, and a feeling of contentment rushed over her; she thanked the gods for her good fortune. They would finish their walk with afternoon tea at the park tea rooms, with soft drinks for the children before returning home.

*

Sunday morning broke with clear skies and just a hint of crispness. After church and lunch, Margaret, their nanny, readied the children for their outing. Rose had already left. It was a busy day for her and the other ladies of the charity board, as two ships were due at Ellis Island. Before leaving, Rose hugged the children telling them to stay close to their Papa and nanny while at the Parade.

Riding in the carriage, Lucas and Isabella never stopped talking about all the animals they would see. Nanny Margaret, and their father, tried to keep them calm but couldn't help but laugh. Ivy, the cook, had offered to look after Tobias being too young to take.

Leaving the carriage at Macy's, they went to Main

Street. Thomas found an ideal position, standing on steps leading up to a hotel — giving them a great view away from the crowds already gathering along the sidewalk. In front of them, a stall keeper had set up selling hot chestnuts.

As time passed, the groups grew until, eventually, a mass of people justled high spiritedly, waiting for the parade to start. Then, finally, the sound of trumpets and tambourines grew nearer — everyone began to cheer. Tumbling acrobats followed trick riders as they leapt on and off the horses backs, some disappearing under their stomachs before reappearing to stand on the saddles and wave. Clowns ran up and down, tossing sweets at the children, some carrying buckets pretending they were heavy with water before throwing them at the masses who squealed, trying to back away only to be covered by colourful confetti, causing gales of laughter.

All too soon, the parade stars arrived; the elephants were enormous. Lucas jumped up and down, squealing with delight. Isabella was not so sure and hid slightly behind her Papa.

"Papa," she whispered, "they're so big I don't think I'll ride one." Her father laughed, putting a comforting arm around her shoulders. The elephants came to a standstill in front of them. With encouragement from their keepers, the elephants knelt and bowed to cheers and applause from the spectators. A baby elephant sat on its haunches and threw a ball using its trunk. With the help of the adult elephant's trunk, a scantily clad young woman climbed up, to sit on its neck just behind its ears and waved. The cacophony of noise is deafening. Isabella covered her ears and began to cry, the noise too much. Suddenly loud bangs and firecrackers danced around people's feet, making them jump and shout. The young lady grabbed hold of the rope around the elephant's neck, fear in her eyes for all to see. The elephant trumpeted loudly and began to stamp and sway. As its keeper tried to control the elephant, it finally took off, and panic ensued. Screams fill the air. Thomas turned, grabbed the children and shouted at the nanny to move. He pushed them back towards the building's double doors, which fortunately swung open; they collapsed in a heap in the foyer just as one of the elephants collided with the food stall outside, sending debris into the air and flying through the window, covering them with glass. Thomas protected the children with his body as others rushed through the doors trampling on them, trying to escape. Thomas pushed them away, and, getting to his feet, he gathered the children. They are crying with fear.

"It's alright, you're safe now," he reassured them. Both were trembling. Then, looking around, Thomas gasped. The nanny unconscious on the floor, he pushed the children behind him; he knelt to help her. She was deathly pale, and the nasty cut on her head was bleeding profusely.

"Margaret, Margaret!" Thomas shook her gently. Then, taking out his handkerchief, he carefully held it to her head.

"Nanny, nanny," the children cried. Suddenly a familiar figure rests his hand on Thomas' shoulder.

"Allow me, Sir," Ely bent down, scooping up the nanny, moving her to the side of the foyer away from the chaos surrounding them. Thomas is glad to see Ely.

"Where the hell did you spring from?" asked Thomas. "Not that I'm pleased to see you."

"I was just across the street and saw you move into here. So I came to help." Nanny moaned as she lifted her head. Thomas breathed a sigh of relief.

"Margaret, lie still. You're bleeding."

"The children, the children," she muttered.

"They're quite safe, Margaret, don't worry yourself," replied Thomas. Isabella moved forward and hugged the nanny. Lucas followed.

"Oh, my little ones, you're safe," she cried. Ely moved to the door and looked out. He returned and informed them that the crowd had dispersed, but many lay injured.

"We should leave, Sir," Ely announced, "before the children see too much."

"Margaret, can you stand?" asked Thomas.

"Yes, I think so; my legs are ok. It's just my head that hurts." Helped up by Ely, the nanny swayed slightly. "Ooh dear, I feel a little dizzy."

Ely wrapped an arm around her, and Thomas took the children's hands as they headed for the door. Outside, it looked like a war zone.

"Papa; papa," cried Isabella as she grabbed her father's coat. Scooping Isabella into his arms and shielding her eyes. Thomas looked down at Lucas, who was holding tight to his jacket,

"Don't let go, son," Thomas spoke quietly, not wanting to frighten them further as they hurried from the scene.

CHAPTER FORTY

Unaware of the chaos in Main Street, Rose, and Veronica, with the other ladies from the charity, returned to Toynbee Hall with three carriages. The young ladies they'd collected from Ellis Island were distressed. Due to the ship's late arrival and steerage, they only had water and a little meatless soup for the last week of their journey. Also, they had been unable to wash due to the water shortage. The young girls gathered in the kitchen and gratefully took bowls of hot meaty soup with a chunk of bread. Three were causing concern. One was heavily pregnant, and Rose believed she had been in labour for some time and was about to deliver.

"What is your name?" asked Rose.

"Betsy," she whispered before folding over in pain.

"Try and have some soup. It will help." Rose held the bowl before her, but she shook her head.

"NO, no, I can't. It hurts so much — please, please help me!"

"Take her into the room next door," Veronica whispered, "there is hot water on, and I'll get some clean towels." Veronica disappeared while Rose gently took her arm and led Betsy into a small room. A single bed sat under the window, with two chairs against the wall, and a fire was lit, making the room warm. Helping Betsy to undress and covering the bed with an old sheet, she laid her down. Betsy curled into a ball and cried, followed by a scream.

"The baby's coming!"

"It's alright, just hold my hand," Rose tried to soothe her. Just then, Veronica arrived with clean towels, along with Dot, a helper from the kitchen.

"Don't worry, pet. I've delivered plenty of babies in my time. We'll soon have this little one out." Dot patted

the young woman, using soothing words. Rose and
Veronica were glad of her help. "You won't have heard
about the Circus Parade on Main Street, elephants the
size of houses ran amok, killing dozens of people and
injuring many more. Our lad ran down to tell us." Dot
babbled away while checking the young girl, oblivious to
the shock she was creating. Rose had frozen to the spot.
Turning, she grabbed Veronica's arm.

"Thomas, the children, and the nanny are there. Oh
my god, what if they're injured? What if..." Veronica
held her hand.

"Stop that thought right now. If I know Thomas, he
would have got them to safety. You go. I'll look after
things here."

"No, I can't leave all this. But, oh, Veronica, what
shall I do?"

Joe from the stables was sent to Macy's to gather
information and return quickly. Rose wiped a tear away
and turned her thoughts to the young girl on the bed.

An hour passed, Rose was beside herself. Joe had so
far not returned, and her mind was in turmoil.

"Where the hell is Joe? What's keeping him?" Rose
muttered to Veronica.

"Give the poor lad time. It's the other end of town
from here. He'll be back. Things will be alright."
Veronica tried to soothe Rose. But, at the same time
frightened that something was dreadfully wrong. Betsy
screamed. She seemed to be struggling. Dot moved away
from the bed, whispering to Rose and Veronica.

"Babes breached. I can't turn it, and she is bleeding
heavily. Where's the doctor?"

"I have no idea. I can only presume tending injuries at
the Parade. All doctors are busy at the hospitals," replied
Veronica. "We'll have to manage, do what you can,
Dot?" asked Veronica.

"Poor lass," said Dot as she moved back to the bed. Just then, the door flew open, and Joe arrived.

"Out, you cannot be in here, out now!" shouted Dot.

Rose turned, to see Joe, who lifted his finger, beckoning her out, she followed him. Veronica moved over to the bed, and Betsy grabbed her hand — it felt cold and sweaty, her face devoid of colour. She whispered. Veronica leaned down to hear what she said.

*

Outside the room, Joe, breathless after running, looked at Rose.

"Your husband said to tell you he and the children are safe and will return home shortly. Nanny got a knock to the head but is alright, and not to worry."

"Thank you, Joe," breathed Rose with relief. "Go to the kitchen, get something to eat, and keep the horse and carriage ready. I shall return home as quickly as possible."

"Yes, Miss," replied Joe, who then ran towards the kitchen.

Stepping back inside the room again, Rose was shocked to see the scene before her. Betsy was lying lifeless on the bed. A tinge of blue on her lips told Rose all. She saw Veronica and Dot trying to bring life into the tiny form lying on the table.

"It's no good. It's joined its mother. We can do no more," Dot whispered.

"Poor little mite, it stood no chance. The crossing won't have helped. Perhaps she had already been in labour too long before we got to her," Veronica sighed.

"Oh, how dreadful," Rose cried with frustration that the doctor had not come to help.

"Leave them to me. I'll tidy up," said Dot.

"Thank you." Rose and Veronica whispered.

"We'll inform the authorities to arrange her funeral."

Veronica opened her hand and looked at the crumpled piece of paper Betsy had given her. On it was the address of her parents. Veronica would notify them.

A short time later, having organised and settled the other girls, Rose and Veronica were preparing to leave Toynbee Hall.

"What a day. I'll be glad to get home." Veronica sighed. Rose hugged her and climbed into the carriage; she dropped off Veronica first and returned home. Rose pushed open the door as Isabella ran down the stairs.

"Mama. Mama, you're back," she threw her arms around Rose and promptly burst into tears. "The elephants frightened me, mama," Isabella whispered.

"I'm here, my darling. All is well." Rose scooped her into her arms, kissing her gently on the forehead. Lucas was halfway down the stairs.

"Mama, we had such an exciting day. The elephants went wild. They trampled PEO…."

"Thank you, Lucas, that is enough. You're frightening your sister." Thomas appeared in the hall.

"Sorry, Papa," Lucas went to his mother and hugged her.

That night as Rose tucked Isabella into bed with a hug and kiss,

"Mama?"

"Yes, my darling?"

"I don't like elephants and don't want to go to the circus."

"Hush now, sleep my darling, don't worry; you're home and safe. We won't be going to any circuses." After tucking Isabella in, Rose entered Lucas' room, where the nanny had settled him. Lucas threw his arms up for a hug, and while Rose kissed him goodnight, he whispered,

"It was so scary, mama. But I looked after my sister."

"I know, my love, you were fearless, and I'm very proud of you," smiled Rose as she kissed him and wished him goodnight. Then, Rose and Nanny left the room.

Rose turned to Margaret and, taking her hand, she asked,

"Are you alright? Did the doctor see you?" That bruise looks very sore on your forehead.

"Bless you, Rose, I'm fine, just a cut from flying glass. It was the little ones that worried me. Thank the Lord, all is well." At that, the two women hugged before Margaret retired for the night.

Sitting on the sofa, Rose rested her head on Thomas' chest downstairs in the drawing room. A tear slipped down her cheek.

"Oh Thomas, when I heard, I feared the worse. I couldn't bear it if anything happened to any of you." Thomas took her into his arms, and there they stayed for some time.

*

Meanwhile, Veronica, glad to be home and exhausted, was bathed and relaxed in her silk gown when a knock on her front door summoned the maid. Tapping her lounge door, the maid appeared.

"Excuse me, Ma'am, there a Captain Friedlander to see you."

After hesitating, Veronica replied, "Show the gentlemen in." The maid disappeared, then reappeared with Captain Friedlander.

"I was in the neighbourhood and thought I would call. I hope it's not too late?" noticing Veronica in her silk gown.

"Not at all, but you must forgive my attire as I have had a rather taxing day; I was not expecting company."

Veronica moved to the sideboard picking up the bourbon. She turned.

"Would you join me in a nightcap?"

"Most kind, my dear," relaxing on the sofa, Willem took the glass.

"You look a little frayed, my dear. Care to share?" Veronica sat on the chair opposite and sighed. She told him of her day and the sad loss of the mother and child. After another drink, Veronica could not hide a yawn.

Willem stood, "You're tired; I must let you rest. Will you join me for lunch tomorrow?"

"That would be lovely," replied Veronica. Willem kissed her hand, holding it just a little too long, then bid her good night.

Snuggling down in bed, Veronica smiled. It was good to see Willem. Would the love blossom? Only time will tell. She picked up the picture of Robert, holding it to her chest and cried.

CHAPTER FORTY-ONE

Christmas time at the Blackwood family was a hive of activity. Isabella and Lucas were helping their father and nanny with the Christmas tree. First, Thomas lifted Isabella so that she could place the star on the top. Then, having celebrated his first birthday, baby Tobias pulled at the baubles and streamers around the tree base.

"Come here, young man," laughed Thomas, picking him up and swinging him in the air.

Nanny turned to laugh. "Come along, children. Time for the party; we must get ready." Invited to the children's Christmas Party at the Casino Royale, their mother was already there to help prepare. After giggles and running from the children, the nanny soon had their outdoor clothes on, and they kissed their papa goodbye. Finally, the nanny left with the children. Thomas breathed a sigh of relief as he poured a bourbon and sat in his favourite chair to read his paper.

*

Arriving at Casino Royale, the first thing to greet everyone was the enormous Christmas tree to the side of the front entrance, adorned with wrapped boxes tied with giant bows and lots of glittery stars, including a massive gold-coloured star on the top of the tree. Rose was already at the door waiting. She scooped baby Tobias into her arms as the nanny helped Isabella and Lucas down from the carriage.

"Is everything ready, ma'am?" asked the nanny."

"Oh yes," laughed Rose. "I'm short of breath with all the blowing up of balloons." Isabella and Lucas, unable to stand still with the excitement at the thought of the party, were securely held by the nanny as they followed Rose to the party room. They found Agnes with baby Lilly-Rose, who had celebrated her first birthday, giggling madly and throwing her little arms to Isabella and Lucas. Many other children were racing around the room wildly. Paul had arranged for a children's entertainer. Then, that 'particular person' would also appear at the end of the Christmas Party.

Nanny Margaret moved to join Grazina, now housekeeper and nanny to Lilly-Rose. Then, turning to Rose said, "Leave the little ones with us. There'll be fine. We'll shout if we need you."

"Thank you, Margaret," replied Rose.

Agnes looked at Grazina. "Make sure she doesn't fall."

"I will take good care of her, ma'am," Grazina replied.

Rose looked across at Agnes in the coffee lounge a little while later.

"Ok, going to tell me what's wrong?"

"Wrong? What do you mean wrong? Nothing's wrong," snapped Agnes. Rose raised an eyebrow as she looked over the rim of her cup.

"What's poor Grazina done?"

"Done? Grazina's done nothing," replied Agnes.

"Then why did you snap at her just then? She is a good nanny; she loves Lilly-Rose. Where would you be without her?" Rose looked intently at Agnes.

"Nothing wrong, it's, it's…oh Rose, it's just me. I don't know."

"Is it Paul?" enquired Rose.

"Paul, why do you always think it's Paul? No, it's got nothing to do with Paul. He's a good man, so leave him alone." Agnes snapped as she took a drink of her coffee. Rose sipped her coffee and said nothing while waiting for Agnes to continue. I know my friend too well; she always tells me in the end. Both friends sat quietly for a few minutes until Agnes replaced her cup with a rattle.

"Oh, Rose, well, I miss the things that Lilly-Rose

does, and Grazina sees it all. But I'm sick of coming home to hear that Lilly-Rose has done something for the first time or that Paul has returned early and spent the afternoon with her. I'm her mother. I should be the first to see and hear all this, for God's sake. But, instead, I'm busy with rehearsals or performing. And don't you dare tell me it's my choice, or I'll thump you?"

"Wouldn't dream of it," smiled Rose leaning across and taking her friend's hand. "I miss things too, and sometimes I stop and wonder if I should give everything up and stay home. But I couldn't now I have responsibilities. And just like you, I love what I do. The children have Margaret. I still tuck them into bed each night and spend time at the weekend with them unless a ship comes in on Sundays, which can be annoying. Oh, Agnes dear, it's life. Although you're a good mother, life's never straightforward — we, of all people, know that. I know you are always late for performances because you tuck Lilly-Rose up each night and have stopped sleeping in the morning to spend time with her. You are tired. You sing until late and need your sleep, so take it. Stop trying too hard. Lilly-Rose will still be there the rest of the day. Your daughter knows you love her, just as my children know I love them. You and I are not the sort to stay home like dutiful little wives and mothers sitting in a rocker chair knitting. God forgives!" Rose laughed. Suddenly Agnes burst out laughing. "What, what have I said?"

"You, little old mum sitting in a rocker knitting, where did that come from?'

"At least I've made you laugh," replied Rose.

"Oh, Rose, you're right. For some reason, I've just felt down these last few days; seeing you always lifts my spirits," smiled Agnes.

"Now, promise me you'll stop trying to do too much.

It would help if you had your sleep," Rose looked at Agnes. "Then you can enjoy the time more with Paul and Lilly-Rose, promise?"

"So, my dear husband has been telling tales has he?"

"But of course, Agnes dear. Men are worse gossips than any women!" Rose laughed. "Now, promise me you'll rest more and stop worrying."

Agnes gave a big sigh. "I promise, Rose."

"Good, now where's the cake."

They spent the rest of the afternoon enjoying time together, Agnes showing Rose her new evening gowns for the show and arranging plans for the Christmas period. Then, late afternoon, a person dressed in red arrived, showering gifts on all the children.

"Ho, Ho, Ho, Merry Christmas!" he chanted.

Shortly afterwards, with happy, exhausted children, Rose and their nanny climbed into the carriage for home. Agnes was by the door, Lilly-Rose in her arms.

"See you, Christmas Eve," Agnes called.

Rose leant out of the carriage window. "Remember Agnes. It's our choice."

"Shut up," came the reply, followed by laughter.

*

On Christmas Eve, the Blackwood House was full of guests, Paul Kelly, Agnes and Lilly-Rose, who shared the cot with Tobias in the nursery, and Rose had insisted Veronica bring Willem and Katrien. Nanny had shared lunch and tea with the family and was now quite happy to stay in the nursery with a glass of sherry.

Paul and Agnes had sent Grazina, their nanny, home for Christmas to see her family — so they had decided to stay in the guest room, instead of leaving late with Lilly-Rose now sleeping.

Much to everyone's surprise, Katrien sang carols accompanied by Rose on the piano. Impressed by her singing voice, Paul Kelly enquired if she thought of the theatre.

"No, my mother was an opera singer, but I have no wish to follow in her footsteps. I have already told Uncle Willem that I want to become a journalist. I've already written to the New York papers and have an interview in the New Year. It's so exciting. I can't wait." Paul Kelly frowned.

"Forgive me, my dear, but isn't that a male-dominated, cutthroat life?"

"You sound just like Uncle. I want to be a journalist, and nothing will stop me." Katrien pouted at Paul Kelly, making him laugh. "Now you are laughing at me. Don't be cruel." Katrien's green eyes glowed fiercely under the light.

"Not at all, my dear. I think it's very admirable of you, and if I can help, please don't hesitate to ask."

"My good man, please don't encourage her," Willem smiled.

"I learnt never to argue with women long ago, especially strong-willed varieties. Isn't that right, my darling?" leaning down, Paul kissed Agnes.

"Oh, please don't bring me into the equation."

"Well, I think it's a wonderful idea, Katrien, and I wish you luck," Rose said. "Now, more drinks, everyone, and eat plenty of food."

Everyone enjoyed the rest of the evening.

CHAPTER FORTY-TWO

In January 1901, Katrien stepped down from the carriage in Chambers Street, Manhattan. She was standing in front of the Cary Building, the home of New York Sun Paper. Its imposing architecture climbed high into the sky; nerves and excitement shivered through her. Its façade of Italian Renaissance reminded her of the Waldorf Hotel she had stayed in with her uncle when first arriving. She took a deep breath and stepped through the doors into the light, airy foyer with marble flooring — benches and chairs on either side of the lobby. She noticed only gentlemen were seated, some chatting animatedly with colleagues or reading a newspaper. A security guard stood behind a desk to her left, just inside the door, smiling at her. At the far end of the foyer, an oak desk dominated the corner where a woman with a stern expression was arguing with a rather angry gentleman.

"May I be of assistance, miss?" the guard asked.

"Thank you, but I have an appointment at eleven. I'm to announce myself to reception." Katrien smiled, thanking him.

"The receptionist shouldn't be too long; perhaps you'd like to take a seat." The security guard escorted Katrien nearer to the reception desk.

"Thank you," replied Katrien, as she moved over to an empty chair to wait, the boom of a voice travelled through the foyer.

"Damn you, woman, how dare you put my name in print. I'm innocent. Do you hear me? Innocent! You will hear from my lawyer." Ten minutes passed before the rather irate gentleman was unceremoniously escorted from the building.

"Charlatans, the lot of you," he shouted as he

disappeared. With the receptionist now free, Katrien walked up to her desk.

"Excuse me; I have an appointment with Marie Mattingly Maloney."

Without looking up, the receptionist barked. "Name?"

"Miss Katrien Friedlander." The receptionist raised a long, elegant finger pressing the shiny brass bell to her side twice, bringing a young boy to her desk.

"Miss Friedlander for Maloney." The receptionist spoke without even glancing at the boy. He took off, rushing up the staircase to his right, returning shortly after, taking up his position against one of the pillars, ready for his next call. Moments later, Katrien spotted a petite lady descend the stairs. As she walked over to the desk where Katrien was waiting, she noticed the lady had a slight limp. Reaching Katrien, she extended her hand, smiling.

"Miss Katrien Friedlander?"

"Yes, pleased to meet you." Katrien smiled.

"Come with me, and I'll show you around."

Going up the stairs, they entered a long corridor. On either side were doors. Marie Maloney opened several as they walked down, introducing Katrien to different departments. Not that she would remember them. They climbed again at the end of the first floor and arrived on the second. Marie Maloney pushed open a half-glass door, to a small room with a desk and swivel chair that's sat in front of double windows looking down onto Chambers Street — another smaller desk and chair with cupboards and shelves to her left.

"Welcome to my little abode. It's not much, but it's mine." Marie Maloney laughed as she pushed books off the spare chair, signalling Katrien to take a seat while opening the door and shouting across the corridor.

"Stephanie, get some tea. So, tell me why you want to

be a journalist?" Marie Maloney stared hard at Katrien, who felt slightly intimidated, as she closed the door behind her.

"Because I want to do something productive, not sit at home and be a little lady wasting my life Mrs Mattingly Maloney," Katrien replied.

"Oh god, Marie, please, we don't stand on ceremony here." Just then, the door swung open, causing it to crash against the wall behind. A buxom lady slightly taller than Marie, her brown hair tied severely back into a chignon and wearing silver framed glasses which rested on the end of her nose, carried a tray and slammed it down on the desk, making the cups rattle in their saucers and scowling,

"I'm not your bloody servant."

"Thank you, Stephanie, dear," replied Marie.

"Huh!" sniffed Stephanie, turning and smiling at Katrien as she left, slamming the door behind her.

"Dear Steffi, she's been with me for years and loves to moan." Marie poured each a cup of tea, handing one to Katrien. "Now, dear, you were saying."

Katrien told Marie about her life and how she came to be in New York and lived with her uncle.

"I want to write about the plight of those poor migrants and how they treat them in the squalor that most must live. I want the public to learn about the hard work the ladies of the charity organisations do. My uncle's friends are from the organisation. They do fantastic work for young girls just arriving. I want…"

"Whoa, stop right there, don't run before you can walk, Henny. Firstly, I'm sorry for your loss. It must have been hard to lose one's family. Secondly, you should learn first that ladies in the journalism world must work hard to get into print. That's not to say we don't have a voice because, my God, we do. But, if you want to get into journalism, you've got to start at the bottom. I don't mean scrubbing floors but learning from others. Know what the people out there want to hear and not hear sometimes. You've got guts. I'll be here Monday morning at seven, giving you a month. Then, I shall tell you if I think you're no good."

"Thank you, Mrs... I mean, Marie, I can't wait; I promise you won't regret it."

Marie stood and laughed. "Tell me, child, how old are you? Something I should have asked before starting our interview."

"Seventeen, eighteen in two months," Katrien replied, holding her breath in case this woman told her she was too young.

"And how does your uncle feel about all this?"

"He thinks I'm mad and tells me I should become a governor or teacher. But he knows journalism is my first love, and I don't want to do anything else. Thank you for giving me a chance."

"Don't thank me now; you might find you hate it. Anyway, until Monday morning, don't be late; I hate lateness."

They had walked down the stairs and were now in the foyer. Marie turned, smiled and shook Katrien's hand.

"Until Monday, my dear, unless you change your mind. Goodbye."

*

Out on the pavement, Katrien looked back at the Cary building and smiled, I will be the best journalist this paper had ever seen, laughing as the security man whistled for a carriage.

CHAPTER FORTY-THREE

Paul Kelly stood in Tammany Hall, a stronghold of Democratic Politicians. He had come to see Timothy Sullivan, a prominent U.S. House of Representatives and leader of Tammany Hall. Sullivan ran legitimate theatres, including nickelodeons. He also ran the athletic club owned by Paul Kelly called the 'Kelly's Young Boxers Club.'

Timothy Sullivan was a giant man with a ruddy complexion towering over Paul Kelly, but whose friendship was strong. Standing in his office, Sullivan raised an eyebrow, a glass of bourbon in hand.

"Well, Kelly, my friend, what brings you to my door?"

"Reform, it's time to clean up this state. Eastman and his gang especially."

"Sure you want to cross Eastman?" Sullivan asked. "You got some death wish. You have gone soft since fatherhood." Sullivan laughed as he refilled Kelly's glass.

"It's not that. People get sick to death from street battles twice or thrice a week. Children getting caught in the crossfire, including innocent citizens. A gentleman shot not so long ago, having just arrived here — a friend of a friend, which caused distress. I'm not saying I'm shutting down my organisation. It's just time to tidy up the roughnecks." Paul Kelly downed his drink.

"Your lads, of course, not included, ay?" Sullivan chortled.

"If Eastman's men and the Gophers pick fights, my men have to retaliate; that's all I'm saying." Paul Kelly replied.

Sullivan raised an eyebrow at Paul Kelly. "The only way you're stopping Eastman is by locking him up or..." Sullivan stated.

"…whichever way, simply take him down, and his gang collapses." Paul Kelly interrupted. "You in?"

"What exactly do you hope I can do?" Sullivan raised his hands in question.

"You've got sway, Sullivan. You'll think of something. What's your work here if you can't sort this out? Tell me that!"

"I'll call a meeting but can't promise anything," Sullivan refilled their glasses. "Now, Paul, enough of work; how's this little one of yours?"

*

Sitting in the Casino Suites, Agnes laughed as little Lilly-Rose pulled herself up on the chaise longue. Agnes had a rare morning due to technical issues with stage lighting. She had sent word to Rose, hoping she would join her for coffee — a knock at the door heralded Rose's arrival. Agnes stood, and both women hugged. Rose had brought Tobias with her, leaving Isabella and Lucas to have lessons at home.

"It's so good to see you. I wasn't sure if you could come." Agnes smiled.

"You just caught me. I was about to take Tobias to the park; he's full of energy this morning," Rose laughed as she watched the little ones sharing toys. "Tobias will enjoy this much more. How are you, Agnes? I hope you feel better about yourself and being kind to Grazina?"

"Yes, and Yes," replied Agnes, just as Grazina appeared with a tray of coffee and cake.

"Go on, Grazina, tell my dear friend I've not been the wicked witch."

"You're never that, Ma'am," Grazina replied.

"See, told you." Agnes smiled.

"Stop putting the poor girl into an awkward situation," Rose laughed.

"Would you like me to pour, Ma'am?"

"No, thank you, Grazina, we can manage." At that, Grazina knelt to play with the children while Rose and Agnes enjoyed their coffee.

"Where is Paul, by the way?" asked Rose.

"He's gone to see an old friend at Tammany Hall. He wants to become a politician and put the world in order. Whatever all that means," shrugged Agnes.

"Paul, a politician? I wouldn't have thought that of him,"

"Why not? I know you always think of him as a gangster, but since having Lilly-Rose, he's changed. He keeps going on about clearing the streets of gang warfare."

"Oh, Agnes, will you stop thinking I always assume the worst of Paul? I didn't know he was interested in politics, is all I'm saying. I know he's a good man to you, Agnes. And he's also become a good friend to us," Rose frowned at her friend.

"Sorry, I must stop jumping. I just…"

"It's because you love him, I understand," Rose leaned across and placed her hand on Agnes.

"How's Katrien doing? Have you heard Rose?" Agnes enquired, changing the subject.

"Oh yes," still holding her friend's hand, Rose told Agnes what Katrien was doing, much to Willem's concern. "But I'm sure she will be fine," insisted Rose.

"Veronica spends a lot of time with Willem. Do you think there's any romance there?" Agnes giggled.

"Time will tell, but I hope so. It's time Veronica found love. I would be so happy for her." Rose mused.

Rose and Agnes spent the rest of the morning playing with the children.

"Goodness me, it's nearly lunchtime. I must be getting back. Give my love to Paul, and we'll meet up on Friday. Maybe you'll have more news concerning Paul's bid to become a politician."

Grazina scooped up Tobias and walked Rose to the door, waiting for the friends to hug before handing him over to Rose.

"Bye now, see you soon." Rose waved.

CHAPTER FORTY-FOUR

SPRING 1905

America celebrated Theodore Roosevelt's second term of office. The inaugural parade was the most significant and controversial event ever. Among those present, the Apache Chief Geronimo and hundreds of Native Americans mingled with cowboys, soldiers, coal miners and students. Roosevelt's tone in his second inauguration address to the people was optimistic. He cited good relations with all countries. Roosevelt stated that smaller nations should have nothing to fear from the United States of America.

"Our attitude must be one of cordial and sincere friendship," he assured the American people that the industrial age's growth and new technology would bring tremendous change and to embrace the future. "We have proclaimed a Great Nation." His address was overall warmly greeted by the American people.

*

Two weeks later, the Spring of that year also brought another significant event. The Casino Royal dance hall was heady with fragrances from Lilly of the Valley, white orchids and roses of garlands. Tables covered in white with matching chairs of baby pink sashes tied in bows. Posies of the same flowers with silver tableware adorned the tables. In an adjoining room, there were matching chairs around the table with vases of flowers.

Veronica stood in front of Agnes' long mirror at the Casino Suites. Smoothing her hands down, her dress of lavender satin, edged with ostrich feathers, complemented with matching slipper shoes, cream gloves and toque. Veronica gently touched the necklace pendant of Sapphire and Tourmaline — a gift from Willem.

"You're ready and look fantastic," Rose smiled.

Agnes rushed in, a smile lighting her face.

"Here, something blue and all that," she laughed, handing her a blue-laced garter. Agnes lifted Veronica's leg, bent down and pushed it up her thigh. "I wore it on my wedding day, not that it stayed there long," giggled Agnes.

"Agnes, your incorrigible," Veronica giggled.

Both girls laughed. "Come on, Miss Cormack, time to go," they chorused.

"It sounds strange using my maiden name." Veronica smiled.

*

Thirty minutes later, the wedding couple stood before the presiding judge.

"Willem Friedlander, do you take Veronica Cormack as your legally wedded wife to have and to hold from this day forward?"

Looking down at Veronica, Willem smiled,

"I take you to be my lawfully wedded wife before these witnesses. I vow to love and care for you as long as we live."

"Veronica Cormack, do you take Willem Friedlander as your lawfully wedded husband?"

"I do." Veronica was looking up into Willem's eyes. The Judge presiding over the civil wedding ceremony took their hands, joining them as one.

"Who will present the rings?"

"We do!" Four excited faces stepped forward, each holding a small cream cushion. Isabella and Lucas are holding the rings. Tobias and Lilly-Rose present two posies of flowers. There was a joyful murmur around the room as the children took their roles seriously.

Having exchanged rings, the Judge looked up.

"I now pronounce you Husband and Wife. Go in

God's safekeeping." Veronica and Willem kissed as guests cheered and clapped. The children jumped up and down with excitement.

"Can we still call you Auntie Veronica?" Tobias asked.

"Of course, my darling, Willem will be your new Uncle." Veronica bent, hugging Tobias. Throwing her arms out, the other children crowd in for another cuddle.

The wedding lunch consisted of roast beef with all the trimmings finishing with peach melba. Champagne flowed. After the dinner speeches, the orchestra played the Waltz. Willem took Veronica into his arms, sweeping her across the floor for the first dance amid applause from their guests. The party went on late into the night. Thomas had danced with Isabella, who'd stood on her father's shoes whilst he'd whirled her around with lots of giggles. Even Paul Kelly took Lilly-Rose and Isabella around the dance floor, telling everyone the young ladies were wearing him out.

Eventually, it became clear that Willem and Veronica had quietly left the party to return to the bridal suite. Adorned with flowers, rose petals cascaded across the four-poster bed. They would be travelling to Yellowstone National Park in the morning to start their honeymoon of two weeks.

*

Late that night, at home, Thomas and Rose collapsed onto the sofa with hot chocolate. The children were already fast asleep. Katrien had returned with them to stay — nanny Margaret had prepared the spare room for her.

"What a wonderful day, Thomas," Rose yawned.

"Yes, indeed, my darling. I thought it a wonderful wedding gift from Paul Kelly to lay on the service and reception for Willem and Veronica."

"I do hope they enjoy their honeymoon at Yellowstone National Park. I've heard great things about Fountain Hotel. We must go one day Thomas, instead of our usual mountain haunt," Rose smiled.

"What and miss our barbecues on the veranda at the Catskill Mountains — the kids running free, enjoying the mountain air. We'll think about it for next year, darling. I don't know about you, but I'm exhausted. Time to retire, my dear."

*

Rose rubbed the sleep from her eyes, wondering what had woken her. She looked at Thomas, who was snoring gently beside her. Unable to settle, Rose climbed out of bed and quietly tiptoed along the landing to the children's room, but all was quiet. As she passed the top of the stairs, her body shivered. Rose had a distinct feeling that someone was watching her. With sudden panic, she felt for the light switch, throwing the landing into light.

Rose called out. "Hello?" But looking down the stairs into the dark hall, she saw or heard nothing. Chastising herself for being silly and probably overtired from the day's event, Rose returned to her room and climbed back into bed, where sleep soon took her.

*

The following day cook was busy preparing breakfast when a banging drew her attention to the pantry. Entering, she was surprised to see the small open window rattling in the breeze. Cook frowned. She was sure it was closed the night before. The cook noticed muddy shoe prints leading to the kitchen door approaching the window. She also saw a joint of cooked ham had disappeared.

"Thieving little blighters, I'll have to speak to the master and get a new lock."

CHAPTER FORTY-FIVE

Katrien skipped up the steps, entering the New York Paper Office, waving a cheery good morning to the receptionist who still did not acknowledge her or anyone else after four years at the papers. Miss Thornton was fondly known as the 'Dragon of the print.' Her beady eyes missed nothing, and her fiery breath disintegrated anyone who displeased her.

Entering Marie's office, Katrien was surprised to find it empty. Discarding her coat, she sat at her desk, preparing to start the lady's magazine due on Saturday. Katrien enjoyed her job but somehow wanted more. Finding new recipes, dress fashions, and the latest smelling soaps the ladies of the day might like was fine but, she needed more.

Katrien needed a story to tell. Please, something to get my teeth into, she thought. Suddenly a voice in the hall heralded the arrival of Marie.

"Steffi, get some tea," Marie shouted as she swung open the door and threw her hat towards the hat stand, which landed promptly on the floor.

"Ah, Katrien, want something different to do? Get your coat and head to the Grovers Shoe Factory on Fifth Avenue. Unfortunately, its boiler has blown this morning. There's debris everywhere, and many were injured. Poor things. Get down there and talk to the survivors, especially the women get their immediate reactions. It will be suitable for the lady's magazine this weekend." Katrien jumped up with excitement, thanking Marie. "Now's your first chance, girl; just come back with the human element." Marie laughed. Just as Steffi arrived with the tea, Katrien grabbed her hat and coat and stepped through the door.

"Morning, Katrien, not stopping for tea then?"

"Thanks, Stephanie," for some reason, Katrien always called her by her proper name, "But I have a job to do. I'm sure Marie is gasping." Walking away, Katrien heard the thump of the tray as it hit Marie's desk.

"Anything else, your ladyship?" Katrien did not hear the reply as she ran down the stairs giggling.

*

Arriving on Fifth Avenue, Katrien was shocked to see the devastation. A massive fire engulfed the four-storey factory, rubble strewn everywhere. People lay injured and screaming in pain, many burnt and many others scolded from the central boiler that had caused the explosion. Katrien felt bereft as she watched ambulances ferry the injured away while others waited for help. She stopped one of the firefighters.

"Excuse me, what happened? Any lives lost?" An angry firefighter quickly rebuked Katrien.

"Bloody press, get out the way," the firefighter shouted at her.

"Sorry," she muttered. Katrien knew it was hopeless. Stepping back and watching, taking her notepad out of her bag to write, Katrien suddenly saw movement from her right. A young woman crawled out of the rubble, covered in the dust, her clothes torn, and blood running down her face. Rushing towards her, Katrien bent and spoke.

"Here, let me help you." Two wide eyes looked up at her; taking Katrien's hand, the young woman swayed as she stood, allowing Katrien to put her arm around her middle and slowly cross the road towards an ambulance. Helping her sit on the inside bench, Katrien handed the woman her handkerchief.

"Thanks," she replied feebly.

"What's your name?" asked Katrien.

"Margaret, I'm a stitcher. Ooh, my head bloody

hurts." Then, taking her hand, Katrien soothed her.

"I'll stay with you if you like."

"Will you? Thanks," the girl leaned her head back, closing her eyes.

"Here, what are you doing in my ambulance?" A rather angry ambulance driver glared at them.

"Can't you see she injured? The poor girl just crawled out of the rubble!" Katrien stared at him with angry eyes.

"Well, you can't stay with her unless your relative. We need all the space," just as two men lifted a stretcher into the ambulance.

"That's my sister, so shut your mouth." Margaret hissed without opening her eyes. Katrien said nothing.

A few hours later, Katrien found herself sitting in Margaret's kitchen. She'd had the cut on her head stitched and was well enough to leave the hospital and be allowed home.

"Thanks, it was good to have your company. Your press, aren't you?" Margaret asked while Katrien poured a cup of tea.

"Yes, I work for the New York Press, however, that's not why I'm still here, I did want to help you."

"Yeh, well, I'm grateful. But I bet you want my story, don't you?"

"Only if you feel up to it. I write a column in the lady's Saturday magazine. I'm sure they would like to know what happened to you. Not just from gossip and half a story. You were courageous this morning Margaret," smiled Katrien.

"Here, I like that magazine — read it weekly. God, I thought I was dead, you know," she whispered.

With a fresh cup of tea, Margaret told Katrien about her morning.

"I started early at the Grovers Factory at seven o'clock sharp. I'd been at my workstation for about an hour."

"What did you do at the factory?" asked Katrien.

"I was a stitcher, you know," lifting her shoe to show the stitching that went around, joining the top of the shoe to the sole.

"Gosh, did you do that by hand?"

"No, not now. Used to mind, it played havoc on our fingers." Margaret held her fingers up to show callouses. "We have a machine now that's a bit like a sewing machine. The whole process starts at one end of the bench where leather's cut to shape, sending it down to the next man or woman who begins to assemble the shoe. Eventually, it ends up with me for stitching, then passes to the end man, who puts the soles on the bottom."

"How interesting to think we put shoes on and never stop to think how you ladies make them." Katrien laughed. "Sorry, please carry on; tell me, when did you know something was wrong this morning?"

"When the bloody floors gave." Margaret laughed, touching her head and winching. "Well, that's not quite right. I was aware of rumbling noises. First, the floor seemed to sway, felt it through my feet. I stopped the machine, as did others. We listened for a moment, and then an almighty bang. The next thing I knew, the floor disappeared from under me. I just kept falling; everything fell on top of me. I'm sure my bloody machine hit me on the head. I must have blackout because I don't remember hitting the floor — the next thing I remember is pushing rubble off me, dust hanging in the air choking me. I remember sitting up and realising I was bleeding. I shouted out, but nobody answered. Oh no…" Margaret laid her hand across her mouth for a moment, "…my poor mates are all dead, aren't they?" Margaret wiped away a tear.

"I don't know, I'm sorry; we'll try and find out." Katrien took her hand, encouraging Margaret to go on.

Wiping away another tear, Margaret sighed. "I managed to get to my knees but couldn't stand. It looked like I was in a cave with everything around me. That sounds daft, doesn't it?"

"No, not at all," Katrien encouraged Margaret to continue again.

"I just started crawling through the rubble, and suddenly I was on the sidewalk. That's when you saw me. Thanks for helping, waiting for me at the hospital and bringing me home in a carriage. I've never been in a carriage before. It was almost worth being blown up just for that," giggled Margaret. "I've just thought I've no job, have I? So, what the hell am I going to do now!" Margaret shed a tear.

"Don't worry about that now. The shoe factory will have to start again, perhaps in another warehouse. So why don't you wait until you hear something before worrying too much." Katrien replied.

"I suppose you're right. I'll go down tomorrow and see what's happening."

"Right now, Margaret, you need rest. I'll call again later in the week and see how you're getting on."

"Do you promise?"

"I promise," Katrien smiled.

"Are you going to put it in print? Am I going to be famous?"

"I will write my story and tell everyone how brave you've been. I will drop the magazine in on Saturday. But, again, I am grateful to you for telling me your story." Katrien stood, putting on her gloves, ensuring Margaret was alright before slipping out.

Walking back to Chambers Street, Katrien smiled to herself. She had got her first scoop, and it was a good one. She only hoped Marie would approve.

*

Saturday evening, Katrien sat in the lounge with Thomas and Rose to read her story published in the Women's magazine that week. It had also made the evening paper's front page the day after the explosion. As promised, she had dropped a copy of the report and magazine into Margaret, who had become somewhat of a local celebrity.

"My word, we have a journalist amongst our mist." Thomas laughed.

"Well done, Katrien, it is excellent." Rose looked up and smiled at her.

"I'm pleased with it, although I say it myself. It is just so tragic to hear of all those lives lost. Perhaps I should talk to the widows and widowers next week and get their stories. People need to listen to all sides of this terrible event."

"Quite right, my dear; I shall look forward to reading it," Thomas replied just as Cook popped her head around the door to inform them that dinner was ready.

*

It was now a month since the disaster at the Grovers Shoe factory. As promised, Katrien kept in touch with Margaret and was glad she had started working again in their new factory, a warehouse only two streets away. Surprisingly, it began production within two weeks of the disaster. In an inquiry into the incident, Mr Rockwell, the chief engineer, informed the chief fire officer that he had instructed the workforce at the end of their shift on Friday to shut down the latest high-pressure boiler to cool for its maintenance on Monday. Unbeknown to Mr Rockwell, the owner had started the old boiler allowing it to heat slowly over the weekend, not wanting to lose production. But unfortunately, the seams were weak. On Monday morning, as soon as the men pushed the switch to full power, it exploded, causing the four-storey building to collapse, engulfing everything and nearly everyone in a fire, killing fifty-eight people, including the owner and injuring many others. Katrien also did a follow-up story on behalf of the widows and widowers left to cope with children. She also arranged for the State of Board Charities to provide emergency clothes and food for the bereaved until starting work again. Rose and Veronica were more than happy to assist. The disaster led to stricter safety laws and national safety laws for boilers. Never again should such a tragedy happen.

CHAPTER FORTY-SIX

Willem and Veronica returned from their honeymoon trip, bringing small gifts for Thomas, Rose and the family. They settled into Willem's house on Fifth Avenue. For now, Veronica had decided to rent her property, having been approached by Thomas for a young gentleman just starting work in Macy's wage department. Katrien had returned home and life returned it seemed, to normality.

The following Thursday, while at Ellis Island, the captain of a ship just arrived and called for the assistance of the Charity ladies.

"I'll go," announced Veronica to Rose. "You have your hands full already. I'll shout for assistance if I need it; not sure what I shall find."

She was escorted onboard by the captain, who briefly explained the stowaways. Veronica was shocked to discover twenty small children between the ages of three and eight in a sorrowful state. Their clothes, tattered and hair rife with headlice, they were found hiding in the lifeboats hours after the boat had set sail from Liverpool. They had been cared for by fellow passengers in steerage and were now alone in a strange country. The eldest child, Doris, told them they had escaped from the local orphanage due to their brutality while living there and how they had used the cover of other families boarding the ship and hiding in the lifeboats. Staff found them after the smaller ones had begun to cry due to hunger and cold.

"I tried to keep them quiet," Doris told Veronica.

"It's alright, come with me," Veronica encouraged the children to follow her.

Having taken the children to the medical centre, where they were cleaned and fed, Veronica and Rose discussed the problem with the other ladies, who felt they should all go to the nearest orphanage. However, after Veronica had approached the orphanage, she made it quite clear they did not have the space for them all. So it was unanimously decided the children should stay at the hospital wing of Ellis Island. Over the next few days, after vetting many families, some of the children were offered homes with private residents, sadly leaving only a handful going to the children's orphanage.

After an exhausting day, and still worried for the children at the hospital wing. Rose was glad to climb into her carriage and head for home. She missed the company of Veronica as she had left earlier to attend a meeting of the Child Protection committee. As she drove out of the gate, leaving the harbour behind, Rose flicked the reigns, but before the horse could gather speed, a tall, broad man stepped out, a large hand grasping the reins bringing the horse to a halt causing Rose to fall forward before regaining her balance. Staring at the man in front of her, Rose could not see his face, as a scarf covered his nose and mouth. A cap pulled down, obscuring his eyes.

"Who are you? What do you want?" Rose kept her voice steady, not wanting to tell him how scared she felt.

In a gravelly voice, he told Rose. "I've got a message for your friend. You tell him to back off, or his little precious, might not have a mummy. You got that?"

"Pardon, what are you saying? I don't understand."

"Do I have to spell it out for you? Tell Kelly to back off unless he wants his Mrs to have an accident. Understand now?" Before Rose could reply, he released the reins slapping the horse on its rump, before disappearing down the alley he'd appeared from. Shaken, Rose grabbed the reins and continued, not stopping until she reached the safety of home.

*

The following day, Thomas sat at his desk at Macy's, fuming with Paul Kelly standing before him.

"We have a good friendship, but not if it puts my wife in danger!"

"Sorry, Thomas, but how is it my responsibility for thugs who appear from nowhere? I will investigate it. My Agnes is in danger too, or had you forgotten that bit?" Paul Kelly raised an eyebrow. Thomas stood and sighed as he reached for the bourbon, filling two tumblers and handing one to Paul.

"I'm sorry to take it out on you, but what the hell is happening? We can't have our women threatened. I won't allow it any more than you. So, explain to me what's happening and why the threat." Thomas scowled at Kelly.

"We both know the answer to that," Paul sighed. "Since becoming a Senator in the house. I'm not the most popular, having already passed a decree to clean up the slums and trying to clamp down on street battles. So, I'll send Ely out; he'll soon find the culprit."

"And what? Violence for violence? How can you clean up if all you do is retaliate?" Thomas replied, exasperated.

"The police are about to raid Eastman's establishments if we can't get him for murder. I'm hoping to get him for corruption. In the meantime, my friend, no one will threaten mine or yours without consequences. That's all I have to say about the matter. Please, let's not fall out. It will upset the girls." Kelly grinned.

Both men looked at each other, "Well, that won't do," they said together with a chuckle.

CHAPTER FORTY-SEVEN

Monk Eastman was on the prowl just after six on a bright spring morning. Frustrated by the police raiding his properties — who had once been his ally and Paul Kelly turning Tammany Hall Democrats against him, he felt like he was losing control of what he called his empire. His money was all but seized by the state, leaving him with just a few dollars in his pockets. Two weeks ago, Kelly and Eastman decided to hold a boxing fight, the winner taking control and carrying on as usual. There had been a bare-knuckle fight between him and Kelly on the scrubland near Poughkeepsie Bridge one very early morning with just their seconds as lookouts and assured fair play. Monk Eastman towered over Kelly. He was sure of his win; he had spent his last few dollars on a bet, only to lose. Bloody sly old fox Kelly kneeling in front of him, pretending to take a breath only to come up, hitting him square on the chin knocking him senseless. He swore to get even with Kelly one day. "Yeh, one day, mate, I'll have you," Eastman muttered.

Walking down 42nd Street, Eastman spotted a smartly dressed young man standing like a sore finger on the sidewalk. It was apparent he had visited the whore house. Eastman chose to rob him because the man still might have money. Eastman took off across the road weaving through the carriages. Looking around to check the coast was clear. He lunged and pushed the man into the alley. Eastman's fist hit hard into his stomach, taking the man's breath away and causing him to fall to his knees.

"Please, please take the money," the terrified man pleaded. While standing over him, Eastman rifled his pockets, taking the fob watch and wallet before kicking him hard again.

"You're pathetic." Eastman muttered at him. Then, rushing off, Eastman exited the alley, only to run headlong into the police, who happened to be walking to their station. Shocked at his carelessness, Eastman drew his gun, turned, and ran, firing wildly. Pain suddenly shot through Eastman's left thigh before reaching the corner, flooring him. Who had fired, no one knew.

*

Later that year, at the Monk Eastman trial, Paul Kelly and Tammany Hall refused to help free him. Eastman was given ten years in Sing Sing prison and jailed for attempted assault and theft. Swearing in the dock, he would get even with Kelly.

That evening at Tammany Hall, Kelly shared a drink with Timothy Sullivan.

"Well, we didn't get him for murder, but I suppose assault and theft are better than nothing," said Sullivan.

"Yeh, only ten years, should have gone down for life!" replied Kelly. "But hopefully, things will start to change. Eastman's gang have already gone underground. Ely hasn't seen anything of them since the trial." Paul Kelly stated before tipping his glass back.

"You want to watch your back, Paul. Eastman can still reach you even in Sing Sing. It's not going to stop him," so Sullivan told him as he filled two glasses, handing another bourbon to Kelly.

"I've always watched my back. But, one sniff of threat, I too can reach Eastman," Kelly smiled as he replaced his empty glass. Then, picking up his coat, he headed for the door.

"Must go, promised Lilly-Rose a popsicle for supper. Night Sullivan." Sullivan raised his glass, thinking, take care, my friend.

CHAPTER FORTY-EIGHT

Following the arrest and sentence of Eastman, his gang and their henchmen were at a loss. Their allies, including the notorious Lenox Avenue Gang, dispersed into the cellars and tenement buildings to lick their wounds. With no leader and very little food, they seemed rudderless. Odd scuffles were between the Hudson Dusters, The Whyos and the Gopher Gang; bodies were all but left. The one person to emerge from the chaos was Battle Axe Annie. She rallied her girls, and they became known as 'The Lady Gophers.' Their reputation soon preceded them. Not only did Annie swing her hatchet, but her girls were also armed with clubs and renowned for hurling bricks. They still used Mallet Murphy's Saloon as their base. Battle Axe Annie could recruit several hundred women to fight the police if they dared to step on her patch. The local authority seemed incapable or unwilling to stop her force. Businesses began to hire the Lady Gophers, including the Labour Unions, to settle labour disputes, always ending in dirty street battles. It was a cause of great concern for those at Tammany Hall.

Paul Kelly, meanwhile, had become more decisive in his campaign to clean up the streets. While maintaining his upstanding politician persona, others considered him New York's Godfather. Keeping his business away from The Royale, he set up a new headquarters at New Brighton to protect Agnes and his daughter. Paul Kelly also opened the New Brighton Boys Boxing Club, a café and dance hall above, hoping the young lads had an outlet for their anger, learning boxing skills instead of corner street fights. Paul Kelly was no fool, knowing he had made enemies amongst his men, unsure of their loyalty, especially his long-standing lieutenants Pat 'Razor' Riley and James 'Biff' Ellison. They had promised loyalty, but

Paul's real friend Ely did not trust them. Others in his gang deflected to other bands. Ely became Kelly's main bodyguard and would follow him everywhere.

On Essex Street, at the Silver Dollar Smith Saloon, Eastman's old abode where many gang members hang out, they felt bitter and abandoned. Swimming in cheap moonshine, the name Paul Kelly resonated with hate. Women aplenty soothed their egos while deep down, they plotted revenge on Kelly.

Queen of her domain, Battle Axe Annie offered loyalty to Paul Kelly in return for leaving her free to continue her reign. The offer was never officially accepted by Kelly, preferring to keep Battle Axe Annie at a distance and not interfere, knowing that her girls kept an eye on his family if ever they were out and about. So, life took on an uneasy truce during the next few months.

CHAPTER FORTY-NINE

In the heart of the summer, Morningside Park was a favourite place for New Yorkers. They gathered in their hundreds, enjoying the lush green lawns and flower beds. The laughter of children floated in the air. It was here that Rose, Veronica, Agnes, and the two nannies gathered for an afternoon treat on Sunday. Finding a spot underneath a large oak tree as shelter from the sun, Rose threw two rugs down. Sitting on the grass, Nanny Grazina helped Lilly-Rose to make a daisy chain while nanny Margaret took Lucas, Isabella and Tobias to feed the ducks. Agnes assisted Rose in laying out the food. It appeared Cook had prepared enough food to feed thousands, or so it seemed to Rose.

"Cook certainly didn't want us going hungry," laughed Agnes.

"No, we could invite everyone here and still have leftovers," Rose giggled. Then, a hearty shout made Rose lift her head to see Thomas and Paul Kelly strolling down the path. Seeing their fathers arrive, the children rushed over with excited shouts, hugged them, and pulled their hands for a ball game, leaving the women to enjoy time together.

Rose turned to Veronica smiling, "How is married life, Mrs Friedlander?"

"It's lovely, you know I didn't think I would ever find love again, although I still miss Robert; you must never tell Willem what I've just said, please don't. I did not mean it to come out like that," the girls laughed around her.

"Of course, we won't, and we understand completely. Married life is certainly suiting you." Agnes laughed again as she placed a hand on her heart. "Oh, to have men fall at my feet," Agnes sighed exaggeratedly.

"Behave yourself; you have Paul. What more could you ask?" The girls laughed. "Yes, I know, just don't tell him he's big-headed enough."

Then they spot a figure rushing towards them, her hat in hand waving madly.

"Hello, hello," Katrien called. "Sorry I'm late; I hope you haven't eaten everything yet?" Katrien dropped down onto the rug next to Veronica.

"Where is your dear Papa? He promised to join us," Veronica asked.

"He's coming. He had sudden business at Tiffany's, something to do with diamonds just arrived, you know Stepmother dear, the one's dear Papa has been fretting over that should have come on Friday. The ship anchored a day late, and the poor gentlemen bringing them had suffered terrible sickness. A young messenger arrived just as we were leaving. Papa promises not to belong."

"I wonder what it's like dealing with diamonds all day?" Rose asked.

"Think all that glitter shining in my hands; imagine a diamond ring on every finger. Oh, I should feel in heaven. I would be forever waving my hands around." Agnes sighed as she waved her hands in front of them.

"You already do," laughed the girls.

Calling the children over, they settled down to enjoy their picnic. Relaxing in the sun and enjoying each other's company.

"Oh, it's so lovely to have us all together. We must do this more often," Rose exclaimed. A cheerful shout went up; turning their heads, Willem strolled towards them, pushing a rather unusual contraption.

"Sorry, I'm late. I hope you left me a little food."

"What have you got there?" Veronica eyed the strange machine.

"I was passing the emporium, and this was outside. So

I couldn't resist it, thought the children would love it." The child's penny-farthing was painted in royal blue with a soft cream seat and a red triangular metal piece near the front wheel to enable a child to step on to reach the saddle. The children jumped up excitedly.

"It's a bicycle!" exclaimed Lucas. "Can we ride it? Please say yes." Lucas jumped up and down excitedly.

"Why has it got one big wheel and one little wheel?" asked Isabella.

"It's called a Penny Farthing," Willem told them.

"I don't think that looks very safe," Rose frowned. "What if they fall off?"

"Where's your sense of adventure, my dear?" Thomas laughed. "Comm'n Lucas, let's give it a go," Thomas helped Lucas, and between Willem and Thomas holding the bicycle, they set off down the path.

"Oh, do be careful," shouted Rose.

Isabella, Tobias, and Lilly-Rose run alongside, squeals of delight and shouts.

"My turn, my turn." Eventually, Willem sat to catch his breath and enjoy his picnic. Next, Paul and Thomas took over, running madly up and down to the children's delight until finally exhausted, they both collapsed on the rug, grateful for a glass of homemade lemonade. Lucas and Isabella were now free to ride independently, having worked out how to climb onto the penny farthing. Lilly-Rose and Tobias, with the nannies, were shouting encouragement.

After the picnic, the girls all decide to stroll around the park. The men lounged on the rugs while the nannies set up the skittles for the children.

Meandering past the rose gardens, the girls stopped while enjoying the perfume of the roses. Music from the bandstand drifted across the park. Agnes slipped her arm through Rose's. Katrien took Veronica's.

"Stepmother, dear?" Katrien looked at Veronica.

"Yes?" replied Veronica wondering what was coming.

"Please, can I drop stepmother and call you Mama? I like Mama, and I want you to be my Mama."

"Oh, my dear Katrien, nothing would make me happier."

"Good, Mama, it is," Katrien looked over to Rose and Agnes, "Ladies, can I introduce you to my Mama." Rose and Agnes hugged them both; the girls were lost in their little bubble of joy, oblivious to everyone.

As they wandered through the park, they came to the fountain, where some children sat on the edge, dangling their feet in the water.

"Come on; my feet are killing me," Agnes rushed forward, removed her shoes and stepped over the low wall. Then, holding her skirt up, she paddled, much to the amusement of those around her. Rose, Veronica and Katrien scolded her for such behaviour, but Agnes didn't care.

"Comm'n I dare you," Agnes teased them. Katrien was the first to join her, followed by Rose and Veronica. Several couples walked past with utter disdain, but the girls didn't care — Katrien and Agnes splashed water onto Rose and Veronica, and all too soon, amid lots of laughter, water splashed everywhere. Then, from the corner of her eye, Rose spotted the park warden heading their way. Someone must have told of their rowdy behaviour.

"Come on, girls, I think it's time to go," laughed Rose. Then, stepping out of the fountain and picking up their shoes, they returned to their husbands and the children.

"Good grief, what happened to you four?" asked Thomas, seeing their wet clothes — shoes still in their hands.

"Oh, we've been so naughty, Thomas dear," giggled

236

Rose. Then, having explained their antics, the men collapsed laughing.

"I would have loved to have seen the faces of those passing." Willem laughed heartily.

"Oh, the shame, the shame!" Thomas and Paul announced in mock response.

*

By early evening the group had returned to Thomas and Rose's house, and the party stayed for light supper. Lilly-Rose curled up on the sofa with her father. Tobias was already asleep, cuddled up to Rose. Finally, the nanny Margaret appeared,

"I think it's bedtime for this tired trio," the nanny announced. Thomas scooped Tobias up and, excusing himself, followed Nanny up the stairs with Lucas and Isabella.

"Night aunties, night uncles," the children called. Shortly after, Paul scooped up Lilly-Rose, who was fast asleep. Then, with hugs and goodnights, the friends left. Rose joined nanny Margaret and Thomas to settle the children.

*

In bed that night, Rose snuggled down, resting her head on Thomas' chest.

"What a wonderful day. We really must do it again. I don't think we have laughed so much for a long time. I wish you could have seen us at the fountain. I'm sure you would have disowned me my darling."

"If I had been there, I would have joined you," laughed Thomas as he switched off the bedside light.

CHAPTER FIFTY

Rose joined Agnes for coffee at the Casino Royale Lounge the following Friday.

"So, babe, what are you wearing?" asked Agnes.

"I thought I would wear my blue evening gown. It's Thomas' favourite colour. What about you."

"What? No babe, we are going to the official opening of the Nickelodeon Theatre, where non-other than the Vice President will be present. So, we are going to Macy's for a new dress. Comm'n, I believe our carriage has arrived," Agnes acknowledged the waiter who has just come to inform them.

*

Arriving at Macy's, the Head of the dress department, Miss Turnbull, greeted them warmly. Rose never forgot her kindness years ago when she first came to New York and always sought her advice.

"Good morning, ladies. How may I help you today?" Miss Turnbull smiled as she beckoned a young girl forward.

"This is Liza; she will assist you, but do not hesitate to seek my assistance if required."

"Good morning, Miss Turnbull; always lovely to see you. We are looking for a dress to attend the official opening of the new Nickelodeon Theatre next week." Rose told her.

"The United States Vice President will be there," Agnes interrupted.

"Oh, how exciting for you both," replied Miss Turnbull. "I'll arrange a coffee while you peruse." At that, Miss Turnbull disappeared, leaving them with a nervous-looking Liza. Agnes looked at Liza and laughed.

"Oh, lass, don't look so scared. We don't bite, do we Rose?"

"Not in the least, now, Liza, my dear. I don't know about my friend, but I prefer blue." Rose smiled to try and put the young girl at ease. So for the next two hours, with the help of Liza, Rose and Agnes had great fun trying on several dresses.

"What about this one? Should catch the Vice President's eye." Agnes swirled in front of the mirror dressed in baby pink, with giant bows on the shoulder — the dress was so low Rose was wondering how she would stay decent.

"Erm, I thought you were looking for sophistication?" Rose frowned and laughed at the same time.

"I am, but it would be fun," giggled Agnes, "they would remember me."

"Oh, definitely Agnes, for all the wrong reasons." Eventually, they decide on their dresses. Rose chose the palest blue with silk coverage, short sleeves and a full skirt matching slipper shoes and purse. Agnes in the bright yellow of a similar design with silver slippers and a bag.

They were leaving a heap of dresses strewn over the chaise longue. First, they thanked Liza for her help with a tip. Then, they said goodbye to Miss Turnbull, who had finalised their attire to everyone's satisfaction and let her know how helpful Liza had been. Then, they descended into the foyer, to find Thomas waiting for them.

"Thomas, what a lovely surprise." Rose leaned forward, kissing him on the cheek.

"I asked a staff member to let me know when you arrived. I thought perhaps lunch, ladies?"

"Ooh, yes, please," they both replied.

While enjoying their lunch, Agnes chattered excitedly.

"I do hope we get to shake the Vice president's hand. What a thrill; I shall feel like royalty. What about you, Thomas? Have you ever met the President?"

Agnes asked.

"Not the President, sadly, but I have met the Vice President, a charming fellow. It was for the celebrations of twenty-five years since Macy's opening. A delightful moment."

"Thomas, you must introduce us; he's bound to remember you," insisted Agnes.

"I doubt that Agnes, but you never know. We might be lucky."

After finishing their lunch, Thomas escorted the girls to their carriage.

"See you later, darling," Rose smiled as Thomas waved them off.

*

It was the night of the grand opening of the Nickelodeon Theatre. Rose was with the children helping the nanny settle them down before leaving.

"You look lovely, Mama." Isabella hugged her.

"Thank you, my darling. Now be a good girl and settle down. Your Papa and I will be late returning, so we'll see you in the morning and tell you all about it."

After tucking Isabella in, Rose headed for the boys room. Lucas sat on the rug with Tobias, reading his favourite story, 'The Tale of Peter Rabbit.' Then, finally, both boys jumped onto the bed and hugged their mama.

"Mama, please bring something back. I don't mind what, but something the Vice President has touched, please, Mama," Lucas said excitedly.

"Perhaps I can get him to sign a menu," Rose smiled.

"Oh, yes, that's it, Mama, please ask him to sign a menu, please, Mama, please try." Lucas jumped up and down excitedly.

"I will do my best, my darling, but I cannot promise. Now you must settle, or nanny Margaret will be cross with Mama for getting you all excited." Rose snuggled the boys down.

"Night, night Mama," the boys chorused. Rose kissed them both and wished nanny Margaret a good night before leaving the room and heading downstairs. Where she found Thomas waiting, he looked astute in his Tuxedo.

"Time to go, my darling. Have I told you that you look stunning?"

"Twice already, but I don't mind," laughed Rose.

*

The carriage pulled up outside the Nickelodeon Theatre. As Thomas and Rose stepped down, Agnes rushed to meet them. Rose hugged Paul Kelly, who stepped forward to shake Thomas' hand.

"This should be an excellent night," Paul Kelly smiled.

"Yes, indeed. Let us go in, ladies. There is rather a crowd gathering. We don't want to get caught in a crush." Stepping through the theatre door to join other guests gathered amidst chatter and excitement, they marvelled at the plush red carpet that complemented the cream walls-crown mouldings that embellished the ceilings. Gilded statues and sconces finished the effect.

Waiters served aperitifs with glasses of champagne. Suddenly a loud voice announced the arrival of the Vice President.

"Ladies and Gentlemen, please show your appreciation for the Vice President, Mr Charles Warren Fairbanks and his good lady Cornelia Fairbanks." Huge applause went up as the Vice President entered the foyer, introduced to dignitaries by John Harris, Manager of the Nickelodeon Theatre. On reaching Thomas, John Harris introduced him.

"I believe, Sir, you know Mr Thomas Blackwood of Macy's Department Store?"

241

"Yes indeed, how nice to see you again. You know, my dear wife, Cornelia."

"Good evening, Sir, Ma'am," Thomas bowed slightly.

"May I introduce Rose, my wife?"

"Very pleased to meet you," Cornelia smiled at Rose. "Perhaps you will accompany me tomorrow while I shop at Macy's. We could have coffee after. Please say you will."

"I should be delighted to," replied Rose. Then, turning, Rose took Agnes' hand. "These are my dear friends, Agnes and Paul Kelly." The Vice President frowned.

"Kelly, did you say? A member of Tammany Hall, I believe."

"That is correct, Sir," replied Paul.

"Splendid, good to meet you. And this charming lady?" Fairbanks took Agnes' hand, kissing it with a flourish.

"May I introduce you to my dear wife and mother to our darling daughter Lilly-Rose?" Paul Kelly bowed slightly.

"Enchanted, my dear," replied Fairbanks. "You must all join our table for dinner after the show."

"We would be honoured, thank you,' replied Thomas and Kelly. At that, the group moved on.

"Oh my God, he kissed my hand; I shall never rewash it, you do realise that!" whispered Agnes.

"Hush, behave yourself. Let us find our seats," Rose laughed.

The evening was a wonderful experience, the performers were unique, and the curtain fell to raptures of applause all too soon.

Rose sat at dinner next to Vice President Fairbanks and his wife, Cornelia. Agnes, to her, left, and Thomas and Paul sat opposite. Rose picked up the gold-edged menu during the evening, remembering Lucas' plea, smiling as she handed it to Mr Fairbanks, explaining her young son's request.

"I should be delighted, my dear." Charles Fairbanks signed with a flourish and included Lucas' name before returning the menu. "So nice to have a fan." Fairbanks laughed as twitter went around the table. Rose slipped the menu into her bag.

As the evening ended with farewells, they found themselves on the sidewalk as the carriages arrived. Rose hugged Agnes.

"What a wonderful evening," Agnes said as she pulled her gloves on, waving her hand at Rose. "I shan't wash it."

"Idiot, well, I'm not offering you a sandwich again," Rose laughed uproariously. Thomas helped Rose into the carriage, shaking Paul's hand before joining Rose.

"Good night, dear friends," they chorused before the carriage disappeared.

*

Arriving back at Casino Royale Suites, Ely stood waiting, accompanied by Swampo and Razor Riley — Kelly's bodyguards.

"Good God, men, how long have you been here?" Paul Kelly looked at them. A sudden uneasy feeling coursed through his body.

"I said we would wait for your return," muttered Ely. Ely had become concerned at the rumours he had heard during the day.

"Problem?" Kelly frowned as he stepped down from the carriage; Ely didn't reply, just nodded. Paul held his hand out for Agnes, who looked up at Ely.

"Oh, Ely, I have met the Vice President. He has kissed my hand," Agnes giggled.

"A good night by all accounts then," replied Ely as he

ushered them towards the door without being obvious. Suddenly Paul turned upon hearing a shout; a volley of shots rang out, disturbing the night air before silence fell. Ely was shot in the shoulder, dazed staggered to his feet. The carriage horse lay dead, as did the driver. The pain in Ely's shoulder was unbearable. But what he saw in front of him was far, far worse.

Slumped against the door, Swampo already dead, Otto, his faithful Jack Russel, at his side bleeding from the loss of an ear. Razor Riley was bleeding heavily from a leg wound and crawled towards Paul Kelly, who lay motionless. Ely dropped in front of Agnes, calling her name, but there was no response. Instead, the sand colour of the sidewalk turned red. Tom, the concierge, rushed out.

CHAPTER FIFTY-ONE

"Mama, Mama, please don't cry." Isabella hugged her mother. Rose was in a world of grief. Her dear friend was gone forever in such a brutal way. On the funeral day, even the sky cried, rain had bounced off the sidewalk. The pastor's words could offer no comfort as Agnes' coffin was lowered into a water-filled grave. Rose could not bear it. It was the day after the funeral, and Rose tried to gather comfort from Isabella, her poor child trying to understand her mother's loss. Rose thought back to when she first met Agnes, so full of life, vibrant, fun, and naughty all rolled into one. And now, now nothing. Rose would never hear her laugh again. Never see the mischief in her eyes. No more morning coffees. Oh, Agnes, dear, dear Agnes. Why couldn't she have survived instead of Paul? Dear God forgives me, Rose thought. Kneeling on the floor, Rose took Isabella into her arms and cried. Nanny Margaret silently slipped into the room, taking Isabella by the shoulders; she gently extricated her from her mother.

"Go and play with your brothers, dear," the nanny whispered.

"But what about Mama?" Isabella sobbed.

"You leave your Mama with me. It will be alright, now run along, child."

"Yes, nanny." Isabella took another look at her mother before leaving the drawing room. Nanny Margaret knelt in front of Rose, gathering her into her arms; she let her cry.

*

At Macy's, Thomas sat ashen faced, looking at Ely, who seemed as if he might drop at any moment.

"For God's sake, man, how was this allowed?" Thomas hissed through clenched teeth. Ely cradled his left arm, which was in a sling and winches. The bullet had gone straight through his shoulder, leaving him numb in his fingers — Ely hoped the feeling would return.

"Sit man, before you fall," snapped Thomas. Ely slumped on the chair with relief.

"It was one of our own," Ely muttered. "I should have seen it was coming, but, well..."

"Well? Well, what?" Thomas frowned at Ely and took a deep sigh.

"Whoever was responsible, find them. Deal with it. Make them suffer. I don't care how. I don't want to know." Thomas stood, walking over to the cabinet. He poured two bourbons, handing one to Ely. Taking the glass, Ely gulped it down in one.

"Sorry, guv, I will find out and deal with it. How's Rose?"

"What do you think? So inconsolable? But, Christ, man, how could this happen?" Thomas rubbed his eyes. "What of Paul? Is he feeling a little better? I should visit him."

"He was lucky," replied Ely. "The bullet missed his heart by inches. But God helps them if Paul gets to them first," Ely muttered.

"I want it dealt with before Paul recovers." Thomas frowns. "Was it Biff Ellison?"

"Could have been, but I think it more likely Razor Riley, his henchman. Whichever, they will answer for it." Ely winced as he held his arm.

*

Two days later, Thomas arrived at Bellview Private Hospital in downtown Manhattan. A large circular reception desk stood on the right through the main doors. After ascertaining the whereabouts of Paul Kelly, Thomas entered his room on the second floor. He is shocked to see Kelly's ashen face, darkly circled eyes, sweat glistening on his brow, and heavily bandaged chest.

Hearing his door open, Paul opened his eyes and grimaced. "Thanks for coming," he whispered.

"I won't ask how you are, man. It's a bit obvious." There was a moment of silence.

"She's dead, Thomas; I've lost her. What will I do? What will Lilly-Rose do without her mother?"

"I'm sorry, Paul, I don't know what else to say. Rose sends her love."

"How is she?"

"Distraught."

"I loved her, Thomas; she was my world. It should have been me, not Agnes. Lilly-Rose needs her mother. Oh god. Damn it, man, damn it. I'll kill them when I get out of here." Paul became agitated and appeared to struggle for breath.

"Calm yourself, Paul. Ely and I will sort this out. Those responsible will answer. I give you my word."

"I feel so bloody useless laid here," Paul Kelly's voice was hoarse. Thomas was shocked to see tears stream down his face. The man was known as The Godfather.

"You need rest; I'll call another day again. I'm sorry, my good man, I wish I could say or do more, but..." Thomas quietly left the room, leaving Paul Kelly still weeping.

CHAPTER FIFTY-TWO

It had been a month since the terrible loss of Agnes. The charity ladies, including Rose, were busy at Ellis Island. The RMS Umbria had arrived from Liverpool. It was full of mothers and children. The child in front of Rose was crying.

"Oh, for god's sake, child," Rose shouted at her in frustration. Veronica laid her hand on Rose's arm.

"You're shouting, my dear. The child is only asking a question." Rose took a deep breath. Kneeling, Rose smiled at the child. "I'm sorry, sweetie. What's your name?"

"Millie," the child whispered.

They discovered her mother died during the crossing. Her brother was lost somewhere in the registration building.

"I want me, mam," the child cried. "Please, Mrs, I've lost my brother in that big building." Millie pointed towards the main registration building. Snot tangled with the child's tears, wiping it away with the cuff of her dress with patches on top of patches. The child looked up at Rose. She was no more than four or five years of age.

"Please, I don't know what to do, and now I've lost Kenny."

"Is Kenny your brother?" Rose asked.

"Yes, my mam told him to look after me. But my mam's dead. The ship's captain put her over the railings with a prayer a few days ago." The child leaned forward, trying to take comfort from Rose. Gathering the child into her arms, Rose stood — taking her hand, they walked back to the registration building. Veronica and Rose entered the building to find chaos. Parents shouted, mothers trying to comfort babies in arms while children ran around like lost sheep.

"Can you see your brother?" Rose asked as she tried to look for a lost child.

Millie shook her head. As Veronica and Rose headed to the desk in the far corner, Veronica was aware of some commotion.

A rather large, pot-bellied, uniformed security man was holding the arm of a wriggling child around eight — the boy was swearing like a trooper and trying to kick the officer's shins.

"Kenny, Kenny," shouted Millie, releasing her grip on Rose's hand and running forward.

"Excuse me, what's happening?" Veronica enquired.

"What's happening, Ma'am? I'll tell you what's happening," the officer shouted above the noise. "This thieving little toerag stole food off the table and tried to pickpocket a gentlemen's coat. He's going into the holding cage. Stop struggling, your thieving little urchin." The officer shook the boy roughly.

"Get off me. I was hungry and I wasn't stealing from that man's pocket. You're a fat-bellied liar." The boy swung around, kicking out his right foot, which landed on the officer's shin, causing him to swear further.

"Please," said Rose, "He's just a child his poor mother died on the crossing. He was just frightened. Have a little mercy."

"Mercy, with this bit of squirt, I'm not letting him run riot here." Then, holding the boy by the scruff of his collar, the officer shook him again. Millie was clinging to her brother's legs in the middle of the melee and crying.

Veronica stepped forward, firmly taking hold of the boy's hand, and pulled him out of the man's grip shielding him behind her. She glared at the man.

"Officer, that is quite enough, and as to running riot in here, may I suggest you take control of those that already are!" At that, Veronica and Rose turned to leave the Registration Building without further ado, Millie holding Rose's hand while Veronica firmly had her brother. The officer is still shouting above the noise.

"If he comes back here, I'll put him in the cage; you hear me?"

*

Arriving in the quiet of the medical building, Veronica released the boy.

"What now, Mrs?" the boy looked up sullenly at Veronica. "I'm still hungry. That copper took my food."

"You young man will sit quietly on that chair and perhaps learn your manners. You have caused enough problems in the few hours you have been here."

"Yeh, but Mrs..."

"No buts, stay there." Veronica looked at him with a stern expression. Kenny sat, arms folded and pouted.

"What are we to do with them?" Rose queried.

"They'll have to go to the children's home; we have no choice, my dear. You keep an eye on them while I make the arrangements." At that, Veronica left the building.

"Err, Mrs, I need a wee," Kenny squirmed in his seat.

"Why did you not say earlier?" Rose asked, exasperated.

"I tried, but Mrs bossy face wouldn't listen," Rose sighed; why was everything so difficult for her? All she wanted to do was return home and curl up on the sofa. Suddenly feeling a tug on her skirt, Rose looked down into Millie's face.

"Why are you crying?" whispered Millie looking up at her. Rose tried to smile as she bent down to the child. Millie lifted her hand and gently wiped a tear away on Rose's left cheek.

"Kenny doesn't mean anything; honest, he's scared

like me."

"I need a pee, Mrs."

"You look sad like our Mam did when she got ill on the boat. Why are you sad?"

Rose sighed. "I'm sorry, Millie. Unfortunately, I lost a dear friend a short time ago and miss her dreadfully."

"Is she in heaven like our mam? Maybe our mam can look after her if you like." Millie smiled at Rose. Oh, the innocence of children, thought Rose.

"Yes, I would like that very much," Rose whispered.

"I'll ask our mam tonight when I say my prayers." Millie leaned in and cuddled Rose again.

"Er, Mrs, are you listening? Honest, I'm not joking; I need a pee."

Rose wiped her eyes with her handkerchief and found herself laughing.

"Come with me, young man, before there's an accident."

"I never mentioned an accident; I just said I need a pee." At that, Kenny jumped off the chair and followed Rose to the back of the medical room.

Returning to the main room with a relieved Kenny, Rose found Veronica, but not alone. A young man with dark curly hair, cap in hand, which he swirled nervously, stood next to Veronica.

"Rose dear, I found this young gentleman at the registration building looking distressed. He's here for his brother and sister…" before Veronica could finish, Millie jumped off the chair, squealing with delight.

"Amos, Amos," she flung herself into him, wrapping her arms around his middle. Kenny also wrapped himself around his older brother.

"We had no idea that family would be collecting them," Rose replied, looking slightly puzzled.

"I'm their older brother, ma'am. Amos Doyle, my

mother was joining us to settle here. I understand mam died during the crossing. I thought something had happened when I couldn't find her, and the Registration Officer told me you had collected the children. That's when I bumped into your friend here. Thank you for looking after them. I hope they've been good?"

"Yes, of course," replied Veronica.

"Kenny stole food off the table, and the copper was going to lock him in a cage," replied Millie.

"Tell-tale, I was hungry. Sorry, Amos."

"No harm done," replied Veronica.

"Forgive me, but we can't just hand the children over, although they know you. But we must be careful. Are you staying in New York?" asked Rose. Amos slipped his hand into his jacket pocket, producing a letter.

"From mam," Amos replied in hush tones. "She wrote telling me she was coming and which ship she would be on, asking me to be here. She didn't tell the kids it was to be a surprise for them. I don't live in New York; I'm a cowhand at Briarcliffe Farm Manor…"

"…Oh, we know it well." Veronica interrupted.

"I have a message from Mr Tyron, instructing me to find Rose and Veronica and tell them that 'he and his wife, Minnie, look forward to seeing them both. It's been a while.' I have a note from him that explains. I showed them in the Registration Office, asking for the ladies' whereabouts. Mr Tyron and his wife are happy to take the kids. It will be much better than what they've had. I wish our mam could have seen it. She would have loved the open plains, the cattle. The fresh air. Poor mam." Amos rubbed his hand across his eyes.

"Oh, how fortunate, I'm Veronica. Yes, we know Mr Tyron; please give him and his wife our regards and tell him we shall visit before the end of the month," replied Veronica.

Amos looked up. "Beggin your pardon, but you must be Rose?"

"I am."

"Oh, then I have a letter from Mrs Tyron, Minnie. I was to give it to you if I saw you."

"Thank you," Rose took the letter and slipped it into her pocket.

"Well, we better get going. It will be dark before we get back. Once again, thanks for looking after these two." Millie extricated herself from her brother to hug Rose again.

"Don't worry; I won't forget. I promise I'll ask mam tonight, then you won't have to cry anymore," she whispered to Rose.

"Bless, you child. When we visit, I'll look out for you," Rose said with a catch in her throat. At that, Amos and the children left.

"Well, my dear, It's late. I think it's time for home." Veronica picked up her bag.

"I'll drop you off, Veronica. It's silly getting two cabs."

"Are you sure it's a little out of your way Rose?' replied Veronica.

"It's only around the corner. I shall enjoy the journey, just the two of us."

Sitting in the carriage, Rose flicked the reins. Veronica looked across at Rose.

"How are you, dear?"

"I'm glad the children had a family. It was such a relief," Rose replied, ignoring the question she knew Veronica was asking.

"Yes indeed. But that wasn't quite what I meant." Veronica placed her hand on Rose.

"Oh Veronica, I know, and I'm sorry, it's just Fridays coming and no coffee with Agnes, no catching up with gossip. I miss her terribly. We've both had losses, but it's not easy."

"I do understand, my dear." Veronica gently squeezed Rose's arm. They travelled the rest of the way in silence until dropping Veronica off; both hugged and agreed to meet the next day.

"Perhaps we could start our coffee morning on Wednesdays together," suggested Veronica. They decided to try.

Rose took a slight detour home, pulling into Morningside Cemetery and guiding the horse down the side path before pulling up and stepping down. Walking down the third row, Rose stopped at Agnes' stone. Beside her stood Freda's. Rose and Thomas thought it would be nice to have them together. Rose felt a salty tear slip down her face, resting her hand on Agnes' headstone. She told her about her day and laughed a little when describing the young rascal Kenny.

"A bit of a rebel like you," Rose smiled. It was then that Rose remembered the letter from Minnie. Taking it out of her pocket, she opened it.

'Just a few lines for you, dear Rose. Hold tight to memories. Lean on friends for strength. Always remember how much we care. With much Love, Minnie.' With her hands on each headstone, Rose let the tears fall.

*

That night as Rose sat on the sofa with Thomas, she felt lighter in her heart, knowing she would never forget her dearest friend or Freda. But she would always think of the happy times they'd spent together. Taking Thomas' hand, she smiled.

"I feel better today, darling." Thomas took Rose into his arms and held her tight.

CHAPTER FIFTY-THREE

Cyclone, the alligator surged upwards, its jaws open, trying to reach the two bodies dangling precariously over the wall. Ely's accomplices had caught Razor Riley and Biff Ellison the previous day. But unfortunately, Ely's men had shown them no mercy, leaving them alive to suffer the final blow. Ely and his accomplices had brought them to The Bronx Zoo in the early morning hours, which had recently opened with exotic animals from bears, giraffes, lions, and alligators. Ely looked down into Cyclone's enclosure and smiled. He could think of no better way than to exact his revenge for Paul Kelly, Agnes, and his mate Swampo. Otto, his faithful Jack Russel, had refused to leave Swampo's grave, until Ely eventually put him out of his misery.

Ely quickly learned who fired the gun from his men and Battle Axe Annie. She wasn't one to rat on her own, the loss of Paul Kelly would not have bothered her, but the shooting of Agnes caught in the crossfire, and the fact she was a mother, would not be allowed to pass without consequence. Also, unbeknown to others, Battle Axe Annie had a soft spot for Swampo; they had been friends for many years. Her Gopher Girls had caught Razor Riley, who was still recovering from his gunshot wounds — leaving Ely's men to capture Biff Ellison as he travelled back to the gay bar and brothel at Columbia Hall. Pathetic groans came from Razor Riley, his teeth broken and his mouth swollen. Biff Ellison remained silent, but the fear in his eyes as he looked down on Cyclone made him throw up onto the alligator. Biff Ellison gathered what little strength he had left, offering money in the hope of release.

"Come on, mates, please, I'll give you a grand each. Think about all those bucks in your pocket — just let me up, mates. Come on, please, please!" Those holding Ellison's legs look at Ely, slightly hesitant in their movements.

Ely gave them a steely glare.

"Do you want to join him?" He hissed. At that, Ely nodded. Razor Riley dropped into the enclosure, followed seconds later by Biff Ellison.

*

Later that morning at Macy's, Thomas looked across his desk at Ely.

"Is it done?"

"Yep." Ely nodded, "Let's say Cyclone, the alligator at the zoo, won't be hungry for a while." Thomas shuddered at the thought. The zoo was one place his children would never attend while he was alive. Pouring two bourbons, Thomas handed one to Ely. This time, he took a gulp leaving a drop for later. Going back to his desk, Thomas opened the drawer, removed an envelope, and passed it to Ely. No words, just a nod from each. Tossing back the remaining bourbon, Ely stood, acknowledging Thomas before leaving the room.

*

Late afternoon, Thomas arrived at Casino Royal Suites, and Tom, the Concierge, greeted him.

"Good afternoon, Sir, a lovely day?"

"Yes, indeed, Tom. Is Kelly at home?"

"Yes, Sir," Tom touched his cap.

Standing outside Paul Kelly's suite, Thomas smiled at the burly chap standing guard. A bit after the horse bolted, Thomas thought with a wry smile. Thomas knocked on the door. Grazina, the housekeeper, opened it and welcomed him.

"Mr Kelly is in the lounge, Sir."

"Thank you, Grazina," Lilly-Rose rushed forward as Thomas entered.

256

"Uncle Thomas," she cried, throwing her arms around him. He scoped her up for a hug.

"Hello, sweetheart. You've grown since I last saw you."

"But you only came last week," laughed Lilly-Rose.

"Exactly," replied Thomas. Then, from his pocket, Thomas produces a bar of candy. "Don't eat it all at once, or you'll get me into trouble." Thomas patted her head smiling.

"Thank you, Uncle Thomas!"

Kelly rose stiffly from his seat, extending a hand. "Good to see you, my friend."

"And you. Glad to see you're improving."

"I shall be even better if you've come with news."

Paul invited Thomas to sit. He noticed the cashmere shawl thrown over the sofa, a Christmas gift to Agnes from Rose. Thomas looked across where Lilly-Rose was playing with her doll.

"Grazina, we could do with coffee; perhaps Lilly-Rose would like to help you," called Kelly. Grazina smiled as she took Lilly-Rose's hand.

"Come, poppet, let's get tea and cake for Papa and Uncle Thomas." They disappeared into the kitchen, closing the door behind them.

"Well, what's the news? You're the first to call." Paul Kelly looked at Thomas. "Tell me revenge is sweet."

"I don't know about sweet, but the matter has been taken care of," replied Thomas, telling Paul what had transpired.

"I hope they suffered long," Paul said bitterly. "Little one still cries for her mother. She drew a picture the other day only to remember she would not be coming home."

"It's only been a month; give it time. How are you?" asked Thomas.

"I'll survive, but I'll never get over her loss. I miss

her every waking morning. It's torture sometimes. Thank Rose for coming. Lilly-Rose loves playing with the children; it's good for her."

"Anytime, Paul, remember our door is always open. So that reminds me, Rose has invited you both for Sunday lunch; please come. But, perhaps without the heavy at your door, don't particularly want him stood outside ours, too big a reminder for Rose."

"Ely put him there, but it's time he left. So frightens Lilly-Rose every time she goes out with Grazina," Just then, the kitchen door swung open as Lilly-Rose rushed in carrying the plate of cakes, while Grazina placed the tray on the table, and for the next hour, they enjoy pleasantries, while Lilly-Rose showed Thomas her toys.

On leaving, Thomas hugged Lilly-Rose, and Kelly promised to come for Sunday's lunch.

CHAPTER FIFTY-FOUR

In the spring of 1906, a devastating earthquake in San Francisco rocked New York City. A few days later, the tremors in New York City caused alarm.

Thomas woke early that spring morning to feel the house move. Waking Rose, they gathered the children, nanny and cook onto the sidewalk. Residents from the other properties were also out.

"Is it an earthquake, Papa?" asked Lucas.

"Tremors from the earthquake, my boy, nothing to worry about." Isabella and Tobias cuddled up to Rose.

"Will we be alright, Mama?" they both asked.

"Of course, my darlings. Nothing more than a little excitement." Rose laughed to make light of it so as not to frighten the children.

"Well, I don't like it." Isabella frowned as she kept a tight hold of her little brother. The neighbours next door, Susan and Ricardo from the Remalde household, brought out their violins, followed by Roberta with her cello — daughter of Mr Fred Arnold, a banker and his wife Francesca, who lived opposite.

Before long, music filled the air and the children began skipping and dancing. Neighbours chatted. And maids arrived with trays of tea and coffee. About an hour later, residents returned to their homes, deciding that all was clear. Nanny Margaret took the children upstairs to dress. At breakfast, Ivy, their cook, was indignant that some plates, cups and saucers had fallen off the kitchen dresser. Rose smiled, telling Ivy to replace them, and she wasn't to worry.

"Let's hope we don't get any more tremors," said Rose. "I found that quite unsettling. Oh, Thomas, those poor people in San Francisco, how terrible it must be." Rose had been reading the daily paper and was horrified at what she had read.

"I must talk to Veronica and see if the Society can do anything."

*

Over the weeks and months, the Christian Association, the Quakers and Red Cross sent help to San Francisco to bring back those who wished to leave and seek refuge in New York City. As a result, Rose and Veronica were kept busy from morning until night. So many children needed homes, not just adults. By Christmas, life began to settle, and Rose invited friends to share Christmas with them. Her only sadness was the loss of her dearest friend Agnes, so strongly felt at Christmas. The New Year was heralded with fireworks in Town Square, bringing a welcome cheer to everyone.

In the spring of 1907, the San Francisco devastating earthquake caused another catastrophe, the Panic of the Knickerbocker crisis. The New York Stock Exchange fell by fifty per cent; Panic ensued throughout the nation, causing bankruptcy to many, including the collapse of the Knickerbocker Trust Company. The financier J P Morgan pledged large sums of his own money, encouraging other New York Bankers to follow to help stabilise the economy. Fortunately for Thomas and Willem, they had invested wisely and were not struck. Thomas' only concern was the sales downturn at Macy's, but he knew it would survive in the long term.

In July, Thomas, Rose, and Nanny Margaret travelled to their hideout in the Catskill Mountains to celebrate Rose's twenty-seventh birthday. Rose had told Thomas she would love nothing better than to celebrate her birthday under the clear pine air of the Catskill. The children were excited to return to their favourite place, knowing it would be many late nights, with barbecues under the stars. Rose was amazed at how quickly the years had gone since arriving in 1897, fleeing home at sixteen, and having her seventeenth birthday two months after arriving in New York, something she had never told anyone.

They enjoyed exploring the mountains, paddling in the stream that ran down to the waterfalls and beyond, and watching a large brown bear as it meandered past their cabin early one morning, demolishing the barbecue in search of food. Tobias thought he was great and wanted to go out and play with him, making his parents laugh and firmly lock the cabin door.

Sitting on the veranda one evening, Rose inhaled deeply, filling her lungs with pine air and sighed. For the first time in a long time, Rose felt at peace. Taking Thomas' hand, she smiled at him.

"You look refreshed, my darling," Thomas smiled at Rose.

"I am, and thank you for my lovely present." Rose held up her wrist to reveal a silver bracelet.

"Where have ten years gone, my darling? And so much has happened. Lucas is now fifteen and told me he was interested in banking."

"He is becoming a young mane has bec." Rose sighed.

"Cheeky with it," Thomas laughed. "Isabella was now twelve, and Tobias eight; time has just flown. Are you happy, my darling?" Thomas suddenly looked earnestly at Rose.

"Oh, Thomas dear, need you to ask?" Rose turned to face him, and they kissed.

"Mama and Papa are kissing, don't look." Then, a giggle burst into laughter as three heads appeared at the veranda door.

Nanny was calling from inside. "Come along, children. It's nearly eleven o'clock. Bedtime."

"You heard you little horrors, shoo." Thomas swiped

playfully at them with the newspaper he'd taken from the table beside him. Then, still giggling, the children hugged their parents before disappearing into the cabin.

Lucas was singing, "Mama and Papa are kissing."

"You young man will have your mouth washed out with soap," laughed the nanny.

*

After returning home from their break, life settled into a peaceful routine. Philip Carmichael, Veronica's, ex-husband, remained friends and on hearing Lucas' interest in banking, had invited him to City Bank as a junior filing clerk on Fridays, hoping to start full-time when reaching sixteen. Veronica was also delighted to hear Philip had acquainted a young lady called Evelyn, whose father was involved with the New York Stock Exchange. Veronica hoped things would progress, and Philip settled down, to find true love with a new wife.

CHAPTER FIFTY-FIVE

It was a gloriously sunny day in September 1907, and Katrien had arrived at the New York Harbour. Maloney had sent Katrien to cover the arrival of the maiden voyage of the Lusitania. She was the most luxurious ship ever built and arrived on her maiden voyage that morning, flying decorative signal flags from her masts as she sailed into Pier 54.

As many as a hundred carriages were lining up on the quayside, waiting for the disembarkation of their passengers. Stepping down from one of the carriages, deafened by the cheers of hundreds of thousands of jubilant Americans greeting her arrival, Katrien looked up in awe at the Lusitania as she stood proud and gleaming under the sun.

Katrien made her way to the gangplank to be escorted by Mr John Piper, Chief Officer.

"Welcome aboard, Miss Friedlander."

"Oh Katrien, please, and this is Gus, my photographer." Gus stood smiling like a cat who had just got the cream. Then, holding his 4A Folding Kodak Camera, its strap around Gus' neck, he offered his hand to the Chief Officer.

"I'm, um, I'm very pleased to be here. It's so big! It's beautiful." Gus stuttered, feeling overawed with the occasion.

"Thank you, Gus. She is, isn't she? But please, she is called The Lusitania, not it." Mr Piper corrected, smiling.

"Yeh, sorry, it's just her magnificence, and I've never seen anything like this before. Sorry, I'm just so excited."

Katrien frowned at Gus, "Get a grip of yourself," she hissed through gritted teeth. Katrien wouldn't let on that; she felt the same excitement, making her shiver slightly.

Then, gesturing with his hand, Mr Piper led them onto the deck, and their tour began.

Entering the first class, the magnificent grand staircase wrapped around two gilded cage elevators connecting all six decks of passenger accommodation, with spacious lobbies on each level. Given half a chance, Katrien would have just gone up and down in the elevator all day.

"Here we have the saloon lounge and music room designed in the Georgian style with an inlaid mahogany panel," Mr Piper told them, stepping aside to allow Gus to take photographs. A fourteen-foot-high green marble fireplace dominated the far wall with enamelled panels. Mr Piper tapped Katrien on the shoulder.

"Look up, my dear," he smiled. Katrien gasped at the barrel-vaulted skylight with stained glass windows.

"How high is it?" she asked.

"Twenty-foot tall at its apex. The stained-glass windows represent one month of the year." Mr Piper replied. A jade green carpet with a yellow floral pattern finished the room.

"Oh, my god," whispered Gus. "Swanky man!"

"This way," Mr Piper moved on, opening double oak doors to reveal a relaxing room. "This is the reading writing room. It is just for ladies. It has panels of grey silk and cream silk brocade. Rose carpeting with Rose du Barry silk curtains and upholstery. A glass dome overhead."

"Blimey, man," Gus muttered as his camera clicked away.

The smoking room was exclusively for men in Queen Anne style, with Italian walnut panelling finished with red furnishings. "Crikey must have cost a fortune."

"Will you shut up?" hissed Katrien.

"Yeh, sorry. But bloody hell Katrien," he hissed back. Katrien flicked her heel back, catching Gus on his shin while smiling as she moved forward with Mr Piper.

Outside on the promenade, Mr Piper showed them the Veranda Café public room for everyone.

"We have Staterooms. Allow me to show one." Mr Piper opened a door into Stateroom Two. "We call this The Port Suite."

"Jeez, man, it's bigger than our bloody house," Gus gasped, unable to stop himself.

"Gus, please just take the photos and shut up!" ordered Katrien.

"It's quite alright," laughed Mr Piper. "To be perfectly honest, I had the same response when I first saw it."

With two bedrooms, a dining room, a parlour room and a bathroom — the whole stateroom was in the style of Petit Trianon at Versailles. They carried on to the dining room decorated in white plaster, gold leaf, and mahogany panels with Corinthian-style pillars crowned with a dome over the well in the centre of the room, all decorated in the style of Louis Sixteenth.

"Man, this is insane," Gus mumbled to himself.

In the second class, the rooms were slightly more modest in design — russet carpets and curtains with smaller chandeliers adorned the lounge: oak tables and chairs, a white tablecloth cover, and no adornments in the dining rooms.

Third-class accommodation was comfortable and spacious. Rooms in a light solid pine. Same layout in the dining room but without tablecloths. Still, for third-class passengers, it was looked upon as a luxury.

"More my style," Gus laughed. "Plain and simple, that's me."

"How many passengers does she take?" asked Katrien.

"There is a total of two thousand, one hundred and sixty-five, not including staff." Mr Piper informed her.

"Now, let me show you the radio room." Heading for the navigation deck, seeing a cream door and a sign saying radio room Mr Piper pushed it open.

"Good morning, Leith. I've brought you visitors." Having introduced Katrien and Gus, a young steward arrived.

"Excuse me, Chief. The captain is looking for you."

"Thank you, perhaps Leith, you can introduce our guests to your beloved radio. I shall return shortly."

"Certainly, Sir, my pleasure."

"Is it alright to take photographs?" Katrien asked.

"Yeh, sure, no problem. Here hang on; I'll put my cap on doing it correctly. By the way, my name is Stanley, Stanley Leith from Liverpool.

"Miss Friedlander," Katrien extended her hand, "but please call me Katrien, and this is Gus, my photographer. We work for the New York Paper. I'm doing a scoop for the weekly ladies' magazine." Stanley Leith was undoubtedly in love with his Marconi Radio explaining in detail its workings.

"How fascinating I've never sent a telegram. My Papa has on odd occasions." Katrien smiled.

"Would you like to send one? We're not supposed to while in the dock, but the Chief is away. Just a short one, mind."

"Oh, I would love to — what fun."

"Who to, Miss?"

"Oh, home, of course. I can't wait for my parents to open it. What do I do?"

"Give me the name and address and a few lines, that's it. Then I'll send it. The telegram boy will deliver it on his bike before you get home." So Katrien sent the telegram informing her parents that she was on board the Lusitania, which was magnificent.

"Can I send one, please?" Gus looked hopefully at

Stanley.

"I shouldn't send any more, sorry mate." Katrien saw Gus' face drop; she knew his mother would have loved one.

"Oh, please, Stanley, Gus' mother is a widow; it would mean much to her. Then, of course, I'll mention you by name in my article," smiled Katrien looking appealing at Stanley.

"Go on then, but let's be quick and not tell the Chief, Ok?"

"Not a word." Katrien laughed. Moments after sending the second telegram, Mr Piper appeared at the door.

"I hope Leith hasn't bored you to death?" he asked, smiling.

"Not at all; it has been most enjoyable," replied Katrien.

"The captain has invited you both to join him for an aperitif. Please follow me." Having thanked Stanley Leith for his exciting life in the workings of the Marconi radio, they followed Mr Piper to the first-class dining room. Mr Piper introduced them to Commodore James Watt, who greeted them warmly.

"How does it feel to captain such a ship?" asked Katrien.

With a twinkle in his eye, Captain Watt smiled. "A great honour and privilege, my dear."

"Do you hope to have many years at the helm?" Katrien smiled.

"Alas, I am to retire upon my return, handing over to Captain William Turner a worthy successor." After spending more time with Captain Watt and Chief Officer Piper, and Gus taking several photographs, Katrien wished them a good day leaving the Lusitania, determined to sail on her as soon as possible. Indeed, she was sure Papa would have business in England.

Travelling back in the carriage, Katrien smiled at Gus.

"What a ship! She is magnificent. I cannot wait to sail on her."

"Yeh, well, we don't all have wealthy daddies. Perhaps I could offer to wash the decks for a free passage," Gus looked a little peeved.

"Oh, Gus, I'm sorry I didn't mean… I'm sorry, forgive me." Katrien laid a hand on Gus, looking pleadingly at him.

"Nah, don't worry, I meant no harm. But tell you what, my Ma sure will love that telegram; bet all the neighbours have seen it by now," he laughed.

"One day, Gus, you will travel on her. I know it," Katrien smiled.

"Yeh, dream on, sweetie," Gus laughed.

*

That night over dinner, Katrien could not keep the excitement out of her voice as she told her parents about her day on the Lusitania.

"Oh, it was just magnificent!"

"I must say, my dear, I was thrilled to get your telegram earlier today." Veronica smiled at Katrien's excitement.

"Please, Papa, say we can sail on her. You must have diamonds to view in England." Katrien giggled, looking at the astonishment on her father's face.

"I may deal in diamonds, my dear, but I cannot just drop everything to sail to England on a whim," her father sighed. He did not tell her he had been invited to London, England, early the following year to visit the store in Regents Street. Tiffany's will introduce the Tiffany Blue Box presented to those purchasing rings for their loved ones. No, Willem will keep that little surprise for Christmas. Even his darling Veronica was not aware of his plans. I must book tickets for the Lusitania to travel in January. Willem smiled to himself, thinking of the secret he would keep. After Katrien had retired and Willem and Veronica enjoyed a bourbon, Veronica looked up at Willem.

"What mischief are you up to, my dear?" she smiled.

"My love, why nothing? Cheers, my dear," Willem raised his glass before downing the remaining drink.

CHAPTER FIFTY-SIX

December 1907 arrived, with it, a grand celebration for the country. Theodore Roosevelt decided to send the US Navy Fleet, known as The Great White Fleet, to circumnavigate worldwide, visit ports internationally, and send goodwill gestures globally. Thousands lined the harbour to see them leave. Thomas, Rose, and the family watched the fleet sail out of the port on its two-year mission.

"I think, Papa, I shall join the Royal US Navy and sail the seas." Lucas proclaimed as he looked on excitedly at the disappearing fleet.

"My dear boy, perhaps your Mama may have something to say about that. I thought banking was in your blood?" remarked Thomas.

"You don't see the world in banking, Papa."

"Fair point, son."

The snow had fallen hard by Christmas, leaving many stranded in their homes, and food became scarce, especially amongst the slums. However, those more affluent could afford the price of food. So, at the Blackwood home, Paul Kelly, Lilly-Rose, and nanny Grazina had joined Thomas, Rose and Family, including Willem, Veronica and Katrien, to stay over Christmas. The sound of laughter resonated through the house. The aroma of roast duckling, spices, and Christmas pudding filled the kitchen and permeated throughout. The Christmas tree adorned the lounge, and also one in the hallway, to greet visitors. The children helped make Christmas decorations and placed presents under the tree. Rose had put a special card tied with two red ribbons on the tree for Agnes and Freda, something she had always done since losing her friends. Fires roared up the chimneys, and contentment filled every room. Katrien had brought her certificate to acknowledge her journalism work on the Lusitania, received at the yearly Christmas banquet, held for all journalists of the different newspapers.

*

On the day of Lucas' sixteenth birthday, a hive of activity in the kitchen where Ivy had baked the birthday cake and prepared the birthday dinner. Veronica, Willem and Katrien attended and a couple of friends Lucas had made at the bank. Paul Kelly, with Lilly-Rose, was the first to arrive, and to the surprise of no one, Lucas had taken Lilly-Rose's hand, and lead her into the drawing room to show her his presents received earlier that day. Lilly-Rose, now eight, was the spitting image of her mother, Agnes. Sometimes Rose would catch her breath when she looked at her, but it was also calming to think that Agnes was there, although only through her daughter. Rose had also noticed that Lilly-Rose looked up to Lucas, treating him like a brother. Rose knew that Agnes would have been happy to know that.

Willem, Veronica and Katrien arrived bearing gifts, and before long, everyone enjoyed their meal, including Ivy, their cook. Ivy had become part of the family over the years. Although Rose had argued with her earlier in the week that she would join them and not be left out and would not take no for an answer. Thomas handed Lucas an envelope to open after dinner. It was a letter from Philip Carmichael offering him a full-time job as a bank's junior clerk. Philip Carmichael had been pleased with his part-time work and knew he would become an asset to the firm over the coming years. Lucas had smiled and taken the congratulations from everyone but said nothing more. Rose had noticed her son's reluctance and would chat with him another day.

*

The snow continued to fall over the next two months, and life took a sedate time in the Blackwood household. Then, as March blew in, the snow melted, and the first signs of spring began to show. It was a relief for everyone. But sadly, many deaths occurred, especially in the slums. Rose, Veronica, and the Society's ladies had done their best to ease the situation. But much to Thomas' concern, cholera had broken out amongst the migrants. Rose constantly changed her clothes on the porch attached to the kitchen before entering the house. Ivy would always boil Rose's clothes and sometimes even burnt them rather than risk disease. So, it was a great shock to Veronica and Rose when two of their YWCA ladies contracted cholera. Sadly, their eldest lady, Tilly, lost her life to the disease and took Tilly's eldest daughter too, who suffered from chest weakness.

*

It was Sunday, and the weather was fair, with a gentle breeze as they sat in Morningside Park. Isabella, Tobias, and the nanny were feeding the ducks while Lucas sat with his mother on the bench.

"How are you settling in at the bank, my dear?" Rose glanced down at her son.

"It's ok, I guess."

"Talk to me, dear; I know your thoughts are elsewhere," Rose spoke gently to Lucas.

"It's ok, Mama, really, but..."

"But what, my dear?"

"Oh, Mama, I did something mad. Well, not that mad. But I went down to the US Naval recruiting office last week. They have given me papers. But, unfortunately, I'm still underage and cannot join until seventeen. But I can become a trainee seaman on the US Coast Guard Ambrose. They train young people before moving on to proper US Ships, as they call them. Only Papa will have to sign and give his consent. I'm not sure Mama if he will. After all, I know he asked Philip for a favour to get me work at the bank. It's not that I'm not grateful; some days, I enjoy it. But it's just…" Lucas lifted his hands in the air with a bit of frustration. "I'm not sure what to do." Rose put her arm around her son's shoulder.

"You, my dear child, must follow your heart. Of course, I will miss you terribly, but I wouldn't want you doing something where you are not happy. There's nothing worse than that. But, if it's what you want, you must try it. After all, you can always return to your job after training if you feel it's not for you."

"But Mama, what about Papa? What would he say?"

"Since when could you not talk to your father? Talk to him this evening; I'm sure he will understand. But, Lucas, dear, we both want you to be happy. Although I will miss you if you leave, remember that my love will always be with you, my darling, no matter where you are."

"I know that Mama, but I will come home for shore leave. You can't get rid of me that easy," Lucas laughed, "Thanks, Mama, I love you."

Lucas jumped up and ran over to join his sister and brother. Rose sat looking across at her children. They are growing up too fast. Oh, Lucas, she thought, remembering him as a shy child all those years ago, and now he is venturing into the world every inch a young man.

Wrapped up in her thoughts, Rose did not see Thomas walking toward her. Instead, she was suddenly aware of someone sitting down next to her. Startled, she turned, looking up into Thomas' eyes.

"You were miles away, my darling, penny for your thoughts," linking arms, Rose leant against Thomas' shoulder. "He's spoken to you, hasn't he?" Thomas asked

273

without looking at Rose; he was busy waving at the children who suddenly noticed him arrive.

"Oh, Thomas darling, how did you know?"

"Because I know everything,"

"Don't be smug, darling; who told you?"

"Drat, I thought I could impress you with my knowledge. The Navy recruitment contacted me shortly after Lucas had left the recruitment office." Although a small tear ran down Rose's face, she wiped it away quickly.

"Oh, Thomas, he's suddenly a young man, and I'm proud of him. Will you let him go?"

"Of course, if it's what he wants, I'll let him sweat a little while he asks me." There was a twinkle in Thomas' eye as he looked at Rose.

"Don't you dare be horrid to him, my poor child?" Rose scolded, giving Thomas a thump on his shoulder.

"Don't be soft, woman," laughed Thomas taking her hand and standing; he called to the children.

"Teatime, let's head home."

"Coming," they chorused.

CHAPTER FIFTY-SEVEN

Two months later and Thomas relaxed while driving his carriage to Macy's on a bright early spring morning. There was little traffic on the streets of Manhattan, cleaned after the washdown from the early morning street cleaners. He was flicking the horse's reins, and the rhythmic sound of the horse's hooves on the road lulled Thomas into a feeling of peace.

Elsewhere four hundred souls prepared for a new day as they travelled on the six forty-five train crossing Pelham Bay Bridge, many enjoying the glistening water of the Hutchinson River below. A freight train left the Bronx, joining the Hell Gate Line earlier. Then, gathering speed, it quickly headed for Pelham Bay Bridge. The signalman on the south side, removing the note of kisses his new wife left inside his lunchbox. Then, checking his watch against the station clock — he still had another twelve minutes before throwing the switch, which would divert the commuter train onto the north line.

Noticing Zeb, his friend, riding past, they called out to acknowledge each other. It is then that the signalman heard a long whistle. Looking over his shoulder, he saw the freight train bearing down at speed towards the bridge. Dropping his cup and sandwich, he rushed to the switches, pulling them to change the points.

"No, no, no!" he shouted in panic. "Stop, stop, you're too bloody early. What the hell?" It was too late; the passenger train arrived at the south end. There was nothing he could do.

Running down the steps from his signal box, he never made the bottom step before being thrown into the air and down the embankment.

*

As Thomas turned into Sixth Avenue, an enormous

explosion shattered the peace. Thomas struggled to gain control of his horse, panicked by the noise it reared up in its harness. Glass from several windows broke in the aftermath of the boom, showering Thomas and others on the sidewalk, all rushing to find cover. Some believed it to be another earthquake.

Gathering his thoughts, Thomas helped those around him injured by flying glass. Thomas was unsure what had happened but felt sure it was not an earthquake. Having waited for help to arrive for the wounded and leaving them in safe hands, Thomas climbed into his carriage, eager to get to Macy's, fearing it may have suffered damage. Unable to go his usual way due to glass and debris on the road and concerned his horse would be injured, Thomas drove the landau through Pelham Bay Park. Many people in the park looked around, wondering what the boom was. One or two stopped Thomas to enquire, but he could not tell them, explaining that he was on his way to the main street, hoping to get more news.

As he was leaving Pelham Bay Park, seeing smoke in the air, Thomas pulled up sharp, travelling to the end of the road and rounding the corner. He was almost unable to take in what he saw. Only recently built, the middle section of Pelham Bay Bridge had collapsed into the Hutchinson River, taking the early morning passenger train with it. Leaving his carriage, Thomas ran to see if he could help; the nearer he got, the louder the screams. So many people were already helping, as were the emergency services which had just arrived. The mangled mass of steel jutted up from the ground, the rear end of the passenger train half-submerged in the river. As Thomas looked, it was clear there was more than one train. The back end of a freight train remained on the bridge; a section hung precariously over the edge.

The other end of the freight train had concertinaed

while tumbling off the bridge down onto the tenement buildings below. Fire erupted quickly, killing the screams from the rubble — so many bodies. Then, again more fire erupted from the flattened tenement buildings. No one could survive that.

Thomas joined others stumbling over metal pieces and other things he'd rather not see, in his effort to help. So far, each person Thomas had found was already dead or dying. The feeling of utter helplessness swept through him. Then, hearing a shout, he turned just as an enormous piece of metal fell from above.

*

Meanwhile, Veronica, Rose and the other ladies are busy at Ellis Island. When they heard of the tragedy, a messenger from Quaker Pennington House asked them to return as quickly as possible. Those slightly injured and who had lost everything were sent to Quaker Pennington House for care and had their wounds seen.

When Veronica and Rose arrived, they found men, women and children standing like statues in the hall. Eyes glazed, bewildered and shocked, but it was the silence that Veronica and Rose found hard to understand. Even the children did not cry. Instead, the ladies offered tea and biscuits — some ministering first aid and comfort. Two small children sat huddled together under a blanket.

Going over to them, Rose asked quietly. "What are your names, sweethearts?" They seemed unable to answer; instead, the little girl held out her arms, and Rose hugged her automatically. The boy sat staring at the wall. Then, slowly, very slowly, the muttering begins. Finally, gentle weeping filled the room as people understood what had happened. It was many hours later before Rose and Veronica headed home. Willem had been concerned, and arrived at the hall, hoping all was well. Neither Rose nor

Veronica realised it was already past midnight.

*

Arriving home exhausted, Rose closed the front door behind her, closing her eyes and leaning against it with a big sigh. She still struggled to understand what those poor people were going through. She hoped that what help they had given would ease their pain a little. Only then did Ivy and Margaret appear in the hall waiting for her.

"Oh, Rose, where have you been? We've been so worried. Mr Erst from the accounts department called early this evening to enquire if Mr Blackwood was ill." Opening her eyes, Rose saw Ivy standing in front of her, a worried expression across her face behind her nanny Margaret stood.

"I'm so sorry; I should have sent word only...wait, what do you mean Mr Erst called from Macy's? Where is Thomas?"

"He's not home," they both replied. "We haven't seen him or you all day; we were getting worried."

"But Thomas should have been home hours ago!" replied Rose. A feeling of panic started to creep through her body.

"He never made it to Macy's this morning Rose." Margaret moved to take Rose's hand in hers.

"What? But I must go out and look for him, stay here with the children." Rose turned, her heart pounding and all tiredness gone, opening the front door. Lucas appeared on the stairs, still dressed and throwing on his coat.

"Wait, Mama. I will come with you."

"Oh, Lucas, you should be asleep," replied Rose.

"Mama, I am sixteen, not six; we will go together; I've been waiting for you to return." Rose didn't argue as the two of them left the house.

CHAPTER FIFTY-EIGHT

"Mama, where do we start?" Lucas looked sideways at his mother as she flicked the reins, setting the horse off on a quick trot. "Please, Mama, stop. Let's think." Lucas implored. Bringing the horse to a stop, Rose covered her face with her hands.

"Oh, Lucas, I don't know, I just don't know, but we have to find your father," she cried.

"Let us try Uncle Willem; perhaps he can help."

"But Lucas, it's the middle of the night!"

"Comm'n Mama, we can't ride around, not knowing where to look. Uncle Willem may have an idea. But, please, Mama, it's worth a try. Here give the reins to me." Lucas gently took the reins from his mother; flicking them against the horse's rump, they set off a quick trot once again.

*

The hammering on the front door awoke Veronica — first startled by the noise, she pushed Willem to wake him.

"Willem, Willem, someone's banging on the front door," slipping on their dressing gowns, they met Katrien on the landing.

"Papa, whatever is it, who could be knocking at this time of night?"

"Only one way to find out, my dears, before we have no door left," Willem rushed down the stairs, throwing back the bolt on the front door and opening it to find a distressed Rose and Lucas.

After settling them in the lounge, a stiff bourbon was in their hands. Rose explained what had happened.

"You don't think he got caught up in the rail disaster?" Veronica whispered to Willem.

"My thoughts entirely," Willem frowned.

279

"No, no, he can't have been on the train. Thomas would have been nowhere nearby. He used the landau this morning." Tears slipped down Rose's cheeks.

"We don't know that my dear. Perhaps Thomas changed his mind. A meeting perhaps somewhere else," replied Willem. "Please stay here with Veronica. Lucas and I will see what has happened and if we can find Thomas."

'No, I must come. I refuse to stay here waiting when I can be out looking." At that, Rose stood, heading for the door. Veronica knew there was no arguing. Katrien and Veronica went for their coats.

"Come along, and we shall all go!" insisted Veronica.

*

Their first stop was at the New York Hospital. Approaching reception, Willem enquired if they had admitted anyone that day with severe injuries, perhaps unable to tell them who he was. After a brief enquiry, it became apparent they had not. Just as they were leaving, having heard the conversation, a nurse called them back, explaining those injured in the train disaster earlier that day would perhaps be better trying Pelham Memorial Hospital, where most of the wounded had gone. Willem thanked the nurse as they left, climbing into the carriage.

"Willem, he can't be there. Thomas wasn't on the train." Rose said, her whole body shaking and tears streaming down her face.

"No, my dear, but maybe he could have been caught up in it somehow," said Willem.

"Oh no, please don't say that. Oh, Veronica, what if…" Veronica held Rose's hand, soothing her as best she could. Nearly twenty minutes later, they were in the reception of Pelham Memorial, bombarding a poor nurse on night duty.

"I'm sorry," the nurse replied curtly. "But it would be

best if you come back tomorrow. We cannot disturb patients this time of night." While Willem and Lucas explained to the nurse the reason for their call in the early morning hours, Rose and Katrien, followed by Veronica, had already slipped through the doors into a long corridor.

"He must be here," whispered Rose.

"I'll take the left side; you check the right," Katrien whispered.

Katrien, Veronica and Rose quietly opened each door until they reached the end of the corridor. Rose was dismayed that she had not found Thomas.

"Oh, Veronica, why is he not here!" exclaimed Rose, her voice rising to hysteria. The nurse Willem and Lucas were talking to followed in quickly behind them.

"I really must ask you to leave immediately. How dare you enter our hospital without permission." The nurse looked sternly at Rose, Katrien and Veronica. "I shall call the guards if you do not leave," the nurse hissed.

"But you don't understand my husband could be lying here seriously ill. I can't find him; please, you must help me." By now, Rose was almost beyond calming. Willem stepped in.

"Please, you cannot let our friend leave without checking if her husband is here; we only ask for your understanding. Can you not see how distraught our friend is, also her son?"

The nurse pursed her lips. "Very well. This is very irregular, but we have four rooms to check. So I must ask to do this very quietly."

"Thank you," whispered Willem.

The nurse opened the door at the end, leading to a square corridor where four doors lead off. Quietly opening the first door, they found a very elderly gentleman snoring loudly. The second, an irate gentleman, was sitting in bed reading.

"Can't you leave me in peace, woman?" he shouted. Then, apologizing, the nurse closed the door quickly.

"A young gentleman is in the third room. His mother is with him. Sadly, he doesn't have long in this world," the nurse whispered.

"There is no need to disturb them," replied Willem.

Opening the fourth door, they found the bed occupied by a man who was grey in the face and heavily bandaged around the head. A nurse was already attending to him.

"This gentleman came in before I started night duty," the nurse told them. "As you can see, this nurse is tending to him because of his injuries," Rose stepped gingerly into the room. Then, tiptoeing to the bed, Rose gasped.

"Thomas!" she whispered, taking his hand in hers; he did not respond. Lucas stood with his mother sliding his arm around her shoulder; he felt tears slip down his face, then quickly wiping them away. He must be strong. His mother needed him.

"Please let me stay with him!" Rose cried softly.

"Very well, but you must be very quiet. I shall leave the night nurse with him in case he regains consciousness. I shall return later and will notify the doctor."

"Thank you, we are most grateful," replied Willem. At that, the nurse quietly left the room. Veronica, Willem and Katrien sat on the chairs against the wall, while Rose and Lucas sat on either side of the bed, holding Thomas' hands.

*

Just after seven o'clock the following day, a young doctor entered the room and smiled at Rose and Lucas, who had not left Thomas' side since arriving.

"Good morning, you must be Mrs Blackwood. I'm Doctor Kelsy."

"Good morning, Doctor. How is my husband? Will he wake up? We've been here since the early hours, and nothing. Please, what's wrong?" Rose stifled a tear as she looked directly at Doctor Kelsy.

"I'm afraid your husband suffered a severe blow to the head by a metal object; only time will hopefully heal. We believe the more he sleeps, the more time the brain must recover from the trauma."

Laying a hand on Rose's arm, the doctor frowned but smiled, assuring her he was in good hands.

"Have faith, my dear," he whispered. Shaking his hand off her arm, Rose grimaced with annoyance.

"Please do not patronise me. I want to know the facts about my husband's health."

"Forgive me, Mrs Blackwood. I had not meant to patronise. My wish is not to worry you unnecessarily," Doctor Kelsy replied. Then, about to open her mouth to speak again, Willem stepped forward.

"Doctor Kelsy, just be frank with Mrs Blackwood is all she meant."

"Thank you, Willem, but I can speak for myself," Rose snapped.

"I think," said Veronica, "we should leave Rose and Lucas with Thomas and return later. There are too many of us in this room." Rose turned, taking Veronica's hand in hers.

"I'm sorry. I didn't mean to snap,"

"Hush, no need to apologise; we will leave you both to spend time with Thomas and will return later. Who knows? He might have woken up by then." At that, Veronica hugged Rose. Then quietly left the room, followed by Willem, Katrien, and Doctor Kelsy.

CHAPTER FIFTY-NINE

Over the next few days, the papers told of the train disaster and the loss of lives. Katrien was sent to Quaker Pennington House to talk to the survivors and tell their stories. She wrote about children orphaned by the disaster, many losing entire families. Katrien worked with Veronica and the Society ladies in helping to find accommodation for those left homeless. Grieving for the loss of husbands, wives, parents, and children, many found themselves alone and, with society's help, found work in the factories and a roof over their heads. Although some women would never tell, they were glad to be free of brutal husbands or tied to parents, never free to do what they wanted. Their only genuine grief was the loss of a child.

*

Four days had passed since Rose and Lucas found Thomas at Pelham Memorial Hospital, who remained unconscious. Rose brought Isabella and Tobias, hoping that hearing their voices would help awaken their papa, but it only ended with tears and distress for everyone. Veronica had also called in daily. Finally, on the third morning, much to Rose's surprise, a somewhat nervous nurse, followed by Ely towering over her, escorted him into the room. He was gentle and kind, telling her whatever she needed to let him know. First, Ely stood, hat twirling through his fingers, looking down on Thomas.

Then, before turning to leave, he bent down, whispering into Thomas' ear. "Wake up, you bloody fool."

Anxious as she was, Rose could not help but smile. So that told you, darling. Then, finally, after acknowledging Rose, he left the room.

The following morning after dashing home earlier to freshen up and change clothes, Rose persuaded Lucas to stay home and keep his brother and sister company while she returned to the hospital. On entering the room, she was surprised to see Paul Kelly.

"Paul, I wasn't expecting you."

"Forgive me, Rose. I just thought I would call to see how things are. But then, I thought I would wait for your return before leaving."

"How kind. Please don't rush off on my account." Paul moved forward, taking Rose into his arms.

"If there's anything I can do, just ask Rose."

"Oh, Paul, I want Thomas to wake up and come home."

"He will, my dear, have faith." If I hear that word again, I shall scream, thought Rose. Saying nothing, she returned a smile.

Kissing Rose on the forehead, Paul gathered his coat and headed for the door.

"Remember, my dear, anything at all, just ask."

"Thank you, Paul."

After Paul left, Rose sat wearily on the chair. She was taking Thomas' hand in hers. Rose talked to him, willing him to move and speak anything.

"But, please, Thomas," she whispered, "come back to me."

Feeling exhaustion wash over her, Rose rested her head beside him on the pillow. It felt good to be with him. Then, closing her eyes for just a moment, sleep took her.

She walked hand in hand through the pine trees, fresh mountain air against her face. Thomas bent, kissing her gently before they continued their walk. She could hear Lucas, Isabella and Tobias squealing with laughter as they splashed in the cold mountain stream.

"Papa, papa," they shouted, "come and join us." Rose laughed as Thomas rolled up his trousers, stepped into the cold water, and splashed the children. A mist suddenly fell, taking away the laughter as it engulfed them. Rose stretched out a hand, calling them — she felt a sudden flutter against her hand, a gentle stroke down her face, soft as a feather.

"Thomas," she whispered. He appeared through the mist smiling. Holding out his hand, but Rose could not reach it. Thomas called her name, but it seemed so far away. And then he'd gone, disappearing into the mist. Rose woke suddenly feeling disorientated. She looked up into Thomas' face to find him smiling.

"Thomas, my darling! Thomas, you're awake!" Rose cried as she gently hugged him.

The following two weeks went quickly. Doctor Kelsy was pleased with Thomas' progress and arranged daily walks to strengthen his legs and regain balance, which worried Rose. Thomas seemed to sway as he walked; he leaned to his left when standing still. Doctor Kelsy assured her this would improve and had been proved right by the second week.

Lucas had been his mother's rock notifying the Straus brothers, owners of Macy's, who, in turn, Isidor Straus visited Thomas, assuring him to take his time before returning.

At the beginning of the third week, much to everyone's relief, Thomas was discharged from the hospital to recuperate at home.

Their cook Ivy prepared her unique broths to which the ingredient was a secret; they were so delicious. Rose and the children joined Thomas in the bedroom to eat their meals. Lucas was due to enrol at the Naval base on the first of September and had been allowed compassionate leave. His enrolment would now be two weeks later.

*

As Thomas recovered, Rose returned to her duties at Ellis Island. However, the arrival of ships never stopped, bringing with them an influx of migrants, all hoping for a better life. Rose, Veronica and the ladies were sometimes dismayed at the arrival of children, many sent without parents, something they found hard to understand. Was it that parents no longer wanted their children or sheer desperation that they could only afford a child fare, hoping the authorities would take pity on these orphans?

*

Over the following weeks, an inquest opened as to the train disaster. And construction work had also begun to clear the site and rebuild Pelham Bay Bridge. The terrible loss of life was over one thousand. At the inquest, it came to light that the freight train left the station under the wrong signal, with its twenty-five cars filled mostly with dairy products, groceries, and general merchandise. The timing should have been 06:54, not 06:45. Those ten minutes meant the freight train ran unheeded onto the single track, meeting the southbound passenger train, which had left on time. The papers described it as "Like Monsters tearing into each other demanding their right of way." The passenger train conductor told of his last moments with the engineer as he lay injured beside the track, asking,

"Was it my fault? Had I mistook my instructions?" The Conductor took out his book and showed it to the engineer, telling him the instructions given by another had not been correct.

"It was not your fault. Rest in peace, my dear friend." Many other similar stories of bravery and heroism among the many who rushed to help.

The Chief of Police and the railway authorities

exonerated all blame from both train operatives. Instead, they concluded that the fault lay entirely with the Bronx Operator, Mr Lane, who confused the date and number of the train with the departure timing. Mr Lane was only twenty years old and had worked at the Bronx station for only three months. A few days later, after leaving a note at his station, the body of Mr Lane was found floating in the Hudson River. The public, and those who had lost loved ones in the disaster, were appalled that the Bronx railway authority should solely blame a young employee still learning with such an important decision. With the help of the local paper, many donated monies for Mr Lane's funeral. The people made clear that the Bronx Railway should be ashamed.

CHAPTER SIXTY

Early fall had arrived, and Thomas, now fully recovered, stood with the whole family, including Willem, Veronica, Katrien, and Lilly-Rose, waving Lucas off on the New York Station platform. How smart he looked in his Naval uniform.

"No, Mama, you must not cry. I'm happy. I cannot wait for my new adventure to start," Lucas laughed as he hugged his Mama goodbye. His father hugged him, reminding Lucas to write, or his dear Mama would never survive. They both laughed.

"Remember, my dear boy; we're not so far away if you need us." At that, Thomas slipped a small box into Lucas' hand. "Open it when you get there."

"Thank you, Papa."

As the whistle sounded, Lilly-Rose stepped forward shyly, holding out a friendship wristband of many colours made from silk; she slipped it onto Lucas' wrist.

"I'll miss you. I made this so you won't forget me."

"Silly goose," laughed Lucas. "I shan't forget you. I'll write to tell you what I'm doing. See you at Christmas." They both hugged and then he was gone amidst the flurry of boarding the train and final hugs.

Lucas leaned out of the window and waved until the train disappeared. Tobias, Isabella and Lily-Rose were jumping and waving madly.

"Oh, Thomas, we shan't see him until Christmas. So long to wait," Rose wiped away a tear.

"Come on, my darling, no more tears." Then, with Thomas' arm around Rose's shoulders, they all left the station.

*

Stepping down from the Great Lakes, Illinois train, Lucas made his way to the Recruit Training Command Naval training base known as RTCNB. Lucas felt somewhat apprehensive. But, as he walked through the gates under the American Royal Navy Insignia, the sight of a Navy training ship anchored at the quayside sent shivers of excitement through him.

After registration, he went to find his quarters. Lucas could see six hammocks hanging from the ceiling instead of beds. Lucas headed for the corner one, thankful to have a window overlooking the harbour. After dropping his bag on the hammock, his fingers twirled around the silk bracelet still on his wrist; with a smile, he removed it, slipping it into his inside pocket, then remembering the gift from his papa still in his pocket. Taking it out, unwrapping the paper, he opened the royal blue box. Lucas felt a tear slip down his face at seeing a silver Tiffany Dialled Patek Philippe Wristwatch with a blue leather strap.

"Oh, Papa, thank you."

Lifting it out of the box, Lucas took the note underneath and read.

"My dear Son,

I hope you wear this with the pride I feel for you today. Godspeed. From your loving father. PS. Don't forget to write."

Hearing a commotion behind him, Lucas quickly slipped the watch on his wrist and wiped away a tear. The door to the room flew back, its handle hitting the wall behind.

"Hello there, you new too?" Lucas turned to see a young man with a round smiling face and a shock of red hair. He was no older than himself. Same height but slightly broader in the shoulders.

"Yes, hello, I'm Lucas, Lucas Blackwood," Lucas extended his hand, which was shaken vigorously by the young man.

"Tobias Pempleton. Toby to my friends," he announced.

"Really? My younger brother is called Tobias," Lucas laughed.

"Well, there you are. We were meant to meet. So, you will be my friend, won't you? I don't know about you, but I'm slightly nervous. Well, petrified more like," Toby shrugged his shoulders as he gave a nervous laugh.

"Yes, I would like that very much," instantly liking his new friend. "Here, grab the hammock next to mine. At least we have a window here." Lucas grabbed the bag off Toby, dumping it on the hammock, which swayed.

"Thought at least we'd have a bed. Have you ever slept in one of these?" asked Toby, gripping the ropes and shaking it.

Before Lucas could reply, four more recruits arrived. After introductions and settling their equipment onto the hammocks, two recruits tried them out, only to fall with a thump amid raucous laughter. Then suddenly, they were brought to attention by a loud command.

"GENTLEMEN, good afternoon. I am your Lieutenant Commander Jackson, Sir — when addressing me."

"Good afternoon, Sir," they chorused.

"Pardon?" the Lieutenant Commander raised his voice.

"GOOD AFTERNOON, SIR."

"That's better heard you this time. Welcome to Great Lakes Training Centre. Make the most of tonight. Tomorrow, you will be boarding US Dento for your entire training. The Mess Hall is open for your evening meal to ensure your dear mamas don't think that we don't look after you. So, enjoy and report for duty at 06:00 hours tomorrow morning. Lateness is not allowed." There was a moment of silence as the young recruits

291

stood looking at the Lieutenant Commander.

"YES, SIR, should be your reply," he barked.

"Yes, Sir," the boys chorused in unison.

"PARDON?"

"YES, SIR."

"God helps me," the Lieutenant muttered as he about turned, leaving the boys in silence. Toby broke that silence with a giggle.

"I don't know about you lot, but I'm starving." Then, with nervous laughter from the group, they left the quarters and headed for the mess hall.

*

'Thank you, Papa, for your gift. Tomorrow I shall board US Dento to start my training. I will always treasure it. Then, I shall sleep in a hammock for the first time tonight. Tell Tobias I hope I don't fall out. Mama, I have eaten well. My love to you all. Lucas.' He folded the letter and sealed the envelope and laid it on the tray near the door to be collected. Lucas glanced at his watch before climbing into his hammock. A sudden moment of homesickness hit him.

CHAPTER SIXTY-ONE

Two weeks to Christmas, the Blackwood household felt like it would burst at the seams. Nevertheless, it had become a ritual that friends gathered to celebrate the season. Paul Kelly, Lilly-Rose , and their nanny Grazina, who could not return home because her younger sister had whooping cough, joined them, along with Willem, Veronica, and Katrien.

At breakfast that morning, a letter arrived from Lucas. Rose was always excited to hear from her son; opening the envelope, she read aloud.

"Dearest Papa, Mama, Issy and Tobias. What a busy time I have had. I am well and hope you are also. I have eaten well, dear Mama."

"Oh, that is good news," Rose said, holding the letter to her heart.

"Mama, please carry on," Isabella laughed.

"Sorry, darling," Rose continued to read the letter.

"This last month, I have learnt to tie rope knots... so many different knots. Tell Tobias I shall show him when I return. Our exercises have increased if that is possible? I can now do fifty-three sit-ups and forty laps of the deck in one minute. Toby is a fast runner. But I'm better at sit-ups."

"Show off," Isabella giggled.

"You will be pleased to know I no longer ache initially, which is a good sign. Mama, you will be delighted to hear we have four weeks' leave. I will arrive at the station at lunchtime on Christmas Eve. I cannot wait to see you all. Also, I have exciting news to tell you.

Goodbye for now.

Much love to you all, Lucas."

Putting the letter down, Rose sighed. "Oh, Thomas, does that mean he will go away for longer? Oh, the thought."

"He's finished his initial training, my dear. We shall hear everything when he returns." Thomas smiled.

"Well, I cannot wait for him to come home. I hope it snows, and then we can go sledging and snowball fighting," Tobias said.

"Lilly-Rose will be pleased to see him; I think she's sweet on Lucas," Isabella laughed.

"My darling, don't be silly; she's only eight," Rose smiled at Isabella.

"I don't care; she's sweet on Lucas, and she's nearly nine, Mama." Then, leaning toward her Mama, Isabella whispered, "Lucas tells me he will marry Lilly-Rose when she is older."

"Oh, hush, child, who knows what will happen," Rose put her arm around Isabella, smiling as they hugged.

"Lucas loves Lilly ," chanted Tobias.

"Don't you dare say anything? If you tell, I'll put frogs in your bed," Isabella stuck her tongue out at Tobias.

"Enough, you two. No one will say anything; now I hear your tutor has arrived. So off you go and leave us in peace," Thomas smiled as they left the table.

"Bye Papa, see you at teatime," they chorused. Isabella kissed her papa before rushing out of the room with her brother.

Thomas folded his newspaper, standing he bent to kiss Rose.

"Until teatime, my dear."

"Be careful," she smiled as she gently touched the scar above Thomas' left eye, caused after stopping to help at the train disaster — leaving the jagged red scar. It made Thomas look even more handsome as far as Rose was concerned.

*

Driving his carriage to work, Thomas mulled over the conversation at breakfast. Does Lucas have a soft spot for Lilly-Rose? He had noticed that Lucas always seemed attentive to Lilly, but then he had put it down to brotherly love. She's a sweet girl only, well she is a Kelly. Oh, for goodness's sake, he scolded himself. What am I thinking? It's years away, and anything can happen before then. Lucas will have lots of admirers before he thinks of settling down. Thomas wondered what ship Lucas would have after his training; he already missed his dear son, but he must follow his dream, as Thomas had.

*

Christmas Eve. Rose, Veronica, and the rest of their guests were busy helping decorate the Christmas tree in the lounge. The last items to put on the tree were the two red ribbons for Agnes and Freda. Rose said a silent prayer and quietly wiped away a tear. Thomas and Tobias had gone to the station to await the four forty-five, which should have arrived by lunchtime, only to be delayed by signalling problems. Again, the station was heaving with people waiting for loved ones coming to celebrate the festive season.

"What time is it, Papa?" asked Tobias.

"One minute from the last time you asked," Thomas laughed.

"Listen, Papa. There's the whistle of the trains coming." Tobias excitedly jumped up and down as Thomas tried unsuccessfully to stop him from colliding with the couple in front of them. They smiled at his enthusiasm. Just then, another loud whistle, and amidst belching steam, the train rolled into the station, slowing to a stop. There was a cacophony of noise as carriage doors swung open and people crowded onto the platform.

"I can't see him, Papa. Can you see him?" asked

Tobias. He then shouted, "Lucas, Lucas!" A young man in Naval uniform suddenly appeared from the mayhem. Thomas called out and waved. Thomas felt a lump rise in his throat, surprised by the young man approaching them. Where is the young boy who left in the fall? he thought. Thomas hugged him.

"So good to have you home, son."

"It's good to be back, Papa."

"Hey, Lucas. Hello," Tobias tried to grab Lucas for a hug.

"Tobias, good to see you too," the brothers hugged.

On the way home, Tobias told Lucas all about the Christmas preparations.

"Everyone has arrived, including Lilly-Rose ," Tobias giggled. Lucas smiled. "Are you going on a ship? Are you sailing the seas when you go back?" Tobias threw questions at Lucas.

"Tobias, there's plenty of time to catch up on all the news with your brother when we get home. So, stop asking all the questions," his father called from the front of the landau.

"Will you show me how to tie rope knots? I can't wait to try."

"I will. I'm here for four weeks, plenty of time," replied Lucas.

"I hope it snows; we can go sledging in the park. You will go sledging with me, won't you?" Tobias looked up with a pleading look in his eyes.

"Can't wait. Oh, look, we're home," said Lucas. Thomas reigned in the horse just as the front door opened, and Rose rushed down the steps.

"Lucas, my darling, you're home. I've missed you so much. Come in, come in, tell me all about it."

Lucas stepped down from the carriage to be enveloped by a welcoming hug from his Mama. Then, standing back from him, Rose looked him up and down.

"You look so handsome in your uniform. Come on, let us go in. Everyone's waiting to see you." Rose linked arms with Lucas as they walked up the steps and opening the front door into the hallway, followed by Thomas and Tobias, carrying his brother's bag. Dropping Lucas' bag on the floor, Tobias banged the door shut behind him.

Entering the lounge, Lucas was greeted by his sister and friends, all happy to see him home — soon, they were sitting down to a welcome Christmas Eve meal amidst lots of laughter and chatter.

CHAPTER SIXTY-TWO

Rose awoke early on Christmas morning; she wanted everything to be perfect.

Going into Ivy's kitchen, the cook was already up, and the goose was in the oven. Rose was adamant that Ivy and their nanny join them for Christmas Dinner again. As Rose sat at the kitchen table, Ivy poured tea, placing a cup before her.

"I knew you would be up early. Happy Christmas, my dear," said Ivy.

"Happy Christmas, Ivy. It's going to be a fantastic day. I want it to be perfect for Lucas and all of us." Ivy sat opposite and looked at Rose over her cup.

"Isn't Christmas always perfect here?" Ivy smiled.

"Yes, I know, but…"

"But what lass. Stop trying too hard and let the day happen. Lucas won't think anything different from last year just because he's returned from the Navy. He's still our Lucas." Ivy put her hand across the table, resting it on Rose.

"Oh dear, am I being over motherly?" laughed Rose.

"Yes, now have another cup of tea, and as I said, let the day flow. It will be just fine." Ivy smiled at her.

*

Later that morning, everyone attended the Christmas morning service. Then finally, the party returned home for Christmas lunch with all the trimmings.

After the main meal, Ivy carried the plum pudding ablaze to the table amidst oohs and aahs. All the children, including Lucas, found a silver dime within their portions. Lucas held up the dime.

"Mama, what would you put in a Christmas pudding in England?"

"Oh, it would be a sixpence, or some families pop in a

penny or threepenny bit. All children loved to find them."
Rose suddenly remembered the last Christmas that her
mother was alive, she had helped make the pudding —
the excitement of finding the threepenny bit. Dear Mama,
so long ago, thought Rose.

After the meal, everyone gathered in the lounge,
enjoying coffee. The presents opened, Christmas
wrapping covered the carpet, and squeals of delight from
the children enjoying their gifts — they couldn't resist
pulling more Christmas crackers.

*

Over the next few days, no one rushed to leave, enjoying
each other's company taking walks in the park and
enjoying a light meal around the fire. Tobias followed his
brother around, asking questions about his time in the
Navy, wanting to learn how to tie all the rope knots his
brother had known. Poor Ivy, the cook, would come
down every morning to find her pinny straps tied up into
knots. She would shout and threaten them with no meals
for the day, but the boys just ran off laughing. Even poor
Isabella's doll did not escape; her long golden hair was
tied into knots, making Isabella shout at them too. Even
poor nanny Margaret found her scarf in knots when she
went to put it on. Finally, after several evenings when
Rose went to close the curtains, seeing the tiebacks all
knotted up every time. She, at last, put her foot down and
said,

"Boys, enough! Leave my curtains alone and everyone
else!"

Fortunately, Paul appeared with some rope, giving it
to the brothers to practice. Lucas spent many hours
showing Tobias how to tie a bowline, the square knot, the
reef knot, the line coil, and others.

While in Lucas' room one night, as the brothers sat
talking, Tobias sat crossed-legged on his bed, with rope

in hand as he lazily tied a reef knot. Lucas told him of his time onboard US Dento — his early morning call, always up at 06:00 hundred hours. Exercises included press-ups, sit-ups, and a run around the deck. Then breakfast was served in the Mess room with bacon, eggs and toast and washed down with large mugs of strong tea or coffee.

"You should see the radio room. It is called a Marconi and is just brilliant." Lucas told Tobias. "I think I might train to be a radio operator. But then again, I enjoy training with the guns on deck."

"Guns, wow, are they big?" Tobias sat wide-eyed.

"They're massive, and you feel powerful when you hold them."

"But won't you hurt people if you fire them?" Tobias looked thoughtfully at his brother.

"Well, that's the whole idea, to fight off the enemy," replied Lucas.

"I don't think I like the sound of war. So why can't we all be nice to each other."

"You are too soft, brother," replied Lucas giving Tobias a shove on his shoulder. "Go on, what do you want to do as you age? Are you going to work with Papa at Macy's?"

Tobias looked thoughtful, then looking at his brother Tobias smiled. "No, I want to be a teacher."

"I knew it; you've always enjoyed lessons. I think that's brilliant, brother."

"You don't think it's daft then?" asked Tobias.

"No, of course not. Have you told Papa and Mama yet?"

"No, but I will after you've returned to your ship. That reminds me, where are you going when you leave port?"

"Ah, that's a secret," smiling, Lucas put his finger to

his nose, laughing.

"Oh, come on, that's not fair. Go on, tell, please." Tobias jumped down from the bed and swiped his brother with the piece of rope he had in his hand.

"I shall board USS Alabama and sail the Pacific Ocean to who knows where, maybe fight pirates on the way."

"Pirates, really?" shouted Tobias. Lucas laughed.

"No, silly. I was joking."

*

It was January 24th, 1909, the day before Lucas returned for duty. Everyone enjoyed a stroll in Morningside Park, including Willem, Katrien and Veronica, with Paul Kelly and Lilly-Rose. It had snowed during the night, everywhere glistened with snow, and the trees gently swayed, showering those that passed underneath in white, soft flakes, and with frost in the air, it lay crisp on the ground. Even the ducks found themselves slithering across the pond — squawking with disgust.

Sitting on a bench warmly wrapped against the chill, Thomas, Rose and Lucas watched the group throw bread for the ducks with the nanny. Then, gentle snow flurries begin to fall. Rose slipped her arm through Lucas'.

"I shall miss you so much."

"I know, Mama, but it will be so exciting. I can't wait to board USS Alabama tomorrow."

"Oh, my dear boy, promise me you will wear warm clothes; it will be freezing, especially at sea and have hot food. The food is good, isn't it, and they give you plenty to eat? And promise me you will be careful."

"Mama, stop fussing. I shall wrap up warm, and yes, the food is excellent. I promise not to go hungry," Lucas and Thomas laughed.

"Stop laughing. I'm your mother. I must know these things," Rose scolded them. "Don't you dare mock me, Lucas Blackwood?" Rose gently thumped her son on his shoulder.

"Mama, I love you and promise to write and be careful," at that, Lucas stood, saluting his Mama.

"Behave yourself. Sit down." Rose giggled.

"Leave him be, woman," Thomas laughed.

So that night, the family sat down to enjoy Ivy's special roast beef and all the trimmings, finishing with Lucas' favourite bread and butter pudding.

"I'm so full I think I shall be too fat to sleep in my hammock," Lucas laughed.

*

Slipping downstairs early the following morning, before anyone woke, Tobias quietly pulled the cord of Lucas' bag and slipped a folded piece of paper deep inside, smiling to himself as he pulled the ties closed and returned to his room.

Later that same day, the family, including their friends, gathered at the station to wave Lucas off. Lilly-Rose stepped forward, giving Lucas a card with the words she had sewn in silk. "Take care upon the Seas until we meet again. January 25th, 1909. Your friend Lilly-Rose." They hugged, and Lucas slipped the card into his soft leather wallet, given to him at Christmas by his father. Isabella gave him a crochet scarf in the navy colours she had been secretly doing during the festive break.

"Bye, Sis. See you soon; look after Mama for me."

"Don't forget to write."

"I won't, I promise."

For a moment, they both stood looking at each other. Then, a whistle sounded, and steam engulfed those standing on the platform.

"Miss you," whispered Isabella.

With hugs and kisses over, Lucas stepped into the train, slamming the carriage door behind him. Then, turning, he rolled down the window to leant out, waving as the train disappeared out of the station.

Slipping her arm through Mama's, Isabella whispered, "See, told you they're sweet on each other."

CHAPTER SIXTY-THREE

Spring had arrived, and a feeling of calm enveloped the Blackwood household. Thomas recovered fully from his injuries; the only reminder was the jagged scar above his left eye. He had left early for Macy's. Post had just arrived, and Rose poured herself another coffee. Flicking through the envelopes, she spotted the tell-tale envelope from the US Navy. Her heart skipped a beat as she quickly slit the envelope open. It is the first letter from Lucas since he left in early January — it was already nearly three months. How fast the time had gone. Just then, the door opened, and Isabella popped her head around.

"Anything, Mama?" she asked.

"Aren't you supposed to be with your tutor?"

"Yes, Mama, but I saw the postman come; it is only dull Latin, so I made an excuse for the bathroom." Isabella giggled.

"Oh, you bad girl," laughed Rose patting the seat next to her. She knew she should send her daughter back upstairs but also knew Isabella was anxious. She seemed to have missed her brother more this time.

Opening the letter, Rose read it aloud.

'My Dearest Mama, Papa, Issy and Tobias.

We are now aboard USS Alabama. She is, as we say, "A beautiful Lady." I have settled in nicely, although I suffered from terrible seasickness in the first few days.

My friend Toby appears to have an iron stomach. He could eat enough for both of us and still seemed fine. He says hello, by the way. Thankfully the sickness has now passed, and I am much better.'

"Oh, look, darling, his letter is dated the first of February. So it has taken all this time to get here."

"Mama, please read the letter, never mind the date."

"Yes, sorry darling, now where was I."

'Tell Tobias his picture is hanging above my hammock. My friends think it is hilarious. No pirates yet, tell him.'

"Picture, what picture?" Rose frowned.

"Tobias drew him a parrot just in case Lucas saw any pirates who might like to have it." laughed Isabella.

"Really?"

"Oh, don't ask Mama. It was a joke between them, Tobias told me the first night Lucas had left. I told him we weren't living in the sixteenth or seventeenth century. But never mind, what else does he say? Where is he exactly?" Isabella tried to read the letter.

"He says they are somewhere in the North Pacific,"

'Tell Papa the guns are amazing. We have been training with them. I cannot begin to explain the power I feel when using them. Only in training, Mama. I am sure we shall never need them only in battle.'

"Oh, dear, I hope not. I don't want Lucas involved in any battles," Rose placed a hand on her chest.

"It's alright, Mama, it's just part of training. Please don't worry. Do go on, Mama, what else does he say," Isabella put her arm around her Mama.

'We have been at sea for several weeks and are now in the South Pacific, and it is scorching hot.'

"Sounds very exotic," Isabella laughed.

"They docked yesterday, whatever day that was," informed Rose.

'Sorry, I cannot say exactly where, but The Natives are extremely friendly and the ladies very beautiful.'

"Ooh, sounds as if Lilly-Rose will have a competition," Isabella giggled.

"Stop it, darling. We'll not tell her that bit of news. But, the poor child, I'm sure it's just childish infatuation."

"We'll see," replied Isabella.

"Oh, it's so good to hear from him," Rose placed a hand on Isabella's. "I know you've missed him too, my dear."

"Yes, I have. I don't know why. Maybe it's just that I knew Lucas would be gone for much longer."

"My dear, you must run along. Your tutor's going to wonder where you are." Just then, a knock at the sitting room door.

"Come in," Rose looked up at Mr Harold, their tutor.

"Forgive me, Mrs Blackwood. I was beginning to wonder what had happened to Miss Isabella?"

"Oh, entirely my fault; a letter arrived from her brother, knowing Isabella would be anxious for news. I'm afraid I waylaid her. But Isabella dear, do run along and finish your lessons." Rose smiled at Mr Harold, who nodded his head.

"Quite alright, Madam, I do understand," he replied. Isabella stood smiling at her Mama for not giving her away and left the room with Mr Harold.

*

That evening after dinner, Rose read Lucas' letter to Thomas while they sat enjoying a bourbon; even though Thomas had already read it earlier, he knew she loved to hear from their son.

"This weekend, my dear, I have a surprise for you all," Thomas smiled.

"A surprise, oh, I love surprises. What is it, darling? Do tell."

"If I tell, it won't be a surprise now, would it." laughed Thomas kissing Rose gently on the forehead.

"I have also arranged a short spring break at our ranch in the Catskill Mountains; a break would do us good."

"The children love the mountains. They'll be so excited,"

"Come on, my dear, it's late," Thomas kissed Rose as they left the lounge to retire.

CHAPTER SIXTY-FOUR

Sunday morning was bright and sunny with a clear blue sky. Thomas had left early, even before Rose had risen from her bed.

"Whatever is he up to?" she thought. Then, remembering the surprise he had promised for the weekend. Perhaps a new landau, although there was nothing wrong with the one they had. It was all very mysterious. Dressing quickly, Rose entered the dining room to find Isabella and Tobias at the table. Ivy, their cook, placed the bacon, eggs and kidney dishes on the sideboard.

"Morning, Mama," the children chorused.

"Morning, everyone; you're all up early this morning."

"Well, Papa has gone for the surprise, whatever that is," Isabella smiled.

"Morning Ivy, where is the maid?"

"She is just hanging out the washing for me. I find the sheets a little heavy these days. So, I thought I would bring in the breakfast."

"Do you know where Papa has gone, Mama?" Tobias asked with a mouth full of scrambled eggs.

"Please don't talk with your mouth full, darling."

"Sorry, Mama,"

"And no, I do not know where your father has gone. Please let us eat our breakfast and wait for his return."

"Maybe he's gone for Lucas; perhaps he's home early."

"Oh, do shut up, Tobias. Lucas has not arrived home. He would have sent a telegram first. Stop giving poor Mama palpitations," Isabella kicked him under the table.

"Ow, that hurt."

"Children, please, don't squabble; finish your

breakfast."

"Yes, Mama," they both replied.

*

A short time later, just as breakfast finished, a strange noise like a horn came from outside.   "Aoogah, Aoogah."

"Whatever is that." Rose looked up with a puzzled expression. Isabella and Tobias rushed over to the window, pushing the curtain aside.

"It's Papa; oh, Mama, come and see!" Both children ran from the dining room into the hall, throwing open the front door, still shouting.

"Mama, Mama, hurry," as they ran down the steps just as their father stepped down from his surprise.

"Papa, papa," they call excitedly. Tobias is hopping from foot to foot.

"You've got a car, Papa. How exciting. Do let us ride in it, please, Papa."

"All in good time, children; let your Mama see it first."

Following the children out amid all the excitement, Rose stood at the top of the steps, nanny Margaret and Ivy just behind, crossing her heart with the cross sign.

"Heaven preserves us. The masters brought a metal monster," said Ivy.

"It's a car, Ivy, not a monster," Rose laughed as she ran down the steps to stand with the children.

"Come on, everyone, hop in. Let's take it for a run around the block." At that, Isabella and Tobias were already scrambling onto the back seats.

"What sort of car is it, Papa?" asked Tobias.

"It's a Ford Model T with two forward gears, and it has a twenty-horsepower engine with a top speed of forty-five miles per hour," Thomas told them, beaming joyfully.

"Oh, Papa, we'll be flying. Hurry up, let's go," Tobias was bouncing up and down on the leather seat.

"Shall we, my dear?" Thomas held out his hand to Rose.

"We're not going anywhere without our hats and coats. You'll catch your death," said Rose as she hurried back up the steps past an astonished-looking nanny and Ivy.

"Oh, Rose, you can't go in that you'll all die," Nanny shouted as the children followed their mama back into the hall.

Grabbing hats and coats, they are soon back outside. Tobias tried to hold Nanny Margaret's hand.

"Come with us, nanny," he shouted.

"Err, I'll wait here for you, Master Tobias. You hold on tight now." At that, Tobias and Isabella climbed back into the car.

"Ready, everyone?"

"Blow the horn, papa," Isabella and Lucas shouted as Thomas set off. He squeezed the rubber ball next to the steering wheel. Aoogah, Aoogah went the horn, causing the children to laugh. As they drove past the park, the children were shouting.

"Faster, Papa, faster."

Already holding onto her hat, Rose called above the engine's noise. "Thomas, don't you dare go any faster, children. Hold tight."

"It's okay, my darling. Relax and enjoy the ride." Thomas squeezed her hand.

"Ooh, both hands on the wheel, Thomas." Thomas threw back his head and laughed.

After several turns around the block, they pulled up outside the house. Thomas jumped out, helping Rose down as the children scrambled out of the back seats.

Nanny and Ivy are still standing on the top steps, relief

on their faces at their safe return.

"Ivy dear, I think it's time for coffee," said Rose as she climbed the steps.

"Cook, cook, you've got to have a ride. It's just brilliant." Tobias grabbed her hand, pulling her towards the car.

"No, thank you, Master Tobias. You won't find me in that metal monster." Ivy quickly entered the house, saying, "I'll get coffee for you all," and disappeared into the kitchen.

"I'll help cook," Nanny Margaret told them.

*

That evening Thomas told Rose they would use the new car to take them to the Catskills.

"What about poor Ivy and nanny? You'll not get them in it," Rose giggled.

"I know, my darling; they will have to follow in the landau, which I'm sure they will be happy about."

"What made you think of getting a car?" asked Rose.

"I had been thinking about one for a while. Willem and I chatted about it a month ago," replied Thomas.

"Oh yes, I do remember Veronica telling me. She told me she'd rather stick to horse and cart. At least she can stop a horse when needed," Rose laughed.

"It was Paul Kelly who got me interested. He brought Lilly-Rose to Macy's two weeks ago to choose a dress for a friend's birthday party. After that, he couldn't resist dropping into the office to show me his pride and joy."

"Oh Thomas, you didn't get one just because of Paul…"

"No, it just made my mind up," Thomas grinned sheepishly at Rose and then laughed.

"Thomas," Rose smiled.

"What, anyway, as I was saying, we'll use the car for the trip. The kids will enjoy that." Thomas moved over to the sideboard and poured two bourbons, passing one to Rose with a smirk. He bent, kissing her on the cheek.

CHAPTER SIXTY-FIVE

In late spring-early summer, the Catskill Mountains always looked its best. It was the time of year that Rose loved. Everything was awakening from its winter slumber — new leaves on the trees, green grass. Young fawns danced skittishly. The stream glistened, and its waters sparkled like yellow diamonds as it rushed past outside their cabin.

Rose and her family arrived four days ago, and she already felt the stresses of the last few months fade away. Tobias and Thomas are fishing in the boat, determined to bring home tea. Isabella was sitting on the veranda with the nanny, writing to Lucas.

Meandering down to the stream, finding a rock to perch on Rose took off her shoes, slipping her feet into the water, the sudden cold made her gasp. Then, she lifted her feet onto the rock she was sitting on and tilted her face to the sun, Rose quietly reflected on the past year.

There was a rustling sound, and Rose was suddenly aware of movement. She watched a brown bear wander down through the trees to the water's edge. Rose knew that by sitting perfectly still, neither would bother the other. The bear glanced back, sniffing the air and then, to her amazement, a small brown furry bundle of energy bounded up, rubbing its head under his mother's chin. Rose sat transfixed, watching a moment of motherly love. She knew the bear was aware of her presence but seemed calm. After several minutes the bear moved back into the forest, young cub followed.

How wonderful, thought Rose. Just then, her daughter appeared at her side.

"Oh, Mama, did you see the bear? Nanny and I didn't dare move, and the baby cub was sweet." Shielding her eyes with her hand from the sun, Rose looked up into her daughter's face and smiled.

"I did, my darling. I cannot wait to tell your father and Tobias when they return." Isabella sat down next to her Mama.

"Sometimes, Mama, I wish we could stay here forever."

"Yes, me too, darling. But I think our friends would miss us, and I enjoy my work at the Charity Board."

"I've finished my letter to Lucas. I have told him all our news about the new car. I'm sure that will bring him home quickly," Isabella giggled. "Look, mama, I've drawn a picture at the end of the letter of the bear and her cub."

"How sweet, my darling, Lucas will love that."

They sat quietly for a while, enjoying the rippling noise of the water as it lapped over stones — the occasional fish leapt up. Then, finally, Isabella removed her shoes, joining her Mama by dipping her feet into the stream.

"Mama,"

"Yes, darling."

"We won't go and live in England, will we? Only this is our home."

"Oh, Isabella, whatever makes you think that?"

"I don't know it was... Well, Papa reading the letter just before we came from Mr Selfridge inviting us over, I thought, would he ask Papa and us to stay. I know you came from England, Mama, do you miss it? Do you want to return?" Rose turned, looking Isabella straight in the face and taking hold of her hands.

"Stop worrying, my darling. I have no wish to return to England. My home is with you, Tobias, Lucas and your dear Papa. No, if we go, it will be for a holiday. I want to show you England, and I know your dear Papa is keen to see this new store by Mr Selfridge. I hear it is very splendid. Perhaps we could have a girly shop while we are there," Rose smiled.

"Oh yes, Mama, I love girly shops."

*

That evening, the family gathered on the veranda after enjoying an evening barbecue of salmon caught and cooked outdoors by Thomas, with help from Tobias. Rose wondered if the mother bear and her cub would return the next day.

Tobias said he would stay near the cabin in case it does. "I don't want to miss it."

The sky was full of stars twinkling brightly in the night sky. Thomas had turned off the lights on the veranda just in time to see a shooting star.

"Papa, I've been thinking about the letter you read from Mr Selfridge. If we go to England, will Lucas be able to come with us?" Isabella asked.

"I hope so but don't think about it just yet. It's going to be nineteen-twelve before we go if we go. It is not for another three years. But, my dear child, I wouldn't have mentioned it if I thought it troubled you."

"I just don't want to go without Lucas, that's all." Isabella sighed.

"Lucas will come if we go on this new big ship Mr Selfridge told us about," replied Tobias. "It sounds brilliant. Can't wait to see it."

"Do they have a name for the store in London?" asked Rose.

"They call it 'Selfridges,' my dear."

"Of course they do," Rose giggled.

"When we go. Mama and I are going shopping. It will be such fun to look around a new store. Will it be as big as Macy's Papa?" asked Isabella. Tobias interrupted before Thomas could reply.

"Papa, have they given a name yet for this ship?"

"To answer your question, Isabella, I believe it is large and grand." Thomas took out Selfridges letter to read aloud. It says here, Tobias.

"Ah, here it is." Thomas read further.

Although it is still on the drawing board, it has already been named "Titanic." Thomas continued. I have the authority that its maiden voyage will be spring nineteen hundred and twelve. I will reserve two first-class cabins for the return voyage as soon as passenger tickets become available, assuming you will come. Of course, Rosalie would love to see you and dear little Violet. I am sure the ladies will enjoy their time at Selfridges and perhaps your travels around England while you're here.'

"Titanic, good grief, how big is this ship going to be?" queried Rose.

"Enormous as tall as the stars," Tobias threw his arms towards the sky, causing everyone to laugh. After that, they all sat quietly, Thomas and Rose enjoying Ivy's coffee.

"Well," said Rose as she looked at Thomas. Our cabin had better be big enough to take a cot; our little one will only be two by then." There was a moment's silence before Thomas suddenly jumped to his feet, engulfing Rose in a hug.

"Oh, my darling girl, what fantastic news."

"Mama, does that mean I will get a little brother?"

"No, it does not. I want a sister," shouted Isabella as both children rushed to hug their Mama.

The End.

About the Author

I was born and raised in North Yorkshire and worked for the Local Council for many years. I have always been a keen reader. My favourite author is Agatha Christy. Now retired, I live at home with my husband and family.

Since retirement, I joined our local writers' group, 'Stockton Scribblers.' I have contributed stories to their book "Zig Zags." Through them, they have encouraged me to write many short stories; Land of Opportunity is my first novel. I have also had poems published in our local paper.

My daughter and I volunteer at our local hospital radio station, playing music, where I read my short stories. In addition, I enjoy the theatre, walking, swimming, watching my son play golf and shopping with my daughter.

Twitter - Linda@ladro25

www.blossomspringpublishing.com

Printed in Poland
by Amazon Fulfillment
Poland Sp. z o.o., Wrocław

34354008R00183